Fire Line

MAGGIE GATES

Copyright © 2024 Maggie C. Gates. All Rights Reserved

No part of this publication may be reproduced, transmitted, or distributed in any form or by any means including photocopying, recording, information storage and retrieval systems, without prior written permission from the publisher except in the case of brief quotation embodied in book reviews.

No part of this work may be used to create, feed, or refine artificial intelligence models, for any purpose, without written permission from the author.

This book is a work of fiction. The characters and events in this book are fictitious. Any similarity to real places or persons, living or dead, is purely coincidental and not intended by the author or are used fictitiously.

The author acknowledges the trademark status and trademark owners of various products, brands, and/or establishments referenced in this work of fiction. The publication/use of these trademarks is not associated with, or sponsored by the trademark owners.

This book is intended for mature audiences.

ISBN: 979-8-9908378-6-7

Editing by Jordan Loft

Proofreading by Amy Pritt

Cover design by Melissa Doughty - Mel D. Designs

To my husband, without whom I would not have survived the last few months. Thank you for being my partner, and walking with me through the tears and fears.

Fire Line

CONTENT WARNINGS

All of my books include content that is intended for adult audiences. As an author I strive to tell stories respectfully, but authentically. In my books you will find explicit sexual content, profanity, and scenes that may be triggering.

For a full list of content advisories and trigger warnings, visit https://www.maggiegates.com/content-warnings

Treat yourself with care and happy reading!

With Love,
Maggie Gates

PROLOGUE
LENNON

Ten Years Ago

"Get your shoes on," Justin barked as he stomped through our shitty apartment. He grabbed a backpack from the closet and slammed the door. Loose flakes from the sagging popcorn ceiling rained down on the dingy carpet.

My brother was on edge and twitchy. *Just perfect.*

All I wanted was to finish my homework and head to bed. He knew I had to be at work to open up in the morning before school.

The last thing I wanted to do tonight was go somewhere because he needed a fix.

Half the time, he'd vanish for days and leave me on my own. The other half, he was way too insistent on keeping me under his thumb and used his legal guardian status to do so.

"I have shit to do," I grumbled as I turned my attention back to the stupid essay I had been working on for hours.

He threw a set of keys at me. "I don't care. Get up. You're driving."

I caught the keys and let out a sarcastic laugh. "Since when did you get a car?"

"I'm borrowing it. Get a move on."

Whatever. It was easier to go with what he wanted to do than to argue.

I threw on a pair of knockoff fur boots and grabbed a jacket. "We're not going to be gone long, right? I have to be up in a few hours."

"You'll be back in time to open the store."

That wasn't promising.

"If I'm late, Mr. Morelli isn't going to let you use my employee discount anymore," I yelled at him.

Because that's all I had to leverage. A measly fifteen percent off at the bodega down the block.

I knew how to drive, but I wasn't great at it. It was more of a *figure-it-out-as-you-go* situation. I didn't even have my license. It wasn't like my brother and I had a car, and I could walk to most places. If I couldn't walk, I'd take the subway.

Justin was more on edge than usual as we hustled down the sidewalk. He flexed his hands and fidgeted with his pants every ten seconds.

I followed him down an alley that led behind a bar.

The rank odor of trash, old beer, and rancid oil filled the night air. Rodents scurried through the gross haze.

"Get in." He pointed to a small sedan parked in the shadow of a building.

"You gonna tell me what we're doing or where we're going?" I asked as I unlocked it and slid behind the wheel. "Or whose car you're borrowing?"

"Shut up and drive. Go down to Amsterdam and then get on Harlem River Drive. We're taking the bridge into New Jersey."

"New Jersey?" I shrieked, slamming my hands onto the

steering wheel. "I have work and school tomorrow. It's ten at night! What the hell do you have to do in New Jersey?"

"It's when I have the car. Shut your fucking mouth and drive, Len."

At least the traffic wasn't that bad because of how late it was.

Justin kept checking his phone every five minutes like he was waiting for a call. Finally, the screen lit up, and he pressed the phone to his ear.

"Yeah. I'm on my way," he said a moment later.

I raised an eyebrow but kept my attention on the road.

"It'll be where I said it will be. We already talked about this." Justin gritted his teeth so hard I was certain they were going to shatter. "She's driving."

Who was he talking to?

"It'll be fine. We'll meet up tomorrow," he said before hanging up.

"Wanna tell me what that was about?" I sassed as I came off the George Washington Bridge, leaving New York and entering New Jersey.

Lights from passing cars and buildings flashed in the night.

"Take a left down here," he clipped, ignoring my question.

I slammed on the brakes at a red light. "And what if I don't want to? Just tell me where we're going."

He hit me with a sharp look. "Do what I say."

"Why should I?"

"Blood's thicker than water. Remember that, Len."

I rolled my eyes and eased through the green light.

Justin pawed around the backpack, unzipping it and closing it again. "I'm meeting a friend for some business."

A caustic laugh slipped from my mouth. "This late at night? Right."

He pointed to a dimly lit building on a deserted street. "Park along the sidewalk. Cut the lights but keep the engine running. I'll be back in less than ten minutes."

"And if you're not?" I asked.

"I will be."

Justin slipped out and closed the passenger door so softly that I wasn't sure it had even latched.

I sighed and leaned my head back, closing my eyes. If I had to guess, he was going to get some shitty weed from some sketchy guy to push on our block. He'd probably be at least a half-hour. *Might as well grab a catnap.*

Five minutes passed.

Then ten.

I opened my eyes around the twelve-minute mark.

A car slowed as it passed by, the headlights dancing off the building's sign. What was Justin doing at a Federal Credit Union? It was closed.

Dread bloomed inside me, floating up my throat, then sinking down like a rock in my gut.

No, no, no...

I checked the clock again. Thirteen minutes had passed when a loud crack rang out.

BAM!

BAM! BAM!

My blood ran cold.

I knew that sound. I heard it all too often in our neighborhood.

Gunshots.

A dark figure sprinted away from the building and ripped the car door open. "Go!"

"Oh my God!" I screamed at the sight of blood spattered across his shirt. "What did you do?"

"Fucking go!" he roared as he threw a bag into the backseat.

"*Justin!*"

My brother's expression turned lethal. He pulled back his jacket, and the glint of slick, black metal peeked out of the front of his waistband. "I said, *drive.*"

1

CARSON JAMES

A neon glow bathed the Silver Spur in soft blues. The chaos of pool tables, a band, and the clink of glasses as two bartenders mixed drinks blended into a wall of sound.

My palms hit the edge of the polished oak bar as I found an open stool.

A blonde bartender glanced over, her eyes meeting mine for a moment before returning to her work. With practiced ease, she poured two fingers of Jack into a glass and slid it to a customer without looking up.

"Whadda ya want?" she hollered over the ruckus.

"Beer," I said. "Whatever's cold."

"Easy enough." She grabbed a bottle out of the ice chest and dropped it in front of me.

I debated paying cash or starting a tab. I didn't plan on sticking around long—just long enough to disassociate for a while.

But I did drive all the way out here ... If I only drank one beer, it'd be the most expensive drink of my life.

A body pushed against mine and craned over the bar. "I need a towel."

"Ever heard of waiting your turn?" I muttered as I handed the bartender my card to start a tab.

The woman turned to me when the bartender disappeared, flashing a pair of split knuckles. "The last guy got it worse. You wanna be next, cowboy?"

The accent told me she wasn't from around here. Not even close. She said "you wanna" like a true New Yorker. It reminded me of my sister-in-law.

She was a pain in the ass too.

"Pipe down, slugger. Ain't nothing that serious."

The bartender gave the woman a handful of ice wrapped in a towel and asked, "Did you start it or finish it?"

The woman grabbed it and pressed the ball of ice to her knuckles. "Finished it."

The bartender waved her off. "Fine by me. Stay out of trouble."

Brown eyes flicked up and down, tracking from my boots to my beer, up my chest, then to my face. "See how fast that was? Now you can get back to drinking your shitty beer and looking broody."

I took a long pull from the bottle and drank her in with my eyes.

Her hair glowed under the neon signs like it was invisible ink under a blacklight. Onyx hair intertwined with snow-white streaks. Sleeves of tattoos covered both arms. She had a slice through her eyebrow and a stud dotting her nose.

She was hot. And crazy.

I scoffed to try and hide my smile. "You'd run into less trouble if your mouth didn't write checks your ass can't cash."

She let a caustic laugh slip. "You think I go around punching people? He had it coming."

"Sure, slugger. That's what they all say."

She shrugged. "He shoulda known better than to make a bet and refuse to pay up. If you're gonna be a loser, be an honorable one."

She had a point there.

"Tell you what." I pointed around the bar to the pool tables and dartboards. "Pick your poison. You win, and I'll buy your next drink."

Her mouth curved up into a devilish smile. "Sorry, cowboy. I play for money."

"Yeah?" I hooked a finger in the belt loop of her denim shorts and tugged her closer. "Well, I play for keeps."

"Not interested," slipped from her lips, but I caught the way her voice softened. The way her eyes flicked to my mouth. "I'm not from around here anyway."

"Neither am I."

"Pool. Hundred bucks says I'll beat you."

"Fifty."

"Seventy-five."

"Fine." I finished off my beer and pulled out my wallet, showing her the bills. "I'm good for it."

Something wicked lingered in her smile. "Rack 'em up, cowboy."

"What makes you think I'm a cowboy?" I slid my hand onto the small of her back and led her to an open pool table.

She let out a loud, raucous laugh. "You're one 'ma'am' away from the big three."

I lifted an eyebrow as I arranged the balls into a triangle. "The big three?"

She counted off each point by lifting a finger. "Cowboy boots. Cowboy hat."

"So, what's the third?"

"You haven't called me 'ma'am.'"

I chuckled and handed her a cue. "Hate to break it to you, trouble. But this is Texas. You'll find all three just about everywhere."

She stole the cue I had chosen for myself out of my hand and shoved the one I had offered her back at me. "It's Lennon."

I trapped her against the table with one hand on the edge of the wood and my boots on the outside of her sneakers. "Either trouble suits you or it follows you. I'm thinking both."

Lennon smirked. "If you think flirting with me will help you win, you're wrong. But nice try."

I had been a gentleman until now. But since she called my hand, I wasn't going to hide my attraction. I dropped my gaze to the tits that filled the low scoop of her tank top. "Just leveling the playing field."

"I'll let you break. It's the least I can do considering you're about to be seventy-five bucks poorer."

The balls clattered as I took a shot at the triangle, managing to pocket one on the break. I took another shot and dropped two more in, clean as a whistle.

"You wanna rethink that bet?" I asked as I chalked my cue. "We should probably discuss what I want when I win."

"If you win, I'll pay you," Lennon said, sinking two more into the side pocket. "That's how this works."

I moved behind her, planting my hands on the edge of the table to cage her in. "I can think of something else I'd like when I win."

Lennon arched her back, teasing me with her ass. "You're thinking with your dick."

I brushed her long, black and white hair to one shoulder, then leaned down until my chest pressed against her back.

"I don't know about you, but I'm playing to win." I trailed my fingers up and down the goosebumps that flooded her arms. "You cold, sweetheart?"

Her tongue darted out, swiping across her lips as she blinked to refocus. "Trust me, cowboy. There's nothing sweet about me."

I smoothed my hand down the curve of her back to her hip, skirting her ass. "That's all right. I don't have much of a sweet tooth." I wedged my leg between her thighs. "When I eat out, it's the main meal."

Lennon's shot went askew. She missed the ball she was aiming for and accidentally knocked one of mine into the corner pocket.

I chuckled as I backed away, searching for my shot. "Thanks for the freebie."

"Ass," she grumbled.

We went through the next few rounds in silence, both of us picking off balls with each turn. Teasing each other with sensual touches.

I took stock of the table and lined up for my next shot. If I made this one, it would tie us up. If I missed and she made hers, she'd win.

"What are you drinking, slugger?" I asked as I shifted to the other side of the table for a better angle.

She chalked up her cue like she didn't have a care in the world. "Water."

I made the shot, pocketed the ball, and tied us up. "Next drink is on me. It's the least I can do after kicking your ass."

Lennon faced me on the opposite side of the table, leaned over, and rested her arms on the edge.

Fuck.

The neck of her tank top was low and revealing. Her heavy tits hung behind the pocket I was trying to hit. "Come on, cowboy. Take your shot."

"It's CJ."

She flashed a full smile. "I didn't ask for your name."

I chuckled. "Figured you'd wanna remember who bested you."

The shot went wide.

Lennon clicked her tongue. "Pride always comes before a fall." And with that, she cleaned up the table, pocketing the eight ball.

"Best out of three," I said.

She came around to stand toe-to-toe with me and flipped her hair to one shoulder. "How about you pay up and stop being a sore loser?" She flexed her bruised knuckles. "You know how it ended for the last guy."

I smirked and tugged my wallet out of the back pocket of my jeans. "Yes, ma'am."

"And there's the big three. You cowboys are such gentlemen. Did it hurt to hold in the 'ma'am' this long?"

I hooked my finger through Lennon's belt loop and pulled her flush against my body. The gasp that escaped her lips was divine.

Slowly, I slid the folded bills between her tits, but didn't dare touch her skin. "I'm no gentleman."

Her eyes flicked down, watching my every move. "You sure about that?"

"Let me buy you a drink."

"Sounds like something a gentleman would say."

Goddamn. I liked her sass.

"Beer or liquor?"

"Whiskey. Neat."

"I'll be back."

She scoffed and pushed away from the pool table. "So you can slip something in my drink? I don't think so."

I cocked my head toward the bar. "Tell her to put it on my tab. I'll get us a table."

Lennon grinned. "You don't wanna go another round? Afraid I'll take all your money?"

I chuckled. "I know when I've met my match."

Lennon strutted off as I perched on a high stool. The table was on the outskirts of the bar, hidden in a shadow next to the darkened ring surrounding a mechanical bull.

Energy buzzed all around, but it felt like I was watching the actions of the crowd from another dimension.

Lennon turned. Her zebra-striped hair splayed as she clutched her drink and looked around.

I let out a sharp whistle and lifted my hand until she spotted me and came over.

"How's it feel to be seventy-five bucks richer?" I asked.

She smirked as she slid onto the stool beside me, so close that our legs were touching. "Pretty good. How'd it feel to lose after you tried so hard to distract me?"

I rested my hand on her thigh and gave it a squeeze. "Didn't mind so much."

Lennon took a sip. "Let me know whenever you want me to make your wallet a little lighter."

A drop of amber liquor fell from her lip, splashing onto her chest. I reached out and mopped it up with the pad of my thumb, then sucked off the taste. Her breath caught.

"You here alone?"

Her lips lingered on the rim of the glass. "I plead the fifth."

She didn't trust me. That was obvious. Not that I blamed her. Getting her drink straight from the bartender was smart. Not letting on if she had people here who would notice if she was missing was smarter. I respected that.

"Tell me something, then."

Her brow arched.

"Why'd you come here tonight?"

Another sip. Another bead of whiskey on the corner of her mouth. Another press of my thumb, this time against her lips. I wiped it away with my thumb and drank it.

She inched closer and spoke with a deep rasp. "To hustle some gullible cowboys out of their paychecks and have a little fun."

"And now that you've got your winnings, what are you gonna do for the fun part?"

"Who says winning isn't fun?" She took a long gulp, finishing off the glass. "Now, are you gonna get your own drink, kiss me, or keep acting like you don't know which one you want?"

That fucking mouth...

I cupped the back of her neck and slanted my mouth with hers, but I didn't kiss her. Instead, I sucked her lower lip between my teeth and nipped at it. "I'll let you lead this dance, trouble. You tell me what you want, and I'll give it to you like the gentleman you think I am."

The corners of her mouth turned up. "Take me into that back hallway and I'll tell you when to stop. I'm not opposed to giving you a ribbon for participation."

Chuckling, I yanked her from the stool and tugged her along the dim hallway. "Participation ribbon, my ass."

She held her glass as I shoved her against the rough brick wall. I slammed my mouth to hers and ran my tongue along the seam of her lips until she opened for me. Her body softened as she molded against me, letting me lead.

"You have good taste in liquor," I murmured as I sucked in a breath.

Lennon laughed. "Beats my taste in men."

"Is that so?" I worked my hand up the front of her tank top, then tugged on the neckline. "I'm more than happy to make up for whoever broke your heart."

Lennon pulled the cash out of her bra and stuffed it in her pocket. She tipped the rocks glass against her collarbone. The last rivulets of whiskey streamed down her breasts. "Lick it up, pretty boy."

I fisted her hair at the base of her neck and yanked her head back, opening her neck. "That's Daddy to you, trouble."

2

LENNON

Fucking cowboys.

CJ latched onto my throat, nipping his way down to my cleavage. His cologne swirled around us as he left soft, sloppy kisses all over my tits.

A gasp burst from my lips. I hated sounding so needy and desperate, but it had been a while. And goddamn, he smelled good.

I tangled my fingers in his hair, almost knocking his hat off. He adjusted it with one hand as I clung to him.

"You shouldn't taste this good, trouble," he growled.

A calloused hand slid down my arm, scraping against my tattoos. Each touch sent a shiver down my spine.

"Whiskey and sass." CJ sank his teeth into the side of my breast. "Can't get enough of you."

His fingers curled around the edge of my bra and peeled it away. A satisfied smirk grew on his face. He brushed his thumb over my nipple, hovering on the barbell that glinted under the neon glow.

My gaze lingered on him as his tongue flicked, toying with the metal stud.

"Well, aren't you full of surprises?" He cupped my other breast and pressed his thumb over the fabric covering my nipple.

Sparks danced across my chest.

"Here too?" he asked, rubbing his thumb over the other piercing.

My head fell back on the brick. "Uh-huh."

"Is this your weakness, beautiful?" His eyes lifted to gauge my reaction as he uncovered my other breast and pinched both nipples. "Is that what gets you to stop fighting me?"

A soft laugh caught in my throat. "Who says I was fighting?"

CJ rolled the piercings between his fingers, and I nearly lost my footing. His muscular arm shot out, steadying me against his chest.

"I get the feeling a little pain doesn't bother you," he said as he skated his fingers up the sleeves of my tattoos. "Does it?"

I trapped my lip between my teeth to hide my smile, but it was useless.

"Should'a known you'd think fighting was flirting." He pressed the softest kiss to the stud dotting the corner of my nose, lingering as he rested his forehead on mine.

For a brief moment, I melted. And I couldn't let that happen again.

"You gonna stand there all night telling me how I should flirt, or are you gonna fuck me? What's that old saying? Spare some batteries, ride a cowboy."

CJ laughed. "I'm all for saving the planet."

He pulled his wallet out and grabbed a condom, trapping it between his teeth. He loosened his jeans and dropped them enough for his cock to hang out.

Jesus Christ. I was all for saving the planet too, but someone would have to save me.

"Don't look so scared, trouble. I'll take good care of you," he said as he rolled the condom. His chest pressed into me as he stole my breath with another kiss.

"CJ—" His name ended in a sigh on my lips as he flicked open the button to my shorts and slid his hand inside my panties.

"So wet already." Hazel eyes danced with delight as he teased my clit with the pad of his finger. "You needy tonight, Lennon?"

I bit down on his earlobe hard enough to leave a mark. "You're not taking me home, so you'd better wow me right here."

"Challenge accepted." CJ pushed my shorts down and kicked them away from my feet.

I squeaked when he lifted me, forcing me to wrap my legs around his hips.

I was a big girl—tall with thick thighs. No one had ever thrown me around or manhandled me. I usually just laid there through something blasé and missionary.

My back slammed into the bricks as CJ notched the head of his cock inside my pussy and pushed inside.

"You good?"

"Uh-huh." It was all I could get out when I was choking on the fullness.

The kiss was soft. The thrust was anything but. I keened, doubling over and tucking my head into the crook of his neck as he rammed inside of me again and again.

"Eyes on me, Len. I've got you." CJ took off his cowboy hat and used it to shield my ass, covering the place where we were connected from any unsuspecting eyes that passed by.

CJ slowed, taking time to press me against the wall and grind against my clit. "You like that?"

"Uh-huh."

"Is that all you can say?"

I let a lazy smile slip as delicious bubbles of euphoria danced up my body like champagne. "Uh-huh."

He chuckled as he shifted his hold on me, supporting my ass with his arm and keeping us mostly covered with his hat. "If this is my consolation prize for getting my ass handed to me at pool, I'd lose to you every day of my life."

"Big words for someone I'll never see again once we're done here. Did they teach you all those flowery declarations in cowboy school?"

"You keep running your mouth, and I'll show you a better use for it."

I clicked my tongue. "Promises, promises."

CJ's eyes darkened as they locked on mine. He braced his feet wide, keeping our bodies tight against the wall for support. Slowly, he rocked his hips, stimulating my clit as he stayed buried inside of me. He dropped his hat back on his head and teased my nipple piercings, circling and tugging on them until I was a desperate, writhing mess.

I was on edge and so desperate that I was ready to plead to any deity that was listening to make him keep going.

"You gonna come, cowboy?"

CJ smirked. "You got the big three, but you missed the fourth."

"What's that?"

He tipped his head to the side and sucked my piercing between his teeth. "Ladies first."

The pull of his mouth against my nipple set me off like a firecracker. I jolted in his arms as my release came washing in like a flood.

CJ grunted, his arms tightening around me. Thick brows furrowed into a groove above his nose as he sucked in a breath. His cock flexed and throbbed as he came into the condom.

I loosened my arms, signaling for him to set me on my feet. CJ only held me closer.

"One more kiss," he murmured against my lips.

It was soft this time, savoring the moment as we came off the high. He raised a hand and brushed my hair away from my face, twisting black and white strands around his finger.

"You okay?"

I nodded. "I should probably go to the bathroom and clean up."

He gently lowered me to my feet, holding on until he was sure I was steady.

Quickly, I wiggled back into my shorts and straightened out my clothes. He took care of the condom and discreetly tossed it in a nearby trash can.

"Can I buy you one more drink?" he asked. The hint of reluctance in his voice told me he didn't want to let the night end.

But it had to end. I had business to attend to.

I ran my hands over his t-shirt, tracing the muscles that had just wrapped around me. "Goodbye, cowboy."

He trailed his finger along the strap of my tank top, straightening it out until there was no evidence of our dalliance. "Goodbye, Len."

I waited in the corridor until he disappeared. A moment later, I bolted to the restroom and locked myself in a stall.

The seventy-five bucks I won off him added to the hundred and fifty I had won earlier in the night. It wasn't a lot, but it covered a motel room for the night and gas to get me to Temple.

"ID AND CREDIT CARD, HON."

I looked across the front desk of the Maren Motel and tried to put on my most innocent face. The clerk's judgmental stare at my tattoos told me no amount of sweet-talking would work, but I had to try.

"I'm just passing through on my way to a new job. I lost my wallet at a truck stop in Tennessee, so I don't have my credit card or license. But I can pay cash for the night. I'll check out first thing in the morning." I tried to soften my voice. "I just need a place to crash for the night before I get back on the road."

She eyed me warily as I tried and failed to play the damsel in distress.

"I don't want to fall asleep at the wheel," I pleaded.

The lady huffed. "If I hear any ruckus coming from your room, I'm kicking you out. And I'm gonna walk through your room to make sure you don't take nothin' that don't belong to you before you leave. We've got cameras, and I'm here all night, so I'll know if you set foot out of your door."

"Yes. Of course," I said as I shuffled a stack of bills through the small cut-out in the plexiglass divider.

She took the cash, counted it out, and handed me a key. "5A is yours. Ice and vending machines are out front."

I hurried out before she changed her mind, grabbed my overnight bag from my car, and scurried into 5A.

I started on my routine as soon as the door was unlocked.

I kept the door open while I cleared each room. It was an old-school motel—simple but clean. There were no devices I needed to check for hidden cameras, but I still checked every nook and cranny. I balled up a piece of toilet paper and stuffed it in the door's peephole.

I locked up, shoved a spare chair under the door handle, and made sure the curtains were closed.

Sitting on the bed, I opened my bag and pulled out my wallet, tucking away the extra cash beside my driver's license.

3

CARSON JAMES

Soot stained my fingers as I worked the charred wood between my thumb and index finger. Black dust covered my hand, but I didn't care. The burned shard I'd held on to the last two years fueled the embers of hate burning inside me.

Hate for all the changes made without giving me a say.

Hate for how everyone seemed so damn excited about building a hotel and restaurant on my land.

Hate for the constant barrage of visitors traipsing over the grass, walking where they shouldn't, and making noise at all hours of the night.

Hate for the lights that dimmed the stars.

The ranch was my birthplace and would be my grave. It was my solace. This land was my universe. Nothing mattered outside the fence. Not a damn thing.

That was until trouble started coming to us.

Trouble. I set the ash-covered wood on my nightstand and grabbed a handkerchief to wipe my hand. That word had been rolling around in my head for the last twenty-four hours.

Trouble.

It's what I had called her. Lennon—the woman I'd fucked in the hallway of the Silver Spur. *Trouble.*

A stupid smile crossed my face. I remembered every soft gasp and desperate moan that had escaped her mouth as I held her against the wall.

The digital clock glared at me, taunting the fact that I hadn't slept a wink, and my day was about to start.

It was still dark out, but that's what I preferred—working sun-up to sun-down. Feeling one with the earth and the animals. Staying away from the trespassers.

But I didn't get to do that today. Maybe that's why I hadn't slept. It wasn't because I'd been reminiscing over a quick fuck in the back of a bar.

Nope. While I sat in a crowded office, forced to listen to my sister-in-law drone on and on about schedules I didn't give two shits about, my guys were free to go out and care for the herd.

The opening and closing of doors in the bunkhouse was my wake-up call.

I tugged my jeans up, buckling my belt as I stepped into my boots. I grabbed a shirt out of the dresser drawer and pulled it over my head as I headed out the door.

Two of my guys were in the kitchen making breakfast while people filtered in and out of the bathrooms, getting ready for the day or going to bed.

I grabbed an insulated cup out of the cabinet above the sink, emptied the remnants of the coffee pot into it, then started a fresh brew for the rest of the house.

If I was going to get through this management meeting without killing someone, I needed to be caffeinated.

Fucking management.

I hated that title.

I didn't want to be a manager. Meetings, business updates, investors... None of that interested me. All I wanted was to spend my time in the fields working with cattle.

My boots squished in the dew-covered grass as bodies floated around the ranch like ghosts. Cars packed the lodge's parking lot as new employees arrived to prepare for the grand opening.

No cattle ranch should have a parking lot. That might have pissed me off the most.

A dust plume rose as a car with out-of-state plates sped down the path as if the driver had stolen it. That pissed me off more than the parking lot.

How was I supposed to tolerate watching outsiders disrespect my land, my family, and me? I yanked the door to the ranch office open so hard it surprised me when it didn't fall off the hinges.

"Oh good. Mr. Sunshine is here," Cassandra clipped as she filled a plate from the breakfast spread my mom had made for the meeting.

I flipped Cassandra the bird and sipped my coffee.

Brooke snickered as she munched on a biscuit and brushed the crumbs off her baby bump. She and my brother, Ray, had married pretty quick after she got pregnant with their first child. Now, baby number two was on the way.

It was strange having little kids around the ranch again. For the longest time, it had just been my two oldest nieces, Bree and Gracie. Now, Bree was about to graduate high school and go off to college. Gracie spent less and less time around the ranch as her fifteen-year-old social schedule got busier and busier.

Charlotte, Becks and Nate's little girl, was starting kindergarten.

Brooke and Ray's son, Seth, had just turned two. And from the look of her blissfully happy smile as she smoothed her hand over her belly, the Griffith baby boom wasn't slowing down anytime soon.

"Morning, honey," Mom said as she handed me a kolache.

"Morning."

She stifled a smile. "I swear, I used to get more words out of Ray. What's got you so quiet these days?"

"Just work," I mumbled as I took a bite.

"We all work," she countered. "I saw your truck leave the other night. You were gone for quite some time. Came back real late."

I shrugged. "Just needed to get out of town and take a breather. Too many people."

That wasn't true. I wasn't entirely opposed to people. I was just opposed to people being where they weren't supposed to be. Namely, my land.

She patted my arm. "You'll get used to it. It's a transition for us all."

"Uncle CJ!"

I looked over my shoulder as the door opened and my niece, Charlotte, bolted in.

I scooped her up and propped her up on my hip. "There's my Charlie Bear," I said as I dropped a kiss on her head. "Did your dad feed you yet?"

She shook her head. "Daddy's sleeping. Mom said Grandma made breakfast."

Becks slipped in the door. "Little Miss was up at four this morning." She yawned. "Jet lag is the worst."

As much as I hated management meetings, at least it was

mostly family. My nieces and nephew were growing up the same way I did, running free, sprouting up like weeds, surrounded by family and legacy.

"Alright. Listen up and we can get through this quickly and painlessly," Cassandra said over the chorus of conversations. "The soft opening for the lodge this weekend went well. Abbey, the manager over there, is working with the lodge employees to iron out a few kinks before the grand opening. Most of the guests have checked out, but we do have a few staying throughout the week, so be on your best behavior."

I withheld an eye roll. I didn't feel like being bitched out this early in the morning.

"Uncle Christian!" Charlie squealed when my older brother slipped into the meeting fashionably late. She reached out, wiggling out of my arms and into his.

"Hey, sprout." He gave her a hug, then guided her to the breakfast spread on Cassandra's desk. "What sounds good?"

"Like I was saying to those who were on time," Cassandra said, pointing the comment at her husband. "Restaurant staff will be arriving this week and begin soft launching. Chef DeRossi got here last night and will be staying in one of the cabins. The other cabins are reserved for VIP guests. On grand-opening night, we're having a family dinner with a few investors. Everyone's expected to be there."

Something about hearing "family dinner" and "investors" in the same sentence didn't sit right with me.

Christian sidled up to me as Charlotte scurried off to her adoring public. "You got back awful late the other night. Something I need to know about?"

"Everything's fine," I clipped.

"You don't usually leave when you have time off. Not that long anyway."

I arched an eyebrow. "Had some errands to run."

A tight smile quirked beneath his beard. "Errands. Right. Any of those errands happen to take you up to that bar out in Maren?"

I chuckled. "I don't go up there for topless bull riding anymore, if that's what you're asking."

Our middle brother, Ray, had ruined that for us when he bragged about Brooke—the newest sister-in-law—taking part in the old tradition.

"Glad you got out," Christian said. "Have a good time?"

I thought back to Lennon. To the way she got my blood simmering in more ways than one.

I'd give my left nut to see her again, but she struck me as a tumbleweed. Not prone to sticking around.

Cassandra droned on. "Brooke has a full schedule with the equine program, and we have a field trip this Thursday. CJ, keep an eye out for any people who look lost or are wandering off. The signage I ordered came last night. Can you get some guys to put it up so we can curb people away from going onto our personal property or near the cattle operation?"

I nodded but didn't say a word.

"Good enough for me," she clipped. "Be helpful and accommodating to the new hires."

I snorted. That was rich coming from her.

Cassandra pointed a raised eyebrow at me. "You got something you wanna say?"

"No, ma'am." A smirk crept across my face. She hated it when I called her "ma'am," but I wasn't above a little malicious compliance.

Cassandra growled. Christian choked on his bite. Brooke and Becks giggled. Even my mom bit back a smile.

"Play nice, you two," Christian said.

I watched the clock through the rest of Cassandra's spiel and the annoying follow-up questions that didn't need to be asked. I kept out of trouble by keeping my mouth full of kolaches and biscuits with strawberry butter.

It wasn't a surprise that Ray's first venture back into hanging out with our family was at a dinner my mom made. She was a fucking awesome cook.

When the conversation pivoted to the wedding and special event space outside the lodge, I bowed out.

My boots ate up the ground as I beelined for the stables. Anarchy was ready and waiting. Gruff blasts of air radiated from her nostrils. She was just as antsy as I was to get away from it all. I tacked her up before anyone else could show up at the barn and demand my time.

"Let's go, Anny," I muttered as I hopped on to the saddle and rode away from it all.

4

LENNON

"Chef Maddox, come to my office when you have a moment. Chef Dorsey will cover you."

I hated that phrase. It could be about something mundane, or I might be about to get fired. We had prepared all week for the grand opening, and things had been going well. Still, I felt like I was being called to the principal's office.

"Yes, Chef," I said as I lowered the flame on the burner and babysat the skillet until Maddie hustled over. The last thing I wanted was for service to slow down.

I pulled off my apron and hung it by the door, uncuffing the sleeves to my chef's coat as I hurried down the hall to the administrative offices. I paused at the door to catch my breath before letting myself in.

"You wanted to see me, Chef?"

Chef Luca DeRossi looked up from the laptop perched on the otherwise empty desk. "Yes, you can leave the door open."

My stomach sank. That was never good. Was HR about to come in? Did the restaurant even have HR yet?

Luca chuckled. "Relax, Lennon. You're not in trouble."

I let out a breath.

I didn't know why I assumed the worst in Chef DeRossi. Maybe it was because I assumed the worst in everyone.

But he had never been anything but good to me. Great, even. His wife was the same—talented and driven as hell, but kind.

People like that were rare, which was exactly why I didn't trust them.

No one was *that* good.

I glanced over my shoulder toward the kitchen. "Is something wrong? I thought you wanted me running the line."

"I do. Chef Dorsey and I are about to go upstairs for dinner with the Griffith family and some opening night formalities. Jessica said the last of the reservations just checked in with the hostess, so—"

"Get ready for another wave for the front line, then start prepping for the staff dinner while the pastry team is doing dessert service."

He cracked a smile. "You're doing great. Are you ready to take over when Madeline and I leave next week?"

"No," I said, quick and firm.

Chef DeRossi, the executive chef and restaurateur for The Kitchen at the Griffith Brothers Ranch, had been hands-on all week. He had been working to the bone to get my team up to speed in a new kitchen. His wife, a badass pastry chef, created the dessert menu and trained the pastry team.

Still, I knew I wouldn't be able to rely on him for much longer. He had other places to be.

"Yes, you are," he said. "You kicked ass for me in New York and everywhere else. I have no doubt you can handle this. The hours are better and the menu is simpler. This is child's play for you, Lennon. And you've got my number and Maddie's. Call whenever."

I clenched my jaw to keep from saying something that would have him questioning if I was the right fit. I knew I wasn't the right fit.

The devil on my shoulder had chipped away at my confidence on the 1,500 mile trip from New York to Texas, reminding me I was nothing more than a pity hire.

I cracked a smile. "You're sure the Griffiths know you hired a jailbird to run The Kitchen?"

His eyes softened. "They're good people. They want good people to work for them. You're good people."

I didn't say anything, and Luca knew why.

His eyes narrowed. "The appropriate response is 'Yes, Chef.'"

He was forcing me to believe in myself, and I hated that. It was also why I had never tried to work for anyone else.

Some chefs spent a year at a restaurant, then moved on for a year-long stint somewhere else to get different experience. I had always worked within the safety of the DeRossi Hospitality Group.

I nodded. "Yes, Chef."

He drummed his fingers on the desk. "Come up to the rooftop dining room before you start prepping the staff meal. I want to introduce you to everyone."

"Yes, Chef," I said as I hurried out before he could get another word in.

I narrowly avoided two bodies as I ran out of Chef DeRossi's office—my future office—like my ass was on fire.

"You okay, Chef Maddox?" Hands clasped around my arms to keep me from crashing into the wall.

I fought the urge to jerk away and forced a smile at

Hannah Jane Hayes. She was an event planner that Chef DeRossi had brought in to assist the front of house manager during the grand opening.

Jessica, the front of house manager, beamed. "I've heard nothing but raving reviews all night. Y'all are crushing it."

"Thank you," I clipped as I hurried back into the kitchen, grabbed my apron, and kicked Chef Dorsey out of my station.

I pressed the top of a ribeye to check its doneness, then added a splash of whiskey, tipping the skillet into the flame. I let out a heavy breath as I dropped a knob of butter and a pinch of herbs into the pan and started basting the steak.

There was safety in the fire.

Fire was predictable. There was no pretense that it was anything other than dangerous. It behaved exactly as expected. If you fucked with it, that was your own damn fault.

I fell into the routine of dinner service, sending plates flying out the double doors.

Thanks to Chef DeRossi taking me under his wing, this was my third grand opening. Launching a restaurant was a strange sort of beast. Chef DeRossi's hospitality company used staff from his existing restaurants to work alongside the new hires until everyone got enough experience. Chefs, managers, and servers formed a dream team of food and hospitality professionals. But this time, I wouldn't be flying back to New York with the sparse team from Nonna's—the Manhattan eatery where I had just gotten my final paycheck. I'd be staying.

This was home now.

I worked behind the rookie expediter, scrutinizing each dish before they went out to the guests.

Jessica popped her head in. "Chef Maddox?"

I glanced up as I used a side towel to clean the rim of a deep-bowled plate. "Yes, Ms. Powell?"

"Chef DeRossi is ready for you to join everyone upstairs."

I held back a groan and put on the stone-cold face of professional indifference. "Be right up."

The last thing I wanted was to waste time playing twenty questions. I'd dodge anything personal, thank everyone for the opportunity to run the restaurant, then hightail it back to the kitchen where I belonged.

After all, I had already met most of them. Cassandra Griffith, a fire-breathing she-beast, was the ranch's property manager. She had made herself available during the week of menu trials and the soft opening.

Christian, her husband, had said his hellos during my second day on-site, and then stolen a snack out of the communal fridge of staff leftovers.

Rumor had it, one of the Griffith brothers was some famous bull rider, but I didn't know jack shit about the rodeo.

As far as I was concerned, if they weren't working in my kitchen or signing my paychecks, they didn't matter. But I owed Chef DeRossi everything. I could suffer through a few minutes of pleasantries.

"Julian, you're on the grill," I said to the new guy who had just joined the team yesterday.

I trudged up two flights of stairs to the rooftop dining area. The sun had set, and a chill bit my neck as I pulled my toque off and tucked it under my arm. I preferred working with a skullcap, but Chef DeRossi had insisted on the obnoxiously tall chef's hats for the grand opening.

First impressions were everything.

String lights glowed overhead while small lanterns illuminated the tables. Standing heaters kept the diners comfortable as they finished their meal under twilight stars.

The Griffith family had a permanently reserved farmhouse table so they could gather for group meals without having to call ahead.

From what I saw on my daily drive, it looked like a lot of them lived on the ranch.

Heads turned as I came around the corner, but the old man at the head of the table continued speaking.

Chef DeRossi sat at the end of the table with his wife, Chef Dorsey, tucked under his arm. They were nauseatingly in love with each other.

Sitting on the other side of Chef DeRossi was Isaac Lawson. He was a billionaire with a capital "B." Everyone gave him a wide berth, probably out of intimidation.

I would have been intimidated, had I not cooked for him a million times at my old job. He was a regular at Nonna's.

Bodies shuffled around as the guy speaking took his seat and Luca stood up.

"There's one more person I wanted to introduce." He turned and motioned for me to join the table. "Chef Maddox, you're just in time."

All eyes were on me as I crossed the rooftop.

Cassandra and Christian Griffith sat together with their daughters squished on either side of them. A man in a wheelchair was corralling a toddler on his lap and had his arm around a very pregnant woman. A red-headed woman and a girl who was her spitting image sat together. The guy seated next to them had a presence that screamed "military."

My gaze fell on the cowboy I hadn't seen around here yet, and I froze.

Chef DeRossi buttoned his suit jacket as he moved to

stand beside me. "If you haven't had a chance to pop into the kitchen before tonight, allow me to introduce you to Chef Maddox. Lennon is my talented sous chef and will be the acting executive chef when I'm not present. Lennon, would you like to say a few words?"

"Lennon—"

But my name didn't come from Chef DeRossi this time. It came from *him*.

The cowboy from the bar.

All eyes turned to him. To CJ.

My cheeks burned, but I gritted my teeth and kept my face neutral. My body didn't get the message that neutral was what we were going for, though. It vividly recalled the sensation of him trailing his hand down my back as I leaned over a pool table. How it felt when he pinned me up against the wall and fucked me senseless. The sound of his rough grunts and the way his brows knitted together. The way his strong lips parted, and how his sharp tongue turned soft when he came.

CJ wiped his mouth, tossed his napkin down, and pushed away from the table. "You've gotta be fucking kidding me."

That wasn't the reaction I expected. Not from the guy who had wanted another drink after our tryst.

"Pipe down, slugger. Ain't nothing that serious," I said with a playful smirk, tossing his words from the bar back at him.

CJ's glare brimmed with vitriol and vinegar. The playful banter we had once shared had vanished. He nearly knocked over an empty chair as he barreled away from the table. "Let me guess. You hustled your way into this job like you were hustling everyone at—"

"Excuse me?" I snapped. It was better than blurting out, *"What the fuck is your problem?"*

"Carson James!" the oldest Griffith lady gasped.

He stalked toward me with a heat and violence in his eyes that I didn't fully understand. Gone was the flirtatious cowboy who had fucked me in a bar hallway.

Lucifer wore a white Stetson.

Whatever his deal was, I didn't care. I'd match his energy and make him regret it. I lifted my chin and met the embers head-on.

"Should've fuckin' known," he growled with a terse shake of his head. "Trouble always seems to find us here."

Chef DeRossi glanced between the two of us. "Len—"

"I should get back to the line," I clipped, then nodded toward the family. "Pleasure to meet you all." I turned and looked at CJ. "*Most* of you."

He clenched his fist and let a derisive sneer slip. "Bullshit."

I narrowed my eyes. "You'd know a little something about that, wouldn't you, cowboy?"

Murmurs rose from the table as I turned and stomped toward the door.

CJ's shout caught me by surprise. "You don't get to storm out. I'm the one who gets to storm out."

"Well, we don't always get what we want, do we?" I snapped.

Cassandra snickered. "I like her already."

Chef DeRossi's wore a calm gaze, but I had been around him enough to know when he was about to smash a plate. "*My office*," he clipped between smiling teeth. "Two minutes."

5

CARSON JAMES

Sweat beaded on the back of my neck. I gritted my teeth as I pinched the wire between the teeth of the pliers and twisted it together. I usually didn't mind the monotony of repairing breaks in the fence. It gave me time to think. To be alone and at peace with myself.

I loved the quiet.

But the quiet had turned to acid, eating away at me today. I regretted sending the rest of the ranch hands to take care of tasks at the front of the property, per Cassandra's request.

A few guys were checking the cattle and monitoring the herd movement as we gently guided them from pasture to pasture, but there was no one close enough to carry on a conversation with. Radio chatter was restricted to business only. I was left with the whispers of wind that carried thoughts of her to me, no matter how far I went to escape them.

Trying to get away from those thoughts was how I found myself on the back line of the property, fixing a fence.

A diesel engine growled over the horizon. I squinted into

the afternoon sun to try and make out who was coming to bitch me out about last night.

I didn't want to be at that fucking dinner in the first place. I had better things to do than wear stiff clothes, eat at a fancy table, and listen to a bunch of suits who didn't know a damn thing about ranching.

Then *she* popped up like a goddamn premonition.

Just like that, my dream girl turned into a walking, talking nightmare.

I should have fucking known.

Good things don't happen to Griffiths.

Like I had conjured it, Nate's truck crested the horizon and rumbled through the field. Anny glared from the spot where she was grazing, and let out a sharp huff.

"You're out quite a ways," he hollered as he hopped out and slammed the door.

Anny grunted out a response, so I didn't have to.

Nate trudged through the soft soil. With each step, he left depressions behind.

Anny bristled at his presence. When he edged a little too close for comfort, she snapped at him.

It wasn't a surprise. If the human wasn't Brooke or me, she'd go on offense.

"Jesus, fuck—" He leaped away, eyeing my horse as he gave her a wide berth and kept walking. "Was she an asshole before you named her Anarchy or did the personality grow to match the name?"

I snorted. "Always been like that. What are you doing out here?"

Nate had retired from the military years ago and traveled with his wife, Becks, supporting her career.

Nate and I had never been close, but he was one of the

only people I'd rant about work with since he didn't work for the ranch. That was the extent of our relationship.

Christian was technically my boss, which knocked him out of the running for my complaints. When Ray was traveling the rodeo circuit, I'd call him up. But he had enough on his plate these days. He didn't need me to add to it.

Nate chuckled as he shoved the sleeves of his Henley up his forearms, revealing deep scar tissue, and grabbed a pair of work gloves out of the bed of his truck. "Asked around. Heard you were out here fixing the fence. Wanna talk about last night?"

"Not particularly."

"Too bad." He grabbed a coil of wire and started on the next section. "I drove all the way out here."

I gritted my teeth as I pinched two ends with the pliers and gave them a sharp twist. "Already got bitched out by Chris."

"Who is she?" Nate said, skirting the comment.

Flashes of Lennon's head tipping back against that brick wall danced in my vision. The way her fight made the yielding that much sweeter. The way she clung to me, curling in when she came.

"An ex?" Nate guessed when I didn't offer anything up.

A person had to date to have exes. The ranch had always been my love.

Nate paused and leaned on the fence post. "Carson. Be straight with me."

I hated it when he used that tone. It made him sound like our father.

Sixteen years sat between Nate and me. I had just turned two when he went off to West Point.

I guess it was the age difference, but Nate and I never felt like brothers.

When I was seventeen, our parents pulled me out of school early, sat me down, and told me that he had been injured in an attack overseas.

They were both crying. Christian was on the phone with God-knows-who, managing the situation. Ray was on his way down from Colorado to be with the family. Gretchen, my late sister-in-law, had finally gotten Nate's first wife, Vanessa, to calm down.

And there I was, sitting on the couch, feeling absolutely nothing.

I was sad, sure. I was worried like any normal person would be. But I didn't feel the gut-wrenching ache of pain for a loved one that everyone else did.

Nate had been there for the occasional birthday or graduation when the military allowed him to be. I didn't fault him for not being around. But I also chose not to feel bad for feeling the same level of affection toward him that I felt for the random relatives we saw once a year at family reunions.

To his credit, he had put in more effort over the years he had been back on the ranch, but time lost was a chasm that couldn't be refilled.

Nate and I would shoot the breeze. I'd complain about whatever dumb shit my new hires had gotten into. He'd tell me about all the places he and Becks had been traveling to. And that was that.

There was a reason he didn't know if I had exes.

I never told him. I never felt the need to. That wasn't the kind of thing a person told a stranger.

My knees sang as I knelt to fasten the bottom strip of wire. "Doesn't matter who she is."

He chuckled. "It sure didn't seem that way when she had you riled up just by stepping in the room. I need to ask Cass if she has the security tapes. That's some good entertainment."

I almost let "she's nobody" slip from my mouth, but it would have been a dirty lie. She was someone I hadn't stopped thinking about.

"Didn't know who she was. Met her at a bar."

"And the fact that you both work on the same ranch didn't come up in conversation?"

"Didn't exactly swap life stories."

I would have if we had made it to that second drink . . .

"So, she's some girl you met at a bar. Big deal. Did she slash your tires or something? Because that's about the only thing I can think of that would—"

"It'll come to you."

He paused. "You hooked up with her?"

Since I wasn't about to offer the details of me fucking her against the hallway wall of a crowded bar, I just grunted.

Nate rested against the fence post. "I'm failing to see the problem here. So, you got some action. Not like workplace romances are forbidden around here."

Yeah, my brothers and their wives were proof of that.

"Not a romance. Not interested. Not with her."

"That's a lot of nots. You sure you're ready to eat three helpings of crow when the inevitable happens?"

I shot him a glare that had him raising his hands in surrender.

"Take it from me," Nate said with a grin. "There's a thin line between love and hate."

"That thin line is my last nerve. And you, Christian, and that whole fucking lodge are dancing all over it. You wanna watch security camera footage of dinner last night? We wouldn't have to have fucking security cameras if there wasn't a goddamn hotel and restaurant on our land. Sketchy shit didn't start happening around here until that fucking revitalization project started."

"Hey," he said in a warning tone. "Cassandra worked hard on that."

"I never said she didn't."

Nate paused. "Have you talked to anyone about that break-in that happened the summer Brooke started working for Ray? When the lodge almost burned to the ground?"

I scoffed. "What a pity that would have been."

He didn't bristle at my sarcasm. "You almost got shot."

I imagined that was the tone he used with new soldiers when he was in the Army. But I wasn't new, and I wasn't under his command.

I clenched my jaw, but he knew he had struck a chord. I kept my eyes trained on my hands.

"Trust me," he said, resting his hands on his hips so I could see the battle scars that warped his arms. "I know how that can fuck with your head."

"But I didn't," I snapped. "And it just proves my point. We don't need this shit around here. It's nothing but trouble."

"Without the revitalization developments, you'd be out of a job."

That one stung, but I didn't let it show. "No one knows for sure that the ranch would have gone under. We were doing fine."

"The numbers didn't lie. I saw the books myself. We were fine until the next drought. Until the next disease outbreak. Until the next market shift or barn needed replacing or piece of equipment broke." He pulled his gloves off with his teeth. "You agreed to it, so you gotta get over it. The lodge and the restaurant and all of it . . . It's here to stay.

The sooner you get on board, the sooner you won't be so fucking miserable all the time."

"You can go," I snapped. "You're not on the payroll anyway."

Nate's demeanor shifted. "I might not be on the payroll, but I live here too. My wife and child live here. So yeah, I have a vested interest just like you do."

I pitched the pliers at the fence post. They hit the wood with a dull, unsatisfying clunk. "Everyone on this goddamn ranch is a fucking sell-out."

"And you think being an asshole makes you the one true Griffith?" he asked with a caustic laugh. "Evolve or die. That's the way it's always been, even before you were conceived."

I packed up my supplies and called Anny over. "Is this where you tell me to make nice with people ruining our land?"

Nate tossed his shit into the bed of his truck and slammed the tailgate. "Don't shoot yourself in the foot trying to pull the trigger on someone else. Sometimes you just have to let it go. She's here to do a job, and so are you. There's hundreds of acres between y'all. I think that's plenty of space."

It wasn't. Because as long as Lennon Maddox was on my ranch, she was in my head.

And I fucking hated it.

6

LENNON

"Chef, the family would like to offer their compliments on the meal," Jessica said as she dipped into the kitchen and grabbed a cup of water.

Seriously, what was with the Griffith family? They ate at the restaurant together way too often. A handful of them would pop in to eat almost every day, and it wasn't just the married couples. It was the brothers eating with the sisters-in-law. Sometimes it was Mrs. Griffith with her daughters-in-law. Sometimes it was Mr. and Mrs. Griffith with their grandkids.

After a week working at The Kitchen at the Griffith Brothers Ranch, I could count on four things: death, taxes, the Griffiths sending their compliments, and CJ avoiding the restaurant at all costs.

I looked up from the expo line. "Do I have to go up?"

She gave me a pitiful look. "Sorry. Chef DeRossi made me promise to make you play nice with them before he left."

Yeah, after he gave me a brutal dressing down for losing my shit on CJ in front of the entire Griffith family.

It wasn't like I could tell him why we went at each other like cats and dogs. I just had to take the warning and choke down the hate.

I groaned under my breath. "Julian, cover expo until I get back."

Julian, the guy I had manning the grill today, moved over to oversee the plates going out. Lunch service was almost over, thank God, which meant he could manage both stations.

"Sure thing, Len," he said. His wandering eyes looked me up and down while I made sure everything was in its place.

Zach, the saucier on shift today, lifted his eyes and looked between us.

"That's Chef Maddox," I said, correcting Julian as I pulled my apron off and mentally counted down the minutes until I clocked out.

Service through the beginning of the week was slow, so we operated on a limited menu. Most of the guests at the lodge checked out on Sunday, returning to their lives. The new wave of weekenders wouldn't show up until Thursday or Friday.

I rushed to the Griffith family's private table and braced myself for well-meaning niceties that would only slow down my day.

Cassandra was dining with Mr. Griffith today. His silver hair rustled in the breeze that danced across the rooftop. An empty chair sat between them with a mostly finished plate at its setting. Probably Mrs. Griffith.

"How was everything today?" I asked as I approached the table, donning the veil of practiced confidence.

I had watched Chef DeRossi recite that question

millions of times. It put everyone at ease and started the conversation, but kept it to the point.

"Excellent," Cassandra said as she dabbed her lips. "How's everything downstairs?"

"Running smoothly."

"Glad to hear it. Chef DeRossi put together a great team."

"I agree," I said, turning to Silas Griffith. "How was your lunch, Mr. Griffith?"

"Spectacular, Chef Maddox. You've got a real gift, sweetheart."

Being called sweetheart made me cringe a little inside, but I tamped it down. The hairs on the back of my neck stood on end as a shadow grew over the table like a bad omen. I knew it was him before he spoke.

"Business must not be too good if the cooks are doubling as servers," CJ clipped, still hovering at my back.

Cassandra rolled her eyes. "Stop being a dick."

I choked down the desire to slap him with a snappy retort and, instead, put on my employee-mandated manners. "I hope you enjoyed your meal, Mr. Griffith," I hissed through gritted teeth.

He crossed his arms and shifted behind me, making my spine turn electric. I could practically see that stupid smirk on his face. "That pained you to say, didn't it?"

His cologne pained me. It's what I smelled on my skin after I left the bar that night. Scent was a powerful memory vault.

I pursed my lips and addressed Cassandra and CJ's father. "If you'll excuse me, I should get back downstairs. You two enjoy the rest of your day."

A hand trailed across my lower back as I turned and

faced the wall of ornery cowboy attitude. "What about me?" he prodded. "You don't want me to enjoy my day?"

A slow smile curled at the corner of my mouth as I lifted my chin so my words stayed between us. "You can have the day you deserve for getting me in trouble the other night."

He chuckled quietly. The sound was dark and promising. "What's that saying? Can't stand the heat, get out of the kitchen?"

"You set foot in my kitchen, and you'll be on the menu. I'm good with knives, cowboy."

He cut his eyes toward me. "I think you're forgetting whose name is on the building, trouble. That name means something around here, and it's one you'll never have."

"Like I'd even want it."

"Go fuck yourself," he hissed.

"I'd say the same to you, but from the way your head is up your ass, it looks like you're already doing a fine job of fucking yourself."

Cassandra snorted, and I realized our hissed jabs weren't at all discreet.

"Stay out of my way, cowboy," I clipped as I brushed past him. Our hands touched for a split second. I cursed under my breath as the sparks between us danced in the afternoon light.

RULE NUMBER ONE: Committing crimes is not a group project. Do that shit by yourself and leave everyone else out of it.

Rule Number Two: Don't start fights. Finish them.

Rule Number Three: Don't try to hustle a hustler.

"I'm sorry, Hon. With your record and no credit history, it's against our policy to rent to ya."

I gritted my teeth and plastered on a pleading smile. "I have references from my employer and my former roommates. I always pay rent on time, I'm clean, and I'm very, very quiet. I work a lot, so I'm not home to make trouble. I don't have any pets and I don't smoke. I moved here for a job, and I *need* this apartment."

I usually wasn't one for begging, but I was running out of options.

The old lady across the desk at the property management office sighed and turned to her computer, clicking through a few pages.

Sweat beaded across my body as I nervously tugged on the long sleeves that hid my tattoos. I had taken out my nose piercing, lightened up my face with a little makeup, and pulled my hair back so it was mostly one color.

The lady turned back and gave me a sad shake of her head. "Sorry. If it was only the credit, I'd give you a pass. But a violent offense is something I can't overlook."

"There's a letter from my former parole officer that vouches—"

"I'm sorry, darling."

I left the rental office with my tail between my legs and headed for my car. The afternoon sun was blazing, even though it was a week past Thanksgiving. Then again, December in Texas was a far cry from December in New York.

I, for one, wasn't complaining.

Three rental company rejections in the span of an hour-and-a-half were cause for a pity party. I needed to figure something out fast.

Someone six-feet tall wasn't meant to sleep curled up in the backseat of a two-door sedan.

Hallmark movies lied. Small towns sucked.

I had always been able to find somewhere to rent or a couch to crash on in the city, even if they weren't the best options.

The rental rejections stung. Maybe I had tipped off some backwoods phone tree that warned every landlord within fifty miles to ignore my application.

Bright red hair had me stopping in my tracks as I hurried back to my car. The color was too specific to be coincidence. The woman was too strikingly familiar. She turned, and sharp eyes met mine. I couldn't quite place her, but a heavy sense of déjà vu cloaked the distance between us.

I darted into a coffee shop, bolted to the bathroom, and locked the door behind me, thankful that it wasn't a multiple-stall situation.

I could still hear that sinister voice that had lodged in my brain since I was a terrified teenager.

There were some acquaintances that I never wanted to see again.

I counted fifty Mississippis, then unlocked the door and opened it a crack. There was a redhead in the lobby with a mini-me beside her, but it wasn't the woman from the sidewalk.

Maybe I had hallucinated.

I blamed it on the unusual autumn heat, and stress about finding somewhere to live.

A bulletin board hung on the wall between the bathrooms and the lobby hallway. I crept out and studied it for a moment, grabbing a few flyers advertising rentals and roommate inquiries.

"Lennon?"

I jumped at the sound of a woman's voice. The redhead had walked over and was smiling at me.

"Depends on who's asking," I hedged.

She laughed. "I'm Rebecca Griffith. I usually go by Becks. I'm Nate's wife. I don't think we've officially met, but I was at the grand opening."

Griffith.

Right. I had seen her a few times around the restaurant, but we had never formally swapped names.

That's when I realized there was a horde of Griffith women in the lobby.

Cassandra was sitting in the corner, regally looking over her subjects. Mrs. Griffith was on the bench seat in the window with Becks's daughter on one side of her and a two-year-old boy on the other. Brooke, the equine program director I had met during orientation, had an oversized muffin resting on top of her baby belly.

Becks smiled warmly. "You should join us."

I didn't have time for coffee, and I was at my limit of professionalism for the day. I wanted to scream, cry, and throw a fucking pity party at how unfair life was. But I didn't have time for that either.

"I should get home. It's been a long day."

"Don't be a stranger, okay?" Becks said. "You work for the ranch. That basically makes you family."

The last thing I wanted was to be "basically family" with her jackass of a brother-in-law.

"It was nice to meet you," I said as I excused myself, and dashed out to my car.

"Home" was a corner of the parking lot at the twenty-four-hour gym where I reluctantly shelled out twenty dollars a month in exchange for a nationwide membership.

I tried to use cash as much as I could, but some things were unavoidable. I wasn't off the grid, per se, but I was cautious. Twenty bucks wasn't bad when it meant I had access to showers, WiFi, and a locker room whenever I wanted.

For once, I was thankful that it wasn't winter in New York. I crossed my fingers and hoped that I'd find something permanent before the chill made its way to Texas.

I pulled down the shades to black out my windows and made sure to lock myself inside.

I grabbed a makeup wipe from my gym bag and scrubbed off the absurdly pink-tinted shades I had dabbed on to look presentable.

When it was dark, I'd go inside, walk a slow mile on the treadmill while my phone charged in the locker room, then call the numbers from the rental flyers I had found at the coffee shop.

I crawled into the backseat, slid into my sleeping bag, and stretched out as best as I could. Endless shifts on my feet at the restaurant had jacked up my back. The seat belt receptacle digging into my hip didn't help.

The shirt I had been wearing that night at the bar was balled up by my head. Earthy notes of nutmeg, cinnamon, and cedar lulled me into a trance. My boiling contempt for CJ Griffith's attitude turned to a gentle simmer as the scent of him chipped away at my stress.

7

CARSON JAMES

"Shitter's all yours, new guy," Jackson, the pain in my ass former new guy, said to the actual new guy, Brady.

I glanced up from the spot at the kitchen table where I had been pushing around the remnants of bulk-batch meatloaf and mashed potatoes. The rest of my appetite vanished at the stench that wafted out of the communal downstairs bathroom.

I grabbed my plate, scraped the crumbs into the trash, and loaded it into the mostly full dishwasher.

"Who's on dish duty this week?" I asked the house.

Murmurs rose from the strewn-about bodies that were relaxing after a long day of working cattle.

"New guy," Cody said. "I had it last week."

"Tell him to start the dishwasher and wipe the sink. I don't want ants coming in."

"Sure thing, Boss Man," Jackson said.

I hated being called boss man, but if it reminded him that I was in charge, I'd let it slide.

The sound from some annoying-ass show on the TV was

way too loud. The voices were grating. Even if I went up to my room and shut the door, the noise would carry.

"You heading out?" Jackson asked, tipping his patchy-bearded face over the edge of the couch. "Thought you were working tomorrow night."

"Just going on a walk," I muttered as I shoved my feet into my boots and headed out the door.

I used to love living in the bunkhouse, even before it was the nice one we had now.

Back when the ranch hands lived in the cabins—the run-down ones Cassandra and Christian had turned into fancy-pants rentals—it was like being in the Boy Scouts.

When we all moved into the new bunkhouse, it was like a frat house. Work hard, play harder.

But I wasn't a kid anymore. I didn't like seeing abandoned beer cans and bottles on every horizontal surface. I yelled at people if they left the lights on. If the TV volume was over twelve, they knew to turn it down. I ruled the thermostat with an iron fist. The chore chart wasn't a suggestion. It was an order.

I used to love the camaraderie of the ranch hands—back when I was just one of the guys working the herd, and Christian was the one telling people to get their shit together.

Now I was the one who had to keep everyone in line. I could see why Christian was okay with taking over for our father as the foreman.

The night air was cool and crisp. I looked up into the black sky, searching for the constellations I usually tracked to calm my mind, but I couldn't see the stars.

The bright lights from the lodge and restaurant obscured them all.

Fuck that. Fuck all that.

Headlights flashed as a car carrying people who had no business being on this property sped toward the lodge. I was half tempted to jump out into the road and scare the shit out of them. We had fucking speed limit signs for a reason.

What if one of my nieces or my nephew had been out for a walk? It wasn't safe for them to wander freely anymore.

Smoke tickled my nose. That smell was usually cause for alarm. Smoke on a ranch was generally a bad thing. Wildfires could wipe out a generational legacy in a day.

But this smoke wasn't a warning. The air carried the scent of slow-cooking beef and a dry rub. Although I had just eaten dinner, it made my mouth water.

I followed the smoke instead of the stars, knowing I was a glutton for punishment.

If my momma had started smoking a brisket, it wouldn't be ready for a day. And if she was still out tending to the fire, I was going to get a piece of her mind.

She hadn't let me off the hook after my little showdown with Lennon at the restaurant during the grand opening.

But in my defense, I didn't want to be there to begin with, and I let it be known.

The tendrils of smoke led me away from the ranch house my parents had called home for as long as I could remember. Even more infuriating was that they led me toward the restaurant.

I saw the glow of the embers as someone stood beside the smoker and prodded around in the firebox.

The person was too tall to be my mom, but the shadows dancing around obscured any other identifiable features.

It definitely wasn't Christian. Cassandra cooked, but wasn't the type to cook outside. If it were Brooke, the ranch would have already gone up in flames.

A twig snapped under my boot, and I froze.

Black and white hair glowed in the firelight like tendrils snaking up from Hades.

Soft features hardened. "What are you doing?" Lennon snapped, wielding the fire poker like a sword.

"Put that down before you hurt yourself, slugger," I clipped in haughty derision.

She didn't.

"Jesus Christ," I muttered as I grabbed the handle of the poker and yanked it out of her hands. "Didn't your parents teach you not to run with scissors or point knives at people? That applies here."

"Actually, they didn't," she said as she elbowed me out of the way and grabbed the poker out of my hand, setting it beside the firebox.

I paused and looked around as one of the exterior lights of the restaurant bathed us in a dim glow.

A lawn chair sat next to the smoker. She had a pillow and blanket, a paperback book, thermometers to check the meat, and a giant insulated travel mug.

"Don't know if you're aware, but there's a whole-ass hotel here now. No need to sleep outside with the animals."

Lennon rolled her eyes. Back at the bar, it had been a turn-on—a signal of good-humored banter and teasing. But the amicable nature of it all was long gone.

She balled her fists, but kept them pinned to her side. "Get lost."

I chuckled, crossing my arms as I moved to stand in front of her. "You really want to hit me, don't you?"

"Yes," she said, lifting her chin. "But if I mess up that pretty face of yours, I'll lose my job."

"And what a pity it would be to never see you again." I looked at the restaurant. "It'd be one person down, seventy to go."

She stepped closer. The smoke mixed with the smell of her perfume made me think of the Angel of Death. Wickedly beautiful, intoxicating, and deadly.

"The bar was a mistake, but it happened. I don't know what your problem is with me. If you leave me alone, we won't have an issue. If you keep trying to get me fired, you'll have hell to pay."

I stepped closer this time, bumping her furry boots with the steel toes of mine. "Is that right?" I smirked. "Because my last name is on the gate you drive through to get to your job. So I think the only person with something to lose here is you."

She eased closer. "Walk away, cowboy."

My gaze fell to the tight workout jacket she was in. The way it hugged every sinful curve of her breasts. The way the zipper was just low enough that I could enjoy the valley of her cleavage. The memory of what those tits looked and felt like was burned in my mind.

"You sure you want me to walk away?" I murmured.

Her eyes were heavy. "More than anything."

Growing up as one of four boys, I found it interesting to see how different we were, even though we shared DNA and had the same parents.

Nate was the type to tell us not to play with fire.

Christian was the one to manage the crisis when someone inevitably did.

Ray would poke at the sparks for the thrill of it.

I was the one who touched the flames, got burned, then always went back for seconds.

I wrapped a strand of long black hair around my finger, tethering her to me as I tipped my head to the side. "Then why did you move closer?"

The outline of the bars that pierced her nipples dotted

the spandex jacket she was wearing. It was an infuriating tease.

"Walk away, Lennon."

"Let me go."

Neither of us moved.

"It was a quick fuck in a bar," she panted. "We didn't even spend the night together. We're both adults. We can let bygones be bygones."

A growl rumbled deep in my chest. "Not when you're on my land, babysitting a smoker all night."

Her breath hitched.

I wouldn't be able to sleep. Not if I was thinking about her out here, alone all night, monitoring the temperatures and the meat and loading more wood into the firebox.

"CJ—"

I tightened my hold on that fucking strand of hair, daring her to move one way or the other. Sharp eyes locked on mine. Her fist was still balled at her side, knuckles clenching in desperate restraint.

"Someone's a little uptight," I murmured as I pressed my chest to hers, teasing those pierced points without my hands.

She sucked in a sharp breath.

"Go ahead, slugger," I teased, lowering my mouth to hers until our lips brushed. "I'll let you get a good swing in."

"If I swing, I'm swinging low."

I chuckled against her mouth. "Still thinking about my dick, huh? It was pretty good, wasn't it?"

Lennon's features turned deadly as she let out a frustrated growl.

"Or maybe—" I rolled my thumb over one nipple piercing "—you need to get that tension out some other way."

She gasped and her pretty eyes fluttered closed.

I let out a pleased chuckle as I felt her nipple pebble under my touch. "That's what I thought."

Lennon melted in my hands as I toyed with her over her jacket, never diving below it to feel the velvet body that had haunted my dreams.

"Wearing leggings can't be comfortable when you're wet for me," I mumbled.

She ground her teeth together. "Who says I'm wet?"

"I'd bet the seventy-five you won from me at the bar that you're wet. You wanna admit I'm right or drop those leggings and let me check?"

Her cheeks flushed in the moonlight. "Fine."

"You're gonna admit that I'm right?"

"Never."

I let go of her hair and cupped her pussy on the outside of her leggings, feeling how damp they already were. "Either you're not wearing panties, or you're going to have to change them."

Lennon whimpered as I teased her slit through the spandex.

"Be a good girl, say my name, and beg me to let you come on my hand."

Her teeth sank into my earlobe. "Never."

The pierce of pain was sobering and arousing all at once. "You've got a long night ahead of you, Len. You sure you want to start eighteen hours out here, all pent up?"

She retaliated by reaching between us and squeezing the outline of my granite cock. "I could say the same about you, cowboy. Don't pretend like I'm the only one who's all worked up."

I grunted as she gripped my dick. "You play dirty."

"Don't try to hustle a hustler, cowboy. A girl's gotta eat."

I pinched her nipple. "Don't test me. I'll get you on your knees and make you choke on my dick."

"I bite," she gasped.

Our weighted breaths were the only sounds lingering in the night air.

"You just talk a big game." I tugged the zipper down on her jacket and slid my hand around her heavy breast.

Lennon whimpered as I toyed with her piercing—teasing her, but never quite giving her what she was craving. Her thighs tightened around my hand as I rubbed the outside of her pussy.

"All you have to do is ask nicely and I'll let you come," I reminded her. "It'll be our little secret."

Her head tipped backward, exposing her throat as she whispered unintelligible pleas to the sky.

"You're soaking these leggings, and I'm not even on your skin."

"Fuck you," she whimpered in desperation.

"Say my name, Lennon."

She shook her head, and I let go of her tit. A distressed whimper slipped out of her perfect lips.

A victorious smile curled at the corner of my mouth, because I had her right where I wanted her.

"I know, baby. I know," I soothed against her lips. "You don't want it to feel good because you want to be right. Just enjoy how fucking good it feels to be wrong. It can be our little secret."

Lennon's face twisted in anger. She opened her mouth to protest, but I rolled my thumb across the divot where her clit lay beneath her leggings, ignoring the ache in my cock.

It was easier to call out her desperation than my own.

"Look at me," I ordered.

Her eyes blinked open, wide and pained. "Please," she whispered.

I shook my head and stepped away, leaving her panting and antsy. "Not good enough."

"CJ—"

"Too late."

Her eyes were pleading, a sharp contrast to the wicked gaze she usually armed herself with.

Lennon swallowed and took a steadying breath. "Either you get used to the fact that I work here, and we figure out how to be amicable, or you leave me the hell alone."

The smoke pricked my senses again. But this time, I didn't think about brisket, good memories, and family around the table. I thought about burning buildings, danger, and threats to the people I loved. I thought about the charred wood I kept on my nightstand as a constant reminder of that night.

"You and I will never be amicable," I hissed. "So, get used to *that*."

Lennon's jaw clenched as I turned and stomped back to the bunkhouse. So much for a walk to clear my head. It was even more fucked up than before.

Like a moth to a flame, I was drawn to her. That kind of attraction never ended well for the moth.

Jackson looked up from the couch when I stormed into the bunkhouse. "You alright, boss man? Thought you went out to get some air? You look pissed."

I ignored the eight sets of eyes in the living room, stalked up the stairs to my room, and slammed the door.

8

LENNON

I snatched the ticket out of the printer and gave it a once-over. "Two ribeyes. One mid-rare. One well done."

Every cook on the line swore in tandem.

Julian groaned. "Why do people want me to cook it like it's fuckin' beef jerky?"

I ignored his complaints and kept barking orders. "Mash on both. Candied carrots with the mid and asparagus on the well. Two brisket corn chowders and two salads."

"Yes, Chef," the kitchen answered like a well-oiled machine.

"Pastry, where are the desserts for table twelve?" I yelled, hoping Javi would hear me over the ruckus.

"Behind," Javi said as he slipped up to the front of the kitchen and slid two perfectly plated dishes onto the expo line.

"Beautiful," I said, giving him a nod as he dashed back to the pastry station. "Where are my starters?"

Brad appeared with two portions of brisket corn chowder and slid them onto the line. I topped the ramekins with a generous helping of gouda and gruyere, and left them under the salamander to broil before delicately placing a cornbread biscotti on the rim.

My mouth watered at the sight. That soup would be my dinner tonight, and I couldn't wait.

The door to the dining room swung open, and a flustered-looking server burst into the kitchen as a new ticket came through.

"Chowder for one."

The bowl appeared in front of me in an instant, and I started the cheese, broil, and biscotti routine again.

"That one's for the roof," the server said. "And the Griffith family would like to send their compliments."

Of course they did.

The thought of a certain Griffith had my blood boiling in the most infuriating ways. I hadn't had a chance to take care of my *needs* after CJ cornered me by the smoker two nights ago.

The lack of an orgasm had me on edge.

I needed to blow off some steam.

The briskets turned out to be award-worthy and had guests raving all day yesterday. The remnants made a kick-ass soup that had Chef DeRossi calling from his restaurant in North Carolina so he could get my recipe.

"Who ordered the soup? I thought the Griffiths were the last table on the roof?" I asked.

The server, Jeremiah, nodded. "It's for Mr. Griffith."

"Mr. Griffith" was a rather vague term when it applied to all four brothers and their father.

I laughed. "Which one?"

"The single one."

That was much more clear. While the older three

Griffith Brothers were married with children, CJ was very much a loner.

I lifted my eyebrows. "The soup is for CJ?"

He nodded. "He practically licked the first bowl clean. You must have finally cracked him."

A wicked thought snuck into my mind. "I'll take his soup up when I go to speak with the family."

Jeremiah raised his eyebrows. "Are you sure?"

I nodded. "Don't worry about it. I'm sure Jessica—Ms. Powell—has side work for you if your tables are taken care of."

He nodded. "Thank you, Chef."

When he disappeared into the dining room, I snatched the bowl out from under the broiler and peeled back the cheese crust. Red bell peppers dotted the pale yellow soup. They added a little heat, balancing the sweetness of the corn.

I dashed into the walk-in cooler and snatched a Scotch bonnet and a ghost pepper off the shelf.

Thankfully, I had ordered a few more than I needed for our array of house-made hot sauces. I swiftly minced them with my knife, wiped the blade, and whisked the cutting board off to the dishwasher to avoid cross-contamination.

If CJ thought I couldn't stand the heat, he was about to get a taste of his own medicine.

I had an extra spring in my step as I strode up to the rooftop with a tray in my hand. "I heard the new corn chowder was a favorite," I said by way of greeting the Griffith family.

Nearly everyone was crowded around their long farm-style table tonight.

CJ's expression fell from neutral to sour when he saw my face.

I waltzed up behind him, savoring how he stiffened as I approached. I cleared his place setting from the right and served his soup from the left without skipping a beat.

My voice was sickeningly sweet as I said, "Enjoy." I clutched his empty plate in my hands as I moved back to the head of the table. "How was everything tonight?"

Murmurs of "excellent" and "delicious" rose from the table. All the attention seemed to be centered on one of the teenage girls at the table.

"Are we celebrating tonight?" I asked, keeping a watchful eye on CJ's spoon as he poked around, drowning the crispy cheese crust in the soup.

Christian Griffith smiled proudly. "We are. Bree got into her first-choice school. She'll be going to college at NYU in the fall." Tears welled up in his eyes. "I miss her already."

"*Daddy,*" Bree huffed with an adoring smile at her father.

"All the more reason to go visit," Cassandra said.

"Congratulations. You'll love New York," I said. "You'll have to try Chef DeRossi's flagship restaurant while you're there."

Cassandra beamed at Bree. "Nonna's used to be a favorite of mine."

As Cassandra and Becks ping-ponged back and forth about Manhattan eateries, CJ lifted the spoon to his mouth.

I held my breath and clung to the dishes in my hands. The first bite must have been safe because he swallowed, cracked the biscotti in two, and dunked one half into the soup.

"How are you liking Texas, honey?" Mrs. Griffith asked.

"Winter is much better down here," I said, drawing a laugh from the table.

CJ stayed quiet and shoveled a heaping spoonful of soup

into his mouth, chasing it with a bite of biscotti. The next bite that nearly cleaned out the ramekin was the nail in the coffin.

His eyes went wide, and he let out a sputtering cough as the heat hit, sending drips of soup spewing from his mouth.

Cassandra grimaced. "Are you dying over there? I don't know the Heimlich."

CJ swallowed and grabbed his water glass, downing it in one gulp. "Holy shit," he heaved.

Nathan, the oldest brother, looked at him curiously. "Yeah . . . I thought the soup was good too . . ."

"So fucking spicy," CJ wheezed as sweat beaded on his forehead. Tears leaked from the corners of his eyes. "I can't feel my tongue. My throat is on fire." He grabbed Ray's sweet tea and chugged it. "Soup isn't supposed to hurt."

"Hey," Ray protested.

"Mine only had red peppers in it," Brooke said, poking around at her empty soup. "But they're the sweet kind. It had a little kick, but it wasn't spicy."

I steeled my nerves as eyes started to turn to me. "She's right. Just red peppers," I said, innocent as a baby lamb.

Becks looked between CJ and me. I was waiting for her to call my bluff, but she never did. A mischievous smile twitched on her lips as she glanced at Nathan.

CJ looked like he was about to die.

"Seriously, man?" Ray said as he took a bite of the remnants from his own bowl. "You think this is spicy?"

"The soup was delicious, Lennon," Mrs. Griffith cooed. "I hope it stays on the menu. I'd eat it every day."

I beamed. "I'll run it by Chef DeRossi."

CJ looked like he was entering a nuclear meltdown as he tried to suffer through the last bites of diabolically hot soup to prove his manhood while his family inadvertently gaslit him.

"Would you like me to bring up a glass of milk?" I asked as I locked my gaze on his bloodshot eyes. "It's not supposed to be spicy, but I suppose some people just can't stand the heat."

"No," he heaved, sucking in a breath as he pointed a finger at me and used a linen napkin to dab the sweat from his face. "I don't want you to touch my food ever again."

"Carson James!" Mrs. Griffith snapped.

I choked on a laugh and nearly dropped the dishes in my hands.

His face turned the color of ripe tomatoes. I couldn't tell if it was from the peppers or his brewing anger, but I definitely knew it was time to get out of dodge. I dashed back down to the kitchen.

Who needed orgasms when there was revenge to be had?

The kitchen pivoted from dinner service to cleaning up before we finally sat down for the staff dinner. Everyone crowded around the stripped-down dining room tables, chowing down on the remnants of tonight's menu.

"I love a steak, but I'm getting burned out," Javi said as he slid his knife through his sirloin.

Julian chuckled. "Already?"

He shrugged. "Must be like working at a doughnut shop. If you're around it all the time, it doesn't sound good after a while."

"Should have gotten the soup," Jessica said as she dabbed her lips with a napkin. "Everyone was raving about it all night."

I hid my smile behind the soup and salad I was demolishing. My diet was severely lacking in green vegetables and I was trying to make up for it all in one night.

"So, where'd you work before this, Chef?" Julian asked.

I kept my eyes trained on my plate. "Nonna's in Manhattan, but I was part of the launch team that helped open the DeRossi Hospitality Group's new concepts all over the country."

"How long you been workin' for Chef DeRossi?" he asked.

I chewed my bite slowly, hoping someone else would change the subject. No one did. "Five years."

Julian let out a low whistle. "Five years and you're running this place? DeRossi must really like you. I mean, you're a good cook. But I'm just saying."

The door swung open and Cassandra cut through the mostly empty dining room.

I lifted my chin and clenched my jaw. "I have earned my position. And if you're insinuating I did it in any manner other than hard work and honing my craft, I suggest you leave my kitchen."

Julian let out a nervous laugh. "Whoa, no. I'm trying to get to know our sous chef. You don't need to get your panties in a twist, Len." He raised his hands in surrender.

I looked him dead in the eye. "I don't understand the joke."

He scoffed. "What do you mean?"

"Well, you're laughing, so you must think what you said is funny." I waved my hand between us. "So, please. Explain the joke."

Utensils clattered as forks fell and jaws dropped.

Julian said nothing. His knuckles turned white as he fisted his fork.

"Let me be clear," I said when the room fell silent. "You

will address me as Chef Maddox every single time. We are not on a first-name basis. And if you ever make a comment like that to me or any other member of this staff again, I will personally walk you out of this building. I don't know what kind of boys club you worked at before, but that shit doesn't fly in my kitchen. Have I made myself clear?"

"Yeah, sure," he stammered.

"*Yes, Chef*," I corrected.

When the staff dinner ended, I checked the stock room and fridges and noted what to order on the next truck while everyone scrubbed the kitchen. When I got back to the office, Cassandra was waiting for me.

"That was quite the speech you gave to . . ."

"Julian," I said as I dropped into the desk chair and pulled up the supplier website.

"Julian," she said, making a note on her phone. "He's now number one on my shit-list."

"Mine too," I mumbled as I started ordering ingredients.

Cassandra sat in the chair across from me. "My first job was at a restaurant. I was seventeen and worked as a hostess, then moved up to being a server. Back then, no one would have balked at a comment about panties being in a twist."

I paused and looked over the computer at her. "Is this your way of saying I overreacted and you're writing me up or telling Chef DeRossi?"

Cassandra shook her head. "Absolutely not. It makes me proud to see that women have stopped laughing off comments like that."

I went back to putting in the truck order because I didn't know what else to say.

"How are things going?" she asked.

"Fine."

"Settling in?"

"Things are running smoothly," I said evasively.

"And you've found a place to live in town?" Cassandra smoothed her hand over the neatly pressed pleats of her trousers.

"Yes," I lied.

"Chef DeRossi asked me to check in and make sure you were doing okay in your personal life," she said. "I have resources and connections if there's anything you need assistance with."

Cassandra Griffith wasn't nice, but she was kind, and I appreciated that.

I nodded. "I'll keep that in mind."

"And if you need help with the Griffith family, or a particular Griffith, you know where to find me."

She stood and slid a dirty soup ramekin onto the desk. Red flecks covered the white porcelain.

A nefarious smirk grew across her ruby lips. "That second batch of soup was really something."

9

CARSON JAMES

"What have I told you damn near a million times?" I snapped as I stomped into the barn and caught Brooke red-handed.

My sister-in-law—my *very pregnant* sister-in-law—had the good sense to look guilty as she clutched the pitchfork to her chest. "Cassandra's in the office today. I'm hiding until the next arena rental starts."

Brooke managed the equine program that I didn't entirely hate. I hated it when field trips came with hordes of barely house-trained preschoolers. But the riding lessons and boarding programs were fine.

I grabbed the pitchfork out of her hand and set it against the wall. "You've worked for her for what—two years now? And you share a last name. You can't honestly tell me you're still scared of her."

"Like you're not scared of her?" Brooke said as she reached for a broom.

I snatched it away from her and pushed her into a chair. "Sit. You do know you can go home and rest, right?"

She let out a heavy breath and rested her hands on top of her belly. "Nope. Ray's home."

I lifted an eyebrow. "If he's back to being a grumpy jackass, I'll kill him."

Brooke laughed. "No, he's fine. Just insatiable when I'm pregnant. I swear, the baby bump turns him into a caveman."

I did not need to know that about my brother.

I set the broom against the old wooden saddle stand and paused when it creaked and swayed. The damn thing looked like it was about to fall to pieces.

I cocked my head. "You remember it being that wobbly?"

Brooke looked like she had been caught red-handed, and I put the pieces together.

"You people are horny heathens," I muttered, shaking my head.

At least Brooke had the good sense to look guilty. "Maybe announce yourself before you walk through here when it's dark?"

I flipped her off as a woman's shriek caught us both by surprise.

"Looks like you're busted," I muttered as Cassandra came stomping in on those ridiculous high heels she always wore.

"I swear if that horse tries to bite me one more goddamn time, I'll—" Cassandra paused when she spotted me and Brooke staring. "There you are. I've been looking for you everywhere. Maybe answer your phone or the radio like a civilized professional."

Brooke swallowed. "Sorry, I was just—"

"Not you," Cassandra clipped. "Why are you out here? You should be resting."

"Told you," I mouthed to Brooke.

She flipped me off.

Cassandra turned her exacting gaze to me. "You're the Griffith I've been trying to hunt down. First, tell your fucking horse to stop trying to bite me."

"No can do, Cass," I said as I snagged a few treats from the bin for Anarchy. Even I had to bribe my way onto her good side sometimes.

"Second, I need you up at the restaurant."

I laughed. "Pretty sure you don't want me anywhere near your little pet project. Not my job, not my problem."

Her features turned deadly. "It will very much be your problem when my size ten Jimmy Choo is up your ass. One of the tilt skillets is broken, and the equipment repair tech can't get out here for a week."

"Do I look like I know how to fix a—whatever the hell a tilt skillet is?"

"Christian and Nate are at the livestock auction, and your father is taking a nap," she said.

I stared her down for a minute, contemplating what I could get out of this. "I want coffee the next time you go into town. Good coffee."

Cassandra looked surprised, then suspicious. "That's it? One coffee?"

I thought back to the second round of briskets that Lennon had been up all night smoking the day after she force-fed me the soup from hell.

I didn't want to admit that I had swapped and taken a night shift so I could watch her from a distance in person instead of watching the cameras.

Spying on Lennon while Anarchy silently judged me wasn't as good as the first night she had been out by the smoker. The night we went tit for tat as I felt her up.

Goddamn, she was something else . . .

"One coffee and takeout from the restaurant."

Cassandra laughed. "I'll pick up your fancy coffee while I'm in town, but you can get takeout anytime you want." She smirked. "Or is your pride bigger than your appetite?"

I glowered. "You want your fancy skillet fixed or not?"

Cass raised her hands. "Fine. I'll even have the food delivered to the bunkhouse."

I wasted time in the shop we used to fix equipment, unpacking and repacking a tool bag that was already neatly organized. Really, I was biding my time, hoping to see Lennon's car disappear down the long drive and head toward town.

When that didn't happen, I trudged to the restaurant, filthy from the day. I waltzed through the packed dining room, to the horror of the staff and guests, and let myself into the kitchen.

"Eighty-six the pork chops," Lennon shouted to a server. "I've got plates for table nine and table four coming up." She snatched up a steak and prodded the top. "Are you aware of what 'rare' means, or should I take the time out of our very busy dinner service to re-educate you?"

A server burst through the doors. "Chef, table seventeen wants to change their steak to medium well."

"Excellent," Lennon said as she plated up the over-cooked steak. "I've got it right here. Let's do our jobs right the first time and keep the food waste to a minimum, folks."

"Yes, Chef," was the communal answer.

"What are you doing in my kitchen?" Lennon barked.

It took a moment to realize that the question was meant for me. I knew she was a force to be reckoned with—I learned that first-hand. But every time my folks had requested the chef come up to our table, she was toned down.

I lifted my eyebrows. A snappy retort was on the tip of my tongue, but that knife in Lennon's hand was too close for comfort. "Cass sent me to fix whatever broke."

Lennon paused. "Oh."

"Show me where it is so we can go back to our separate corners."

"Julian, you're on expo," she said as she wiped her hands clean.

Julian—the guy manning the grill—turned and looked me up and down before muttering, "Yes, *Chef*," at Lennon's back.

I waited until Lennon led me a few steps away before asking, "What's his problem?"

She snorted. "Much like you, he doesn't like me very much at the moment."

"Probably has a good reason."

She cut me with a sharp look, but said nothing more about it. "This is it," she said as she led me to a shiny stainless-steel table with a heavy looking lid. It sat next to a long row of ovens and standalone pots that were large enough to cook a person.

"What's wrong with it?" I asked as I lifted the lid to the giant rectangle and tried to figure out exactly what the thing did.

"The hinges are jammed or something. It won't lift. We've had to scoop everything out by hand, which pretty much defeats the purpose."

There was a wide slanted spout on the front, giving the cooks the ability to make a big batch of something, then lift it and pour it out.

Lennon and I switched places without touching. I opened the machine and tried to tilt the cooking surface, but it wouldn't budge.

"Did you not hear what I said?" she huffed like I was a complete moron. "It's jammed. It won't—"

"Cool your tits. I heard you."

Her expression turned deadly. "You and I can go at it outside this building, but you will not speak to me that way when I'm in the kitchen and my staff are around. This is my job. You don't have to like me, but you will respect me. Have I made myself clear?"

I went silent for a moment, digging my fingers into the handle of my tool bag. "Yes, ma'am."

Lennon stood frozen for a beat. I swore she was about to call my bluff, but instead, she turned and walked back to the front line.

I watched her hips sway as she slipped through the crowd of bodies churning out plates of food. The curt warnings of "behind" she doled out were firm without being overreaching.

She grabbed a large knife, sided up to a cutting board, and started decimating everything in her wake.

It was organized chaos, a well-timed ebb and flow. She was mesmerizing, leading the charge with clear orders and a take-no-prisoners attitude.

Cooks and servers peppered her with questions, one on top of the other. She answered each one with mind-blowing efficiency, never missing a beat with her own tasks.

The kitchen was an Olympic relay, each competitor handing off the baton to the next without fumbling. It was a case study in communication and teamwork.

When those brown eyes glanced my way, I ducked behind the tilt skillet and went to work.

The tilt skillet was mostly fine, but it looked like someone had shoved it into the back wall a bit too hard after pulling it out to clean it. The shove had dented the metal panel that protected the wall from grease and steam. It bent the hinges of the cover and dislodged the tilting mechanism from the track.

"Shit—"

I was lying on my back with my feet sticking out from under the machine as I unfastened the screws when someone tripped over my ankles.

I eased up, trapping the screws between my teeth, and peered out. "Sorry, man," I muttered as I craned forward and dragged my tool bag out of the way.

The guy was carrying an armful of dirty dishes. "No worries. 'Preciate you gettin' that thing working again. Maybe Chef will stop being a bitch when it's not broken."

I wiped the grease from my hands onto my jeans. "What was that?"

He scoffed and cocked his head back toward Lennon. "She's got a stick up her ass or something. I thought workin' here would be chill. Cook some steaks between smoke breaks, ya know? She's running a fucking sweat shop."

Didn't like that. Not one fucking bit.

I chuckled under my breath, because the idiot clearly had no clue who he was talking to.

"I've worked around here for a long time," I said as I rifled around in my tool bag to grab a fresh set of screws so I could replace the old ones. "I'll let you in on a secret."

He grinned. "What's that?"

I looked him dead in the eye. "If you disrespect the women on this ranch, you'll have hell to pay. That includes Chef Maddox."

He sneered. "Nah. Bros before hoes. She ain't one of them Griffiths."

"No, but I am."

He paled.

"So, if I tell you to respect her, you will respect her. Or you can find another job."

I watched as he stormed off to the dish pit and dumped his haul on the kid loading the dishwasher and manning the three-compartment sink.

"What was that about?"

I nearly smacked my head on the tilt kettle beside me when Lennon appeared. "Your guy was running his mouth."

She looked around until she spotted the idiot who made the mistake of speaking to me. "Who? Julian?"

I shrugged.

"What did he say this time?"

"Bitching about you," I grunted as I shoved the hydraulic base of the tilt skillet back onto the tracks and gave it a test lift before securing it.

Lennon huffed. "He needs to get some new material." She paused and watched for a moment as I finished putting the pieces back together and cleared out my tools.

"What did you say to him?"

I packed up my shit and stood shoulder to shoulder with her. "That I'm the only one who gets to bitch about you."

"Boss," Reed yelled from downstairs. "Door."

I swear these cavemen stuck with single-syllable words just to piss me off.

"Hold on," I yelled down as I grabbed a pair of sweatpants and pulled them on. I didn't bother with a shirt.

The only people who came by the bunkhouse were family. The only reason they didn't come in on their own was because a dozen people lived here, and at least one person was always in a constant state of undress.

I never mentioned it to my family, but a while ago, I had started getting quotes from contractors to build my own place. All my brothers had put down roots on their respective pieces of land, but I had always been happy being one of the ranch hands.

Not so much anymore.

I padded down the stairs and skidded to a halt when I spotted Lennon lingering in the open door.

She still wore her restaurant uniform, but she had taken off her hat, let her hair down, and left her crisp white chef's coat unbuttoned. A tight tank top that showed off a slice of her stomach peeked through the open sides.

Lennon stiffened when I rounded the corner, steeling herself for battle. "I always wondered what the devil's lair looked like." She made a show of peering around. "It smells like a sock in here. I have to say, I expected a lot more red and orange. Maybe some pitchforks."

"The pitchforks are in the barn. What do you want, trouble?"

She shifted, lifting the cardboard produce box in her hands. "Dinner delivery."

I crossed my arms over my chest and leaned against the door frame. "Tell me, how was *your* dinner? Crow, right? You're welcome for fixing your equipment, by the way."

She snorted. "Actually, I flexed my baking skills. Made you a humble pie since you had to set foot in my kitchen and not set it on fire."

I reached into the box and peeled back the aluminum foil on one of the disposable metal pans. Slices of brisket with perfect smoke rings and thick bark were lined up like soldiers. Drippings pooled around them.

That was one sexy piece of meat.

"Cassandra put an order in for your house," Lennon said as she peered over my shoulder and looked around. "Apparently, that was the deal you two struck to fix my tilt skillet."

"Bunk house," I muttered. "Ranch hands live here. You know, people who actually belong on a ranch."

Lennon rolled her eyes. "Take the food before I dump it on you. I don't want to waste it."

I lifted the box out of her arms, careful not to touch her, but our fingers brushed.

"How much of this did you poison?" I asked as I walked it into the kitchen and set it on the island.

Lennon never moved from the doorway. "I guess we'll get to see how much you trust me."

"I trust you as far as I can throw you," I said as I wandered back to the front door.

She reached out and squeezed my bicep. "If memory serves, you have no problem putting me where you want me."

God, that felt good. My dick throbbed at the feel of her hand on my body. Sparks danced at her touch, threatening to grow into a blaze if they weren't snuffed out.

"Go home, trouble," I said as I backed away and grabbed the door. "Thanks for the food."

10

LENNON

"We're getting so many complaints already," Jessica whispered as she dashed into the kitchen. "Rock, paper, scissors for who has to go ask Cassandra to do something about it."

I laughed as I scooped spoonfuls of butter and herbs onto the beautifully caramelized New York strip, basting it to perfection. "You're the front-of-house manager. Ergo, customer complaints are your problem. I only deal with complaints about dead cows. Not live ones."

"Ms. Powell," a server said as she pushed into the kitchen. "All the rooftop tables are requesting to be moved to the dining room."

Jessica sighed. "Pull Terry to help you set the dining room tables and reseat the rooftop guests. We'll tell walk-ins and the rest of our reservations that the rooftop has to be closed for maintenance."

"Offer the re-seats a free dessert," I told the server, then looked over my shoulder. "Javi, we're about to have a lot of sweets going out."

"Yes, Chef," he hollered back.

"I'll deal with the customers if you talk to Cassandra," Jessica begged. "She scares me."

She still scared me too, but I had learned long ago that pretending I wasn't scared was necessary for survival.

"Ms. Powell, there's a cow in the lobby," a flustered server said.

The kitchen became too crowded for my liking. Employees kept coming in with customer complaints about livestock.

I handed the steak in my pan off to the expediter to let it rest and started untying my apron. "You handle the situation here," I told Jessica. "I'll deal with the cows."

More like I would deal with the man in charge of the cows.

The proximity of the ranch's cattle herd to the front doors of the restaurant was not a coincidence.

"Zach, keep things moving until I get back," I shouted.

"Yes, Chef," Zach Simmons, the saucier that Chef DeRossi had poached from a local competitor, said as he shifted to cover my station and his.

Julian scoffed. "Seriously?"

I looked Julian dead in the eye as I balled my apron in my hand. "You want my respect? You have to earn it. Chef Simmons stepped up yesterday when we had a rush. He has my trust."

And with that, I strode out of the kitchen. I was past caring if I hurt Julian's feelings by calling him out in front of everyone.

Sure as shit, there was a cow with pool noodles on its horns, taking a nap in the middle of the restaurant lobby.

Waiting guests were both horrified and a little curious.

"You have got to be kidding me," I gasped, then immediately cupped my hand over my mouth.

The stench was putrid. Piles of shit dotted the neatly

manicured lawns and pathways. Cows with rusty-brown and white patches roamed the lodge property, dotting the land all the way to the lake and beyond.

A handful of cows had indulged their curiosity and were seeing what the parking lot was all about.

A shadow of a man on a horse loomed in the distance.

I'd know that Stetson anywhere. It had covered my ass when I was being fucked against the wall of a bar.

"Unless these animals are going to walk themselves into the smokers, they need to leave," I shouted as I stormed over to where CJ lingered beneath a tree.

The obnoxiously large black horse he was riding turned and glared at me.

A slow, nefarious smile curved like a sickle beneath the shadow of his hat. "I'm just giving the people—what's everyone been calling it?" He snapped his fingers. "That's right. *The immersive cattle ranch experience.*" He sucked in a long breath, then blew it out. "Take it all in. You smell that? Smells like putting food on the table."

I laughed in disbelief. "You are such a fucking asshole. Get the goddamn cows out of here."

He let out a loud, caustic laugh. "And why would I do that? My cows gotta eat. How else are you gonna get those fancy, overpriced steaks to cook and serve? Or do I need to explain the food chain to you?"

I glanced down to make sure I hadn't accidentally stepped in shit and pinched the bridge of my nose to stave off the stench. "There's a cow *inside* the restaurant."

CJ grinned. "Inside? That's probably Mickey. He's my niece's pet. Kinda goes where he wants. He's a people person. Might have gotten lonely in Cassandra's office. He probably went hunting for some attention."

He was saying all that as if it were normal.

"I don't give a flying fuck that your pet cow—"

"Gracie's pet cow," he corrected with a grin that annoyed me to the core.

"I don't care whose pet cow it is!" I screamed. "Get it out before someone calls the health department and gets us shut down!"

He looked down from his literal high horse. "And what a shame that would be."

"I don't know what your fucking problem is with the restaurant, but it's above my pay grade. Take it up with someone other than me and stop fucking around."

The horse took a menacing step toward me. My head snapped in its direction, and I glared until it backed away.

CJ bristled.

I stabbed a finger up at him. "I swear, if I see a cow within fifty yards of the restaurant or lodge, I will draw and quarter you and hang your body on a meat hook in the walk-in cooler."

"I'd love to see that, actually."

I jumped, whirling around at the sound of Cassandra Griffith's voice. Her cold demeanor was downright arctic today.

"Three things are going to happen, children." She counted them off one by one on her fingers. "First, all livestock will be removed immediately. Second—" she turned to me "—I will see you in the office at *my* earliest convenience. And third—" she glared at CJ "—we are not playing chess with cattle, Carson. Christian is coming up to help you move the herd since you apparently cannot do your job, and then the two of you are going to have a chat."

The horse opened its freakishly wide teeth and made a move for Cassandra's hair.

"I swear to God, Anarchy—" Cassandra hissed.

The horse backed away.

CJ clenched his jaw, working it side to side. Finally, he tapped the horse with his boots. "Let's go, Anny."

Cassandra turned to me. "Office. Now."

"I was trying to get him to move the cows," I said as I headed back to the building.

Cassandra snapped her fingers. "Not your office. *Mine*." She spun on her heels and strutted off through the field.

I had to jog to keep up with her pace, taking in the scenery as I was death-marched to my termination meeting. There was no way I was getting out of this, even if it wasn't my fault.

He was family, and I was the help.

We rounded the bunkhouse and cut through the grass until we found a dirt path leading to a group of barns and outbuildings.

The trespassing cow wearing pool noodles had been shooed from the restaurant lobby, and was now making its way back to the livestock-friendly part of the ranch.

If I wasn't in the process of being escorted to my own execution, it would have been a beautiful afternoon walk. The land was gorgeous. Grass rolled on for miles and miles on end. I hadn't explored anything beyond the restaurant because I had no reason to. But after a short walk, it felt like we were in another world entirely.

"Are you coming in?" Cassandra asked.

It took me a moment to realize she was talking to the cow. I waited behind her as the massive beast lumbered into the office, where it plopped down on a dog bed.

"What are the pool noodles for?" I asked, lingering in the doorway as Cassandra and her animal friend got comfortable.

"It keeps him from breaking things. Mickey still thinks he's a calf."

"You have a cow that thinks he's a dog."

She cracked a smile. "It gets less weird the longer you're here. Not much less, but a little. Have a seat."

I eased inside and dropped into the chair across from her. "If I'm getting fired, can we make it fast? It's a long drive back to New York."

"You're not getting fired," Cassandra said as she reached down, yanked open a drawer, and pulled out a bottle of whiskey and two shot glasses. Without missing a beat, she opened the door to a mini-fridge and pulled a pint of mint chocolate chip ice cream from the freezer compartment.

She poured two shots, slid one to me, then knocked hers back and chased it with a spoonful of ice cream.

I tossed mine back and hissed at the burn as it slid down my throat. "I could get used to these kinds of staff meetings."

Cassandra pointed her spoon at me. "Stick around long enough and you'll find your coping mechanism. I would kill for this family, but sometimes they drive me batshit crazy."

"So weaponizing cows is normal behavior?"

"No," Cassandra said. "That was definitely a first."

I tapped my shot glass. "In that case, I'm going to need another round."

Cassandra tucked the whiskey back in the drawer and put her ice cream pint back in the freezer. "No can do. You're still on the clock."

"Then why are you feeding me shots?"

"Shot," she clarified. "One shot to loosen you up before this chat."

I narrowed my eyes. "You're not HR, are you?"

She snorted. "Does it look like we have HR? Lord knows we need it. Then again, it would just be me sending the boys to the principal's office all day long and then nothing would get done. Now, what's going on with you and CJ?"

"I already had a talk with Chef DeRossi after the incident at the grand opening dinner. I've done what's required of me."

"I'm aware of the conversation you had with Mr. DeRossi. I want to know what happened between you and CJ that started this little battle of wits."

"He doesn't like me."

"I know why he doesn't like you working here. He's not a fan of the lodge or the restaurant. What happened between the two of you? He ignores everyone else who works for the development, but you two go at each other like cats and dogs."

"We had a—" I hesitated, trying to choose my words carefully "—previous interaction before I started my job here."

Cassandra's eyebrows lifted. "Here on the ranch?"

"No."

She sighed. "I'm trying to help you, but you have to trust me. I'm not sure if you're aware of what my job entailed before I came to work for the ranch, but I am very, *very* good at keeping secrets."

I didn't make a sound. *Snitches get stitches.*

Cassandra pulled open a drawer and yanked out a thick file. My name was on the tab that jutted out from the top.

She huffed and laced her hands together. "I cannot run interference to protect you if I don't know what's going on. I'm perfectly aware of everything in here," she said, tapping a manicured nail on the file. "So, unless you literally murdered someone, just tell me what happened. And if you did murder someone, blink twice and I'll call our attorney."

She had a point. It wasn't like I had done anything wrong.

"We hooked up at a bar. Didn't exchange anything more than first names, so I didn't know who he was, and he didn't know I was coming to work here."

To her credit, Cassandra didn't flinch. She didn't even look fazed. "Workplace hookup. Yeah, that tracks for the Griffith boys."

"It wasn't a workplace hookup. We didn't know—"

She held her hand up to silence me. "I'll be frank. CJ doesn't like the restaurant. Ergo, he doesn't like you. Keep your head down and let Christian and me handle him." Her posture softened a bit. "Chef DeRossi hasn't been back because I've been sending him glowing praise about your job performance. As long as you keep doing good work, I'll have your back."

11

CARSON JAMES

"**B**ring it up in the back." Christian's voice crackled over the radio as we collectively guided the herd deeper into the west pasture.

Anny grunted in annoyance from beneath me as her hooves thundered into the ground.

I didn't blame her.

Granted, it was mostly my fault that we were having to do a herd move.

Sadie, the ranch's retired cattle dog, was in her element. She circled the stragglers as we gently urged the animals to move to more forgeable fields.

We had been rotating them west anyway. I may have just let them move a little farther west than we usually would have. Causing a little havoc at the restaurant and lodge was the icing on the cake.

The chorus of lowing cattle, stamping horses, and yips and barks from the dog was music to my ears. This was how the ranch was supposed to be.

"You ready to talk?" Christian asked as he and Libby slowed up to fall in line with Anarchy and me.

"Not particularly," I said as Anny took the pressure from my boots as a cue to get away from Christian.

It didn't work. Christian was too seasoned a rider to let me get away that easily.

"Too bad. It's time for you to get your head out of your ass. You're acting like a child. And since my girls are almost grown and out of the house, I'm not too keen on parenting anyone else these days. You can throw your temper tantrums all you want, but it's not changing reality."

My grip on the reins tightened. I could feel the shift in Anny's demeanor as she reacted to my energy.

My horse wasn't an asshole by nature. She reacted like one because I reacted like one.

"And when we're done moving cattle, you can get a shovel and clean the shit off the walkways, parking lot, and the grass up front. I'm not making the lodge or restaurant staff pick up after your little prank," Christian said.

Resentment was a quick-acting drug. It flooded my body, pulling me deeper and deeper into an inescapable abyss.

"There are other ranches, you know," Christian said.

I yanked on the reins and Anarchy came to a screeching halt. "The fuck just came out of your mouth?"

Christian knew exactly what he'd said. If I were a betting man, I'd say he threw it out there just to piss me off. The look on his face as he glanced over his shoulder told me that he wasn't bluffing, though.

The ranch hands kept the herd moving, but Christian and I were frozen in a stand-off as we sat astride our horses.

His jaw was set in a hard line. "This ranch is a choice. You don't have to be part of it. Nate chose to go into the military. Ray rode bulls. This land is a birthright, not a death sentence."

I shifted in my saddle and looked away from him.

"Your last name means you will always have a place here, but only if you choose it," he continued. "And right now, you're not acting like you want to be part of the legacy. I know you haven't been happy here for a while. Not since the construction started. But we're not turning back the clock. We won't survive if we do. Would it really have been better if we sold out to a big corporation and became a cog in a giant industrial machine? To become a conveyor belt for beef instead of ethical, sustainable ranching?"

The question lingered in the air for a moment before he continued. "It was that, or we found our own solution. Dad said something to me that hit. If someone is willing to bet on you, maybe you should bet on yourself. So, we made that bet. Doesn't mean it was an easy call. Better the devil you know than the devil you don't."

He took a deep breath and his eyes met mine. "Either you come to terms with the direction of the ranch, or you put in your notice."

"You can fuck off," I muttered, kicking Anny into high gear.

~

Dusk had fallen by the time we got the herd deep into the west pasture and I made it back to the restaurant and grabbed a shovel. There was something humbling about scraping piles of shit off the ground. It seemed like a fitting metaphor for my life as of late.

One steaming pile after another.

Warm lights glowed from the lodge as guests settled in for the night. Muffled music floated through the air, accented by the scrape of the spade on the concrete sidewalk with each scoop.

"Heard about your little stunt."

I spun at the sound of my brother's voice. Ray was pushing his wheelchair up the paved walkway. Brooke walked beside him, keeping one hand on his chair for support and one hand on her belly.

I grabbed the hem of my shirt and used it to wipe the sweat off my face. "What are y'all doing out here?"

"Date night," Brooke said as she smiled at Ray. "Momma's got Seth at her house so we could eat without also feeding a toddler."

Ray gave me a half-cocked smile. "It's kinda nice not having to leave the ranch. It's a lot of effort for both of us these days."

Life had changed so quickly for both of them. Ray went from being a champion in the rodeo circuit to waking up in the hospital, paralyzed. Brooke had come into his life when he was an angry son of a bitch and chipped away at him, piece by piece.

The change in him was night and day. It didn't surprise me in the slightest when they married quickly and didn't waste time starting a family.

"I begged Lennon to keep that brisket corn chowder on the menu. It's the one thing I've been craving all week, and I might cry if it's gone," Brooke said.

I didn't miss the way Ray couldn't keep his hands off Brooke whenever he wasn't actively pushing his wheelchair.

Brooke squeezed Ray's hand. "I'm gonna run inside and go to the bathroom." She offered me a sheepish smile. "I swear, this baby thinks my bladder is a trampoline."

Ray waited until Brooke had disappeared through the stately wooden doors of the restaurant.

I could read the look on his face like a goddamn book. It was the same one Christian had been wearing earlier.

"I already got an earful from brother dearest," I muttered as I went back to shoveling shit.

Ray chuckled. "I'm sure you did."

"So I don't need it from you too."

"I wasn't going to give it to you," he said.

I eyed him suspiciously. Something was on his mind, but if it wasn't Christian's high-horse speech reimagined, I didn't have a clue what it was.

"You know what I appreciated about you after I moved back to the ranch?" he said.

"My great sense of humor and charming personality?"

Ray laughed, and I flipped him off.

"No," he said as he scratched at the scruff on his jaw. "I appreciated that you didn't hover. You knew I was going through shit. Everyone did. But you didn't pester me about it. I always knew in the back of my mind that I could bring it up to you if I needed to."

"What are you getting at?"

"You know where my house is. I've got a deck chair for you to sit in if you want to talk to someone you don't have to work for."

"I'm fine," I muttered.

Ray looked at me for a moment with an acute sadness in his eyes. "'Fine' is the biggest lie we force ourselves to believe. You'll feel better when you admit you're not fine than when you try to pretend you are."

"Don't need to talk. It is what it is."

He shrugged. "Offer stands."

I watched as he wheeled inside and met Brooke in the lobby before peeling my eyes away and getting back to work.

The air was cold as I made the walk back to the barn to drop off the shovel I had pilfered from the stables.

I did a cursory walkthrough, making sure the animals were taken care of and that nothing was out of place.

Brooke ran a tight ship. As cheerfully scatterbrained as she had been when she first came to the ranch, it seemed like leaving the distractions that plagued her behind helped her settle down.

When it came to the equine program, her babies, or Ray, she was always on top of things. Cassandra had taken Brooke under her wing and given her structure and leadership. As far as sisters-in-law went, Brooke was cool. I didn't mind having her around, and we got along just fine.

On top of that, she had Anarchy wrapped around her finger. I swear my horse liked her better than she liked me.

Instead of heading back to the bunkhouse, I let myself into the ranch office. I didn't feel like being around the guys or my family. When my head was loud, I used to go up to the lake when I needed a little clarity. Unfortunately, there was a fifty-room lodge there now.

Sitting on my land.

The office door screeched as I shoved it open. Mickey lifted his head from the corner where he had fallen asleep.

"Sorry, dude. Didn't mean to wake you," I said as I shut the door behind me. "Too loud out there for you too, huh?"

Mickey let out a deep, bellowing huff and went back to sleep.

I dropped down into Cassandra's desk chair and spilled backward when the seat tipped with my weight. I grabbed the edge of the desk and heaved back up.

"You think she's got a screwdriver in here?" I asked Mickey as I rifled through the drawers. "This chair needs to be tightened up."

He didn't answer, but I didn't mind. I probably would have shit my britches if he had.

The first two drawers were a bust. I didn't find anything except throwing knives and whiskey. I glanced over at the wall to see which picture was tacked on the target as evidence of who had pissed off Cassandra this week. A photo of the entire town council was pinned to the wooden target hanging on the wall. The stab marks in the paper were a clear answer.

A file folder on top of the desk caught my eye. *Maddox, E.*

Maddox . . . That was Lennon's last name. The 'E' could've been a typo.

The folder was unusually thick to be employment records for someone who had started work a few weeks ago. It should have only been a few tax forms. Maybe an application or resume.

I abandoned my search for the screwdriver and flipped open the folder. "What are you hiding, trouble?"

12

LENNON

"Vegan order coming through," I shouted. "Chimmichurri steak. Sub portobello and eggplant for the meat. Throw some extra veg on there. I want new pans and utensils. No cross-contamination."

"Heard," Julian shouted over the sizzle of the grill as he hustled to scrape and sanitize it as much as possible.

Echoes of 'heard' followed as everyone acknowledged the change-up. Pans, tongs, spoons, and ladles clattered as they were swapped out.

"Excellent," I said as beautifully charred pieces of mushrooms and eggplant appeared in front of me a few minutes later. I made quick work of dressing the dish and sliding it onto the expo line. "Clear," I called out.

The kitchen let out a collective heave as we returned to business as usual.

"Last reservation just checked in. Julian, cover for Zach. Zach, start closing and preparing for the staff meal. Let's get home before one in the morning, alright?"

"Yes, Chef," the men said in tandem.

"Javi, how are we looking on garde and pastry? You set?"

"Good to go, chef," he hollered from the back.

"Great work tonight, team. Let's keep it moving."

The irony of my gym membership lifestyle was that I never used it to exercise. Working day in and day out in a restaurant kitchen was a workout in itself. On a slow day, I'd log fifteen thousand steps, lift fifty-pound boxes of meat and produce repeatedly, then sweat it out on the line instead of a cardio class.

The door to the dining room slammed open, rattling the glass-front cooler that sat beside it. I looked up, expecting to see Jessica with her ass on fire.

CJ stood in the doorway, braced in a wide stance as he tapped a file folder on his thigh.

"Out," I barked as Jessica nearly ran straight into his back. "Unless you're about to be fileted, grilled, and served, you don't belong in my kitchen."

He didn't smile. There was no playful heat or disgust in his eyes. Just a cold stare that cut me to the bone. "Is that so, *Eleanor*?"

The knife fell from my hand with a clatter and my blood ran cold.

Everyone in the kitchen went silent. The hiss of meat on the grill was a cymbal to the heavy thud of my heart.

I fought the urge to use my side towel to dab at the cold sweat on my neck.

He . . . he didn't. I was hallucinating. I had to be.

But the file . . .

Cassandra had pulled it out earlier when we were in her office.

Protect me, my ass . . .

I was the only one who would protect me. And I wouldn't forget it a second time.

CJ took a step into the kitchen, but paused when I lifted my knife.

"If you come near me, this will not end well for either of us. *Leave.*"

That asshole smile that he used to charm the pants—and panties—off of me at the bar was back. But this time I didn't feel the sparks. I felt the flames.

We were both about to burn it all down.

"Pipe down, slugger. You sure you want to add another charge to your rap sheet?"

I dropped the knife and lunged before he could get another word out.

If I was going to catch another charge, it wouldn't be for *attempted* murder. It would be premeditated, in the first degree.

I took a swing as someone yanked me back, arms banding around me before I could get my hands on him.

CJ never flinched. *Asshole.*

"Chef—" Julian grunted as he struggled to keep me from gouging CJ's eyes out.

How fucking dare he go through my file.

I wasn't sure if I was angrier that he had read through my file or used my unfortunately legal name. *Eleanor.*

I hadn't heard that one in a long time.

Julian pulled me back a safe distance from CJ and let me go, returning to his station to flip the steaks.

We didn't want to mess up the crosshatch, after all. Homicide could wait, but hungry guests couldn't.

"You good, Chef?" Zach asked as he came up behind me.

I didn't answer, because I wasn't good. I wouldn't be good as long as I was in CJ's vicinity.

The kitchen had turned into a stand-off. Us versus him.

"That tattoo on your arm is accurate. Isn't that right, jail bird?"

I swung before I could think better of it. CJ never saw it coming. My fist connected with his jaw, cracking in a swift punch.

Jessica shrieked. Shouts rose up.

I bit the inside of my cheek to keep from groaning at the snap of pain in my hand. That was going to be a bitch to work through.

CJ jolted at the punch, swearing loud and bright as he stumbled back. Whether it was to come at me or to get his footing, he bolted forward. Julian and Zach wedged between us, Julian shoving CJ away and Zach yanking me deeper down the line.

I channeled every ounce of fury that boiled inside of me as my eyes locked on his.

CJ used the back of his arm to wipe the blood that trickled from the corner of his lip. "Looks like you live up to your name, slugger."

"Fuck off!" I roared in anger.

I knew most of the Griffith family lived on the ranch, but the houses were seemingly separated by miles. The only one I passed on my way in and out was the main house at the very front of the property.

If I had any doubt how fast news traveled on a cattle ranch, I had my answer when Cassandra and Christian Griffith stepped into the doorway.

∼

Cassandra sat at her desk wearing silk pajamas that

somehow still resembled office attire. She rapped her nails across the top of my file.

I was right back where I had started this afternoon.

Christian stood behind her. I imagined it was partially as a show of force, but also to keep CJ and me from killing each other.

CJ stood in the far corner, holding an ice pack to his face. It matched the one I had discarded on the desk after pressing it on my knuckles during the walk from the restaurant to the ranch office.

Cassandra had been silent for far too long as she worked through measured breaths and flipping through incident reports.

"I'm not sure where to start with you two," she said as she reached for a pen and scribbled a note to call Chef DeRossi on a scrap of paper.

My stomach sank.

As soon as the punch connected, I knew what my fate was going to be. There was no use arguing it.

"CJ," Cassandra said. "Are you pressing charges?"

"I should," he muttered.

"The correct answer is 'no,'" Cassandra clipped without skipping a beat. "I have a restaurant full of witnesses that say you started it. You will take having your ass publicly handed to you as the consequence of your actions. Especially because we told you to get the fuck over it after your stunt with the cows this afternoon."

At the mention of cattle, Mickey lifted his head and opened an eye.

"Now," she said, turning to me. "Is this going to happen again?"

"Not if he pretends I don't exist. Leave me alone and we won't have a problem."

That's all I could ask for. I couldn't rewind the clock and erase CJ outing my name and past to all my cooks, no matter how much I wanted to.

"Seriously?" CJ shouted. "She punched me in the fucking face and she gets off with a slap on the wrist?"

"Chef DeRossi and I will discuss Lennon's consequences later," Cassandra said.

I wished she would just fire me. I didn't want to see the disappointment in Chef DeRossi's face.

CJ let out a malefic laugh. "You're seriously going to let a fucking murderer work for the ranch?"

"Your reading comprehension skills need work, dumbass," I snapped.

"Shut up, *Eleanor*," CJ hissed.

"Watch your mouth," Christian said as he turned on his brother.

"You're defending her?" CJ shouted in disbelief.

Cassandra slammed her hands on the desk. "We're here because you—" she pointed at CJ "—couldn't keep your dick to yourself."

I choked on a laugh.

Cassandra's terrifying gaze turned to me. "And you couldn't keep your hands to yourself and your temper in check."

"How did he even get my file?" I said. "*You* were the only one who was supposed to have access to it."

She shut me up with a lifted finger. "You are on *very* thin ice. I suggest you change the tone you are currently using with me. Understood?"

I gritted my teeth.

"CJ," Cassandra said. "Why did you go through the employee files in *my* office?"

He didn't make a peep.

"No one's going to talk? Fine." Cassandra stood. "You both have two strikes. If you want to keep your jobs, don't get a third."

CJ's jaw dropped, but he snapped it shut. "You can't fire me."

"No, but I can," Christian said as his gaze hardened toward his brother. "I told you—the ranch is a choice. Either you straighten up your act or you find another job."

He sided up to his wife and put his hands on her shoulders with a gentle squeeze.

"You both think your little spats are harmless. They're not. You two picking at each other is the spark that will start a wildfire. It doesn't seem like it'll affect anything until it's all burning down. You have to sacrifice something when you dig a fire line, but it's necessary to keep the burn from spreading. It's time to decide what's worth saving: your pride or your longevity."

"Fuck you," CJ spat as he stormed out of the office. "Fuck all of you."

I made the drive to the gym in silence.

No radio. No music. No humming or tapping.

I felt like a cat on its tenth life. At some point I would run out, and it should have happened a long time ago.

Christian's words about digging a fire line echoed in my mind.

Once upon a time, I had gotten caught in someone else's blaze, and I paid the price. Like the phoenix tattooed on my arm, I felt like I was cheating death over and over again. I didn't know what my fire line was—that piece of myself I had let go of to stop the cycle of destruction.

Unfortunately, it didn't come to me. Not after my mile on the treadmill. Not after my shower in the locker room. And not as I settled into the backseat of my car for the night.

I wondered how long I could outrun the wildfire front before it consumed me entirely.

13

CARSON JAMES

"How's everything lookin', doc?" I asked as I peeled my work gloves off and shoved them in my pocket.

Martha, the vet who had been servicing the ranch since I was in diapers, was packing up her bag when I walked over. She let out a weathered laugh. "You're gonna be awful busy come springtime. All your ladies look healthy, though. Gonna give you a good bunch of calves."

I offered a hand and braced her elbow as I helped her up. "I appreciate you coming all the way out here." My breath clouded with each word.

Doc rested her hands on her hips and surveyed the herd. "Sharp lookin' bunch. You're doing good work out here. And the ranch isn't lookin' too shabby these days. I might have to grab my better half and take her out for a date night at that fancy steakhouse. Sure smelled good when I was driving in."

I bit my tongue to keep from talking shit about the restaurant. Christian wasn't out with me today. But I knew if I so much as thought a bad word about the lodge or restaurant, Cassandra would pop up like bloody-fucking-Mary and dare me to speak.

Christmas had come and gone, and we were firmly in the new year. I was glad to see the decorations disappear. I hated the garland draping from each window of the lodge. I hated the trees with their twinkling lights lining the walkway to the restaurant.

I hated how goddamn picturesque it was.

January, with its gray skies and bleak temperatures, was a reprieve. For once, my surroundings matched my mood.

Doc said her goodbyes, packed up, and headed out.

Truthfully, I wasn't on schedule today. Not that I would have admitted it to anyone. But I hadn't taken a day off since Christian laid out his ultimatum. Either I spent every waking moment as far from civilization as possible, or I got my ass terminated.

I didn't question whether he was bluffing when he said he would fire me; I knew he wasn't joking.

Ranching hadn't been a choice for our father or his brothers. It was survival. But our parents raised the four of us making sure we knew it was a choice, not a destiny. It also meant everyone had to work hard and keep from bitching about it. We could all walk away, and that's what pissed me off the most.

I didn't want to leave this place, but I also didn't want to toe the party line.

"CJ, you there?" Christian's voice crackled over the radio.

I ripped the radio off my belt and smashed the side button. "Present."

"Head up to the house."

My knuckles turned white as I strangled the radio. He knew exactly what he was doing.

I couldn't argue on an open line. We kept family drama

separate from ranch work. It was a management tactic that kept the family respected among the ranch hands. We presented a united front, always.

"Still working," I clipped in return.

Christian didn't waste a second. "You're done for the day."

A colorful string of curses flipped through my head, one after the other. I dropped the radio to my side, resigned to let him have this one.

On second thought, I picked it back up and pressed it to my mouth. I hesitated, then dropped it again.

Anny glanced at me from where she was nibbling on the threadbare grass. I swear she called me a dumbass in that one look.

"Understood," I muttered into the radio before turning the damn thing off.

I had been summoned.

Anarchy was full of attitude today, and I didn't blame her. She let it rip as we galloped across the plains. Adrenaline rushed from my fingertips to my boots in a tidal wave.

The rush of wind around us flooded my lungs. For once, I could breathe.

We took the long way up to the house, circling the backside of Ray's property and Christian and Nate's houses. Part of the route was so I could stretch the ride out as long as possible and avoid family dinner. The other part was so I didn't have to see the restaurant. So that I didn't have to see her shitty clunker of a car. So, I didn't have to think of her in that building.

Far sooner than I wanted it to, my parents' ranch house came into view.

Christian was waiting on the front porch, sitting in one

of the rocking chairs with his arms crossed. "Took you long enough."

"Had shit to do," I groused.

He let out a displeased huff. "I told you to straighten up, not to work yourself to death."

"Same thing, isn't it?" I dropped off Anny's back and headed up the stairs.

"Dinner's ready," he clipped. "Wash up." And with that, he turned and walked inside.

"Yes, *Dad*," I muttered at his back. Something warm and aromatic floated through the air, making my stomach growl.

I slipped into the kitchen and found my mom tidying up.

Her cheeks lifted when I slid through the door. "Well, hey, sweetie. I was starting to wonder where you were."

"Sorry," I said under my breath as I turned the tap on and scrubbed my hands. "I was out pretty far."

She let out a low chuckle under her breath. "I figured. Doesn't bother me. Unlike children, chili will keep. Go take a load off and eat with the family. There's a place for you."

Of that, I had no doubt. Mom always set a place for everyone, even when we weren't there. When Nate was deployed or stationed somewhere else, there was always a place for him and his first wife.

When Ray was riding the rodeo circuit, there was always a place for him. When he moved back to the ranch after his accident and refused to see anyone, she still set a place for him.

Maybe that's what hurt so much about Christian putting his foot down about this thing between Lennon and me. For years it had been Dad, Christian, and me running the ranch. Then Dad retired and it was only Christian and me.

Now I felt like a lone ranger.

"What's the matter, kid?" I asked Gracie when I dropped into the seat between her and Bree.

The side of the table where my nieces sat, looking rather morose today, was safe. I wouldn't have to hear about whatever shit Cassandra and the lodge and restaurant managers were cooking up.

"Nothing," she grumbled into her bowl as she stabbed a bean over and over with her spoon.

I reached into the cast-iron skillet and snagged a piece of cornbread. "I don't know about that. Why are you murdering your chili?"

"It's about a boy," Bree mouthed from her spot, catty-cornered to me.

"Ah."

"It's not about a boy," Gracie snapped.

Geez. No wonder Christian was on edge these days. Two teenagers were a nightmare and I had barely been sitting between them for thirty seconds.

"Then what's it about? Who do I get to kill?"

Bree snickered, but Gracie ground her teeth together.

I gently elbowed her.

Gracie huffed. "I've been talking to this boy named Jordan, and he invited me to go to the bonfire with him on Friday night, and I got all excited, but then he invited my friend Julie too. So now I don't want to go because he invited her after he had already asked me to go with him. And when I told him I didn't want to go, he told me I was making a big deal out of nothing."

I made a show of mulling it over. "Grace, I think there's only one thing you can do."

"What?" she mumbled in the most sour tone I'd ever heard as she stabbed another bean.

"Change your name, move schools, and never be friends with anyone whose name starts with J."

Bree snickered, but Gracie's cracked smile made my heart soften.

"What's that thing that Cass says all the time? Anyone whose name is spelled weird is a red flag? Add 'J' names to that. Jordan, Julie, Joe, James, Jessica, Jackson, Jonathan, Jenny. Red flags all around."

Gracie let out a soft laugh. "I can't not be friends with people because their names start with J."

"Eat up, kid. You'll figure it out."

She stirred her spoon around in her chili, but it was less felonious than before. "What do you think I should do?"

Not go to a bonfire. Everyone knew what happened at those teenage hormone fests.

But I wasn't her parent. That nightmare dilemma was Christian and Cassandra's problem.

"Go anyway. Have a good time. Find some better friends while you're there. If the J-names want to act foolish, let them. Don't let their actions and choices get to you. Be your own person and what's meant for you will find its way to you." I shoveled in a bite. "And if you need to hide a body, call me."

"Thanks," Gracie said as she finally dug into her food.

"How's the herd looking?" Nate asked from the other side of the table.

I nodded as I swallowed. "Good. Doc said everyone's on track. Should be a busy calving season."

"I bet the lodge guests will love having some baby cows to look at," Brooke gushed. "I love calving season. It would be so fun if you had some bottle-fed calves up close to the property for people to help feed and love on."

My cows did not need strangers to feed them or handle them in any way.

"No," I clipped.

Ray bristled, straightening in his wheelchair as he glared at me for the tone I took with his wife. "You wanna try that again?"

Great. Now he was angry with me too.

I wiped my mouth and shoved away from the table. I had eaten enough to tide me over until I could scrounge up something at the bunkhouse.

"I'm heading out. See y'all later," I grumbled.

Mom's face fell as I stood. "Carson James..."

There it was. The double name everyone always used because I was always the one getting in trouble. Even in my thirties.

I remembered when everyone called me Carson. They'd shortened it to CJ after a particularly trying summer I spent following Nate around while he was home, trying to do what Christian was doing, and attempting to be like Ray.

"Thanks for dinner," I said as I passed Mom and headed out the door.

Somehow, Cassandra was waiting for me on the porch. I hadn't even noticed her slip out. Last I remembered, she was talking to Becks and Brooke about the upcoming Saturday afternoon they'd spend together in town.

"You blew me off."

I kept walking. "When?"

"For our ride this afternoon."

I paused.

When Cassandra first started working at the ranch, we got in the habit of taking afternoon trail rides together. She was shit with horses, hated everything, and needed a reprieve. Kind of like I was, except horses were the only things that tolerated me.

I scoffed. "We haven't gone riding in months."

"And whose fault is that?" she said as she pushed away from the porch and started after me down the stairs. "You're the one who stopped showing up."

"I had work to do."

She let out a terrifying laugh. "Bullshit. You boys like to pretend like it's work, work, work, sun up to sun down. But it doesn't have to be that way, and you know it. You're using those damn cows as an excuse to run away because you're uncomfortable."

"I already got an earful from Christian. I don't need it from you too," I said as I stomped over to Anny.

"I tried my best," Cassandra called after me. "I'm sorry it wasn't good enough."

Two things struck me.

First, Cassandra apologized for something. That made me want to check the weather report for snow in hell.

Second, what was she talking about? What wasn't good enough? I hated to admit it, but she had turned our struggling ranch into a destination. People were willing to pay a mortgage to stay there.

"I know you're unhappy, and it's my fault." Cassandra's expression softened to a state I had never seen it in before. She was always sporting her "hell hath no fury" look. "So, if you want to be pissed at someone, be pissed at me. Not your family."

"You're family."

Her eyes widened.

I shrugged it off. "Got that new last name, right?"

But the truth was, Cassandra was more of a sister than a

sister-in-law. We bickered and picked at each other, but we never meant anything by it.

Something had settled in me when she joined the ranch. Like a missing weight had balanced the scales.

Same with Becks. She had been holding down the fort long before Cassandra came to the ranch.

Brooke felt like the final piece of our family. She was the miracle that brought Ray out of the darkness after his accident.

I loved my sisters. So why did things still seem off kilter?

Cassandra followed me over to Anny and held her hand out, waiting to see if my horse was in an amicable mood or not.

Anny snapped at Cassandra's hand, and Cass jumped back.

"See?" she said as she crossed her arms. "Anarchy used to tolerate me because we'd ride in the afternoons. Now she hates me again."

I shrugged. "She's antsy because of the storm coming in."

My stomach soured as I hopped on Anarchy's back and took in Cassandra's face. She looked genuinely regretful, and that wasn't an emotion she let slip around anyone.

"I know you lost a lot when we built the lodge and the restaurant," she said. "But I hope you'll stick around long enough to see what you've gained rather than what you lost."

Anarchy stood still as Cassandra and I stared at each other.

Finally, Cass backed away. "Have a good night, Carson."

14

LENNON

Frigid smatterings of rain pelted me as I dashed from the gym door to the parking lot. Wind cracked like a whip, snapping at my skin as I kept my head down and ran.

I thought moving to the bottom of the country meant I had escaped cold winters. Apparently, the joke was on me.

Shivers danced through my body as I crawled into the driver's seat and locked the door. I hadn't gotten a chance to fully charge my phone, but it would get me through the night. *I hoped.*

I would have killed to be on the schedule at the restaurant today, but it was my day off. Chef DeRossi had called to not-so-subtly threaten me to take the mandatory day off, so I wouldn't stab someone with a chef's knife.

Particularly, a certain cowboy who had, thankfully, made himself scarce. He avoided the restaurant on his trips to and from the bunkhouse, and had stopped eating there with his family.

I shook off the rain and cranked up my car. I'd run the

heat for ten minutes, then cut it off for the rest of the hour, then repeat.

I cursed the leasing office that had most recently rejected me due to a "clerical error" after initially offering me an apartment. It was probably for the best, though. It came with an asinine monthly lease and required four months' rent as a deposit. The terms were criminal.

Shadows danced across the hood of the car as the trees shook with each gust. The storm howled like phantoms screaming in the night.

I wanted to scream with them.

My fingers had turned to icicles during the sprint from the building to my car. They were stiff and chilled as I stretched them and held them in front of the vents to thaw.

I needed to get my window shades up so people couldn't see in my car; not that anyone else was at the gym tonight. Except for the lone employee keeping the lights on inside to make good on the promise of twenty-four-seven access, the lot was a ghost town.

I was haunted by it.

Vacant memories of the last ten years had tortured me in my sleep. I was running on fumes and staff coffee, and I was damn near out of both.

Something rattled against the outside of my car, and I jumped, nearly knocking my head on the roof.

I hesitated before turning on the interior light. It was generally against my rules of car living, but a moment couldn't hurt.

A small branch had fallen on the hood of my car. Nothing was damaged or concerning.

I let a slow breath leech from my lungs and rummaged around the floorboard of the passenger seat for the window covers. A shadow fell over the seat as I grabbed them and sat up.

If a tree fell on my car, that would be the icing on the cake.

Maybe I should move parking spaces and get away from the tree line. I liked the privacy it afforded, but I wasn't in any position to buy a new car.

I turned to glance out the window and scout for a new spot. Eyes stared back at me through the glass.

Burning pain ripped through my vocal cords as I screamed and clapped my hands over my mouth.

Rain-drenched hair in scarlet red pressed against the window next to a pale palm.

No.

No, no, no—

I had been running for so long, but I hadn't run fast enough.

They'd found me.

Vomit lurched up my throat and filled my mouth. I stomped on the brake and yanked the gear shift into reverse. My tires screeched on the rain-soaked asphalt.

The woman jumped backward, trying not to get hit by four thousand pounds of metal on wheels.

I slammed the gear shift back into drive and floored it, squalling tires as I peeled out of the lot. My heart was in my throat as I gunned it down the road without a single thought about where I was headed. The sweat beading on my skin was colder than the rain outside.

I had been so careful. So cautious. I never stayed in one place too long. I kept my traceable finances as minimal as possible. I went without so I could stay under the radar. And for what?

To be found halfway across the country?

Tears stung my eyes as I hit the service road that led to the ranch. I hadn't even realized I had driven out this far. The route had become a habit, and habits put you in obituaries. Then again, you had to have a family to submit your information to an obituary. People who you were survived by. Loved by.

I didn't have that. I'd be a nameless, unclaimed body in a morgue.

One tire hit the pothole, then two. Mud and rainwater sloshed outside as darkness engulfed the car. The faint glow from the decorative lamps that lined the dirt and gravel road to the lodge was drowned out by the storm.

I pressed harder on the gas as my heart and pulse raced in tandem. Choppy breaths made my head spin. A shriek slipped from my lips as the car slid across the rivers of stormwater, struggling to stay on the path. I white-knuckled the steering wheel, praying to any deity that was listening to let me make it a little closer to the restaurant. I didn't want to have to run two miles in the pouring rain and lightning.

My lungs hitched as the car skidded out of control. A loud *thunk* jolted me out of the terror as the car hit a pothole.

Okay. Take a breath. Breathe.

I let go of the steering wheel and shook my hands to try to regain circulation. The war against fight or flight was an uphill battle.

I pressed the gas, but nothing happened. The crash of rain overhead drowned out the faint whizz of the tires spinning in the mud. I pressed my foot to the floor.

Nothing.

"No, no, no," I muttered as I pocketed my phone and cracked open the door. The front tire was halfway buried in mud. My headlights were barely visible in the torrent. Hell, I could barely see my hand in front of my face.

I grimaced as I yanked the keys from the ignition and slammed the door. My sneakers sank into the mud as I tried to get away from the car. The last thing I wanted was for a guest braving the storm to rear-end my car or flatten me like a pancake.

The field was waterlogged, but it was easier to cross. I kept my head down and counted each breath as I walked, then jogged, then ran.

Everything was dark. The freezing wind was an insulting smack that rattled my bones. I couldn't walk into the lodge looking like this, and heaven forbid the cooks who were still closing up the restaurant saw me.

My sneakers had nearly suctioned to the ground when the faint glow of the bunkhouse came into view.

The only light on in the entire house was at the very top. That light was my beacon as I picked up my pace, focusing on the burn in my lungs to keep from crying.

It didn't help.

The warm sting of tears was a sharp contrast to the frost that coated my skin and cut to my marrow.

Oxygen came in short, choppy gasps like waves lapping at the shoreline as I stumbled up the steps to the front door. Lights began to turn on inside, one by one.

My energy was gone. I wanted to collapse on the stoop and cry. I wanted to sleep for years. The fear would come back tomorrow.

Before I could knock, the door whipped open. I nearly fell into the body that met me on the other side.

CJ's hands shackled my waist, holding me up and drawing me in. "What the hell are you doing, trouble?"

I couldn't help the mix of sniffles and sobs. "I-I didn't

have a-anywhere else to g-go." My teeth chattered as I choked out each pathetic word. "What are you doing?"

"I was coming to get you."

My eyes found his. Those hazel eyes were soft like cashmere but were surrounded by sharp lines of worry and a little mistrust.

"What?"

"We have cameras everywhere," he said as he kept my body firmly against his while he reached around and closed the door behind us. "I know exactly where you are, always."

I wiped my cheeks with my fingertips, not realizing they were flecked with mud from the run. Dirt smeared my cheeks as I tried my best to keep from crying in front of him.

I didn't have much to my name, but I had my pride. And that was the one thing I had to let go of.

My fire line.

I had to cut it down to stop the burn.

"I just need somewhere to crash for the night," I admitted. "Or not even for the night. Just until the storm lets up."

CJ's jaw worked back and forth. "Go upstairs."

My eyes danced over the conglomerate of sectional couches and recliners in the spacious den. "I can wait on the couch."

"I'm not letting you sleep on the couch. Besides, you're filthy." With that, he turned and walked up the steps.

I followed, feeling a little like I was being marched to my own execution. He opened the doors and led me down the hallway.

Men peered out of the rooms at me as I dutifully followed CJ. I had seen most of them working around the ranch, but hadn't spoken to them. Their gaze made my skin itch.

"Inside," CJ clipped as he opened the door at the end of the hallway and waited for me to walk in.

The room was simple and neat with a queen-sized bed, a nightstand, and a heavy trunk against the wall. He had pulled back the curtains on either side of the window, giving him a bird's-eye view of the lodge, the restaurant, the patio where the restaurant's smokers were kept, and the road that led in and out.

In the distance, I could make out the little lump that was my mud-covered car.

He had watched everything.

Every move I made. Every late night I spent babysitting the smoker so I wouldn't have to sleep in my car. All of it.

The click of the door closing shook me out of the exhaustion-induced stupor.

"Bathroom's right here," he said as he opened one of the interior doors and flipped on the light.

The room was tight, but it had a private sink, toilet, and shower that the rest of the house couldn't access.

He opened a narrow closet and grabbed a folded towel. "You're filthy."

I looked down at the mud I had tracked across the floor. "I'm sorry."

He didn't accept or reject the apology. There was no cursory "it's okay." His face remained stoic and unreadable as he pushed the towel into my hands.

"Go on."

"My clothes are in my car," I said through chattering teeth as I looked down at the rain-soaked leggings and long-sleeve shirt that clung to my body.

"You're gonna get pneumonia if you don't get out of those wet clothes and get warm. I'm not going to tell you again. Get in the shower, Len."

I refused to linger on the fact that he had called me Len instead of "trouble." I clutched the towel to my chest and slipped into the bathroom.

I had rules about bathing. I always waited to use the gym showers until at least two other showers were in use. There was strength in numbers and witnesses if something ever happened. I was quick and efficient. I didn't dilly-dally.

Those rules were the same, even behind the locked doors of overpriced truck stop showers. I rinsed off and got out within ninety seconds.

As much as I wanted to linger in the billows of steam and the perception of safety, I wasn't breaking any more rules tonight. Showing up at CJ's door, practically begging for help, was all my pride could take.

I was in and out in record time.

I had just hopped out of the shower and was squeezing the water from my hair with the towel when a knock at the door startled me.

I yelped and wrapped the towel around my body, tucking its tail between my boobs.

"Unlock it real quick," he said from the other side.

I took a slow, deep breath and flipped the latch on the knob.

But CJ didn't come in. He didn't even peek. He stuck his arm through the crack, dropped a stack of clothes in the sink, and then shut it again.

I stared at the closed door, wondering what the hell his angle was. Curiosity got the better of me and I rifled through the stack. There was a pair of sweatpants that would fit if I rolled the waist over, and a t-shirt I'd swim in.

But they were clean and dry.

I dried off and dressed, trying my best not to focus on

the lingering remnants of his cologne as I rinsed my mud-caked clothes in the sink and wrung them out.

When there was nothing left to do but face the music, I opened the door.

CJ was stretched out on his bed, scrolling through his phone. When a floorboard creaked underfoot, he looked over.

"We have a washing machine, you know. We're not completely uncivilized," he said as he took in the damp clothes in my hands.

"I'll take them to the laundromat in town when I get out of here tomorrow."

He sat up and his feet hit the floor. "What were you doing out in the storm?"

I bristled at the interrogation. "None of your business."

"It is my business if you're sleeping in my bed."

I laughed. "Who says I'm sleeping in your bed? I told you I'd wait on a couch. And if that's off the table, I'll walk to the restaurant and wait it out in my office."

Lightning snaked across the sky.

"Sure," CJ said with a dry laugh. "Step outside and get struck by lightning. Be my guest."

I scowled at him.

"Tell me why you were out in the storm, and I'll let you sleep on the couch downstairs."

Fuck him.

I turned and headed for the door. "Thanks for the shower. I'll take my chances with the lightning."

CJ was up and out of bed before I could get my hand on the doorknob. "Lennon—"

"What is your angle?" I snapped. "I don't owe you answers. You're the one who opened the door and let me inside."

He froze in stride. "Why were you going back to the restaurant in the middle of the night? Why aren't you at home?"

"It's barely after ten. It's not the middle of the night."

His eyes flared with sparks and embers. "Might as well be midnight when you have to be up at the ass crack of dawn. Now answer the question."

I worked it over in my mind. I couldn't tell him the whole truth, but that look in his eye said that he wasn't about to let this go. And if he didn't let it go, he'd take it to Cassandra. Or worse, Chef DeRossi.

"I had to move my car," I hedged.

The flames that had pulsed between us that night at the bar were back. Heat roiled between us as we lingered in the standoff.

"Right," he said doubtfully. "You had to move your car. In the middle of a fucking storm."

I lifted my chin. "You asked for the answer. I didn't say you'd like it."

Energy pulsed between us like downed power lines arcing with electricity.

"Take the bed," he said as he grabbed his phone and brushed past me, heading out the door.

15

CARSON JAMES

Rule Number One: When you're holding a grudge, don't think about how attractive the object of your hatred is.

Rule Number Two: When you do think about how attractive she is, ignore it. It will go away. Probably.

Rule Number Three: When you steal a car, it helps to have the keys.

Daylight was breaking as I hopped into my truck and headed for the front gate. I had a travel mug of coffee in the cupholder, an ache in my balls, and trouble in my bed.

I looped Lennon's car keys around my finger as I pulled off the dirt road into the field.

She had done a number on the service road when she tried to come in during the storm last night. Grooves of dried mud created deep canyons. I'd have to get one of the guys to grade it down before one of the highfalutin guests got their fancy sedans stuck in one of the ruts.

I did a quick turn, backing my truck up so the hitch lined up with the front of her car, then hopped out.

I unlocked the driver's side door so I could put the car in neutral, but froze as soon as it was open.

A sleeping bag was laid out in the backseat. Shades to block the sun were fitted over the back windows. From the looks of it, the ones in the passenger's seat were meant for the front windows and windshield.

A duffel bag was wedged in the floorboard of the backseat. A set of crisp chef's whites was on a clothes hanger that dangled from the "oh shit" handle. Snacks and shelf-stable foods were arranged in a hanging organizer that draped behind the driver's seat.

I got the car ready to be towed out and slammed the door. The anger was a better pick-me-up than the coffee.

It took a few tries before the mud let go of Lennon's car. Before I could fully comprehend how—not if—I was going to address my findings, I was pulling up to the bunkhouse.

I didn't know who I was going to bitch out first: my brother, my sister-in-law, or Lennon. But someone was about to get a fucking earful.

The ruckus echoing from the bunkhouse as I hopped out of the truck and unhitched her car was my answer.

The bunkhouse kitchen was mayhem. Music blared from the speakers as every ranch hand crowded around the island. The scent of bacon, cinnamon, and coffee hit me like a right hook.

And in the middle of the chaos was Lennon.

I had her duffel bag in one hand, her keys in the other, and a grim look on my face. Lennon's smile was bright and wide as she cut up with the guys while she piled more and more food onto the kitchen island for breakfast.

I kicked the door shut with my boot, letting it slam like a gunshot.

Lennon looked up as she shuffled pancakes out of a skillet and froze.

"Upstairs," I clipped. "Now."

Her eyes dropped to the things I had in my hands. Fear flashed across her face like a bolt of lightning, but as quickly as it came, it was gone.

Lennon ignored me, turning back to the range to drop more batter into the skillet.

I broke through the mass of bodies vying for a plateful of food, grabbed her bicep, and tugged her away. "I said upstairs, trouble. You and I are gonna have a talk."

"I have food cooking," she snapped. "It'll burn."

"Then let it fucking burn. They know how to use a fire extinguisher."

She wrenched her arm out of my grasp and snatched her keys from my hand. I held her duffel out of reach, forcing her to march up the steps.

When the bedroom door shut behind us, I dropped her bag and had her pinned against the wall like we had been that first night.

"Tell me it's not true," I growled.

"That I made breakfast?" She rolled her eyes. "God forbid I scramble some eggs. You do know I cook for a living, right? I'm not going to burn your house down."

I pressed my body against hers, shutting her up. "Tell me you're not living in your fucking car."

Her sassy sneer turned to stone. "That's none of your business."

"It's my fucking business when you work on my ranch. If you aren't getting paid enough to live, that's a fucking problem."

"Let it go," she hissed, pushing back against me.

"No."

"Let. It. Go. You already know," she snapped as tears welled up in her eyes. "You went through my file. Or was I right about your reading comprehension skills? I'm a felon. I have a record. People will not rent to me. I've been trying to get a place ever since I moved here to work on your fucking ranch, and all I've heard is no."

Her keys jingled as she reached up between us and dabbed her eyes. "Now you know. So, just fucking drop it and let's go back to ignoring each other."

There was no way in hell that was happening.

"What happened?"

Lennon shoved against my chest. "None of your fucking busi—"

"It is my business," I barked as I grabbed her wrists and pinned them to the wall. "My ranch. My land. My last name on that uniform you wear. My business. So if you have a problem, it's my problem too. Now talk."

Something inside her seemed to break. Piece by piece, it shattered behind those haunted eyes. I watched as the shards fell from her gaze, turning from sharp weapons into nothingness.

"It's a long story," she said as her blank eyes lowered to her bare feet.

I loosened my grip on her wrists. "Then you'd better get started."

She pressed against my hold, but the fight wasn't there. I let go, but stopped her with a hand on her stomach when she tried to move away from the wall.

"There is not a place you can hide on this ranch that I will not find you. Don't even try to run from me."

Lennon swallowed and nodded. She began to pace the room and wring her hands, trying to collect herself.

My eyes followed her, but I never moved.

Animals and people weren't all that different. They both spooked easily when they were on edge. If I wanted the whole story out of Lennon, I couldn't scare it out of her. She'd run.

"Chef DeRossi and Cassandra know everything," Lennon blurted out. "It's not like you can use this against me or something. I'm sure Christian knows too."

I worked my hand over the scruff on the side of my jaw. "Who said anything about using it against you?"

"Why wouldn't you use it against me? You've tried to get me fired. *Repeatedly*."

She may have had the slightest point, and it stung.

"I want to know why the hell you're living in your car. You're the one who said it was a long story. Better get started. We're burning daylight."

"I did six years in federal prison for accessory after the fact to armed robbery. I was seventeen, but they tried me as an adult."

I had read that much in her file, but hearing her say it out loud struck something inside me.

"I was assigned a job in the kitchen and that's where I learned to cook. Chef DeRossi started a reentry program with his restaurant group to help inmates build skills and find work in food service when they got out. I started as a prep cook in one of his restaurants and worked my way up."

Lennon's hands began to shake. She breathed through whatever was warring in her mind and centered herself. Her discipline was impressive.

"I served my time," she continued. "I've been a productive member of society. I take pride in my job, and I want to leave all the bullshit behind me."

"Why do I feel like there's a 'but' coming?"

Lennon glanced at the window as if she were waiting for someone to come take her away. "All I did was drive the car."

"What are you talking about?"

"My brother . . . he was the one who did it." She sat on the edge of the bed and picked at the knee of the sweatpants she wore. "Well, my half-brother. We have the same mother. Different dads. Mine was a deadbeat one night stand. His was an alcoholic who came around every once in a while. Our mom went to jail when I was fifteen, and the state decided he was fit to be my guardian."

It felt like I was floating as I strode across the room and sat behind her on the bed, pulling her back between my legs.

Lennon tensed. "It was a school night. I had a part-time job at the bodega near our apartment that I had to be at the next morning. I was working on homework when Justin came into the living room and told me I had to drive him somewhere. He handed me the keys to a car that I didn't know was stolen, and told me to drive him over the bridge to New Jersey. He had me park outside a bank and told me he'd be back in ten minutes."

I swore under my breath as I slipped my arms around her waist and held her against my chest.

"I heard gunshots, then Justin came out of the building with a backpack. He got in the car and—" her voice cracked "—there was blood spatter all over his clothes. I freaked out and he pulled the gun on me and told me to drive." A tear slipped down her cheek, splashing on my hand. "We made it out to the Hudson River and he stashed the bag. But by then, the cops were all over looking for him. The security guard at the bank had pressed the silent alarm before Justin . . ." Lennon sucked in a sharp breath as she tried her hardest not to cry.

"Before Justin shot him. Instead of making it to school the next day, I got arrested."

I rested my forehead on the back of her head, feeling like utter shit for everything.

"I'm sorry," I said as contritely as I could. "I'm so fucking sorry, Len."

"I did six years. He went away for thirty. Armed robbery and attempted murder. He lucked out that the security guard lived. Probably would have been life."

"Should've been," I muttered.

"Having a record sucks. It makes finding places to live really fucking hard. I usually end up subletting or agreeing to shitty lease terms. My credit is trash." Her pause was weighted. "I'm still working on finding somewhere local to live. There aren't many options in town."

"I know I'm going to regret asking this, but where have you been sleeping?"

Lennon was halfway to picking her nails to death. I wrapped my hands around hers to still her nervous fingers.

"My car," she said with measured caution. "Nothing I haven't done before. I'm a pro by now. I have a gym membership that gives me amenities all over the country. If I'm desperate for a bed, I'll get a cheap motel room with cash."

"Why cash?" The words were out before I could stop them.

Lennon chewed on her lip for a long moment. "Remember when I said my brother stashed the bag of money he stole?"

I nodded.

"My public defender got the judge to agree to time off my sentence if I helped them put Justin away. I told them everything. Every detail down to the phone call and where he hid the money. Except, the bag was already gone. I ended up still serving time because they thought I had lied since they couldn't find the money."

"What phone call?"

She sighed. "Before the robbery happened, Justin got a call from someone, and it sounded like they knew what he was about to do. I only heard Justin's side of the call, but he said, 'It will be where I said it would be.'"

"Did the cops ever find out who he was talking to?"

"No." Her hands tightened in mine. "They thought I faked a third person so I could hide the money. But it had already disappeared while I was still handcuffed to a table, getting questioned. I used to wonder if I had hallucinated the phone call."

Lennon lifted the t-shirt I had loaned her and showed off a sickle-shaped scar that curved over her hip. Two nickel-sized scars dotted the skin beside it.

"I didn't hallucinate it," she said a little more firmly. "When I got to the facility I was going to serve my sentence in, a woman in my block shanked me. Some guy paid her off to send me a message. He thought I had the money."

I traced the ridged silver skin with my fingertips. "If you don't have the money and the guy from the phone call doesn't have it, that means your brother has to have it, right?"

She shrugged. "I always wondered if my brother double-crossed his guy and had someone hide the money from everyone when he stashed the bag by the river. Honestly, I don't give a shit where the money is or who has it now. I just want to put it all behind me. I'm constantly looking over my shoulder. I can't explain it, but I've always had this feeling that someone was waiting for me to get out so they could track me down. So, I pay for most everything in cash. I travel with Chef DeRossi's launch team that opens his new restaurants, so I'm not in one place for too long. Everyone always called me 'Len' when I was younger, so I started going by Lennon instead of Eleanor. I always hated my name, so that wasn't a loss. It sounded too stuffy anyway."

"Lennon fits you." I pressed a kiss to the back of her head. "What happened last night? Why'd you have to move your car and come back to the ranch?"

She wrenched her hands from my grip and pressed her fingers to her eyes. She looked exhausted.

"Someone knocked on my car door when I was getting ready for bed. This woman I've seen around town a few times."

"Did she tell you to leave or something?"

"I think I did time with her." Lennon closed her eyes. "And running into someone you met in prison once you're out is generally a very *bad* thing."

I tightened my hold on her. "Was it the woman who stabbed you?"

"I don't know. They both had red hair. Like, really bright red-velvet cake colored hair. I'm not sure if it's actually her, but I'm not about to find out. I need to lay low, change up my routine, and find somewhere else to crash."

"Here," I said without a moment of hesitation. "Stay here."

Lennon peeled away from me and stood up, running a hand back through her black and white hair. "No. I'm not staying somewhere I'm clearly not welcome. I'm fine on my own."

I jumped up after her. "Len—"

She turned to me with hostile, red-rimmed eyes. "Thanks for the hospitality and the heart-to-heart. But I learned long ago that I'm the only one who can protect me. I'm not falling for you, Cowboy."

16

CARSON JAMES

I watched the grainy feed from the trail cameras as Lennon dashed out of the bunkhouse, grabbed her things from her car, and hurried back inside. For once, I wished we had cameras inside the bunkhouse so I could watch her.

My head was spinning after her confessions this morning. I hadn't wanted to leave her, but the ranch didn't wait for anyone.

I was a piece of shit.

The feelings I had been ignoring since the night we hooked up at the bar had come back with a fiery vengeance. My suspicions that she was hiding something had been spot on.

She was hiding herself.

Frankly, the ranch wasn't a bad place to get away from the world. It's what I did.

"Thought I'd find you out here." My father's voice cut through the rustle of grass and the low din of the animals.

It was rare to see him up on a horse these days. A double hip replacement a few years back had put him out of commission for a while, but it was good to see him getting out. He had saddled Dottie, the sweet girl Cassandra always rode.

Anarchy flicked an ear their way, then decided she didn't care that others were present.

"I'm always out here," I said as I rested my hands on my thighs.

Anarchy shifted beneath me.

My dad held the same posture, surveying the herd without much commentary.

He chuckled. "You're right. I figured after last night you'd come out here to do some thinking."

"What are you talking about?"

"I was up last night when Chef Maddox came back. Saw her slide off the road and get stuck. Almost made it out to offer her a hand, but she took off. When I saw you tow her car out this morning, I figured she'd gone to you."

I didn't delve into the details of Lennon showing up at my door last night, or what she had told me this morning.

All I knew was that I had some work to do.

"I messed up," I admitted as the words clouded around me in the chilly morning air. I had said those three words as a kid more times than I could count, but my father was unfazed as usual.

Dad cracked a smile. "I'll say. But that's all right. Nothing you can't fix, right?"

I recalled the hurt on Lennon's face when I stormed into the restaurant kitchen and outed her identity to the staff like an asshole. She had hidden her fear behind anger and retaliation.

"I don't know if I can fix this."

"Take it from someone who has to do a lot of apologizing to his sweetheart on a daily basis. Saying you're sorry is a good start. Flowers don't hurt either." He took a pull from an insulated thermos and offered it to me. "Coffee?"

I took it and downed a gulp, then sputtered. "Jesus! What the hell?" Liquor burned my mouth worse than the bitterness of the coffee. "Why are you drinking whiskey at seven in the morning?"

He took the thermos back and snickered. "What? I'm retired. It's five o'clock somewhere. Having a little whiskey in my coffee and riding a horse isn't drinking and driving."

He and I apparently had different definitions of what "a little" whiskey meant.

"I don't think this is a *flowers and apologies* situation," I admitted.

"I didn't say it was a fix. I said it was a start."

"Doesn't matter if I get her forgiveness." I sighed and gave Anny a little tap to get her going.

My father followed beside me on Dottie.

"She said she's not falling for a cowboy."

He chuckled. "Sounds like your Momma. I heard that exact same thing outta her."

"Len . . . She's not like Momma."

He let out a blustering snort. "Really? She's not hardheaded and argumentative? She's not a workhorse who refuses to take time off? She's not—"

"Fine, you have a point."

He grinned.

We wandered in silence for a while, checking on the bred and springing heifers. After that, we made sure the gates and fencing were secure.

"Took me a year to convince your momma to give me a chance, and we were starting on even ground. You've gotta dig yourself out of a hole first."

Didn't I know it . . .

"I don't know how to handle her."

He raised a wary eyebrow. "Well, there's your first mistake. You don't 'handle' a woman, so get that out of your vocabulary. You work with each other. You learn how to read her and meet her where she is, and she'll do the same for you. It's a partnership. You don't 'handle' Anarchy. It's a team effort, even in the courting."

"I don't know how to handle any of this shit. Everything changed so fast. One day we were cattle ranching and the next we're a fucking tourist hotspot."

He sighed. "You and me both, Son. I miss not having cars passing the house all the time. I even thought about putting up a fence for some privacy."

"Say the word and the guys and I will get it up."

He nodded. "But I also think about what it brought us. We've got the girls now. Becks, Cassandra, and Brooke. All the little ones. Though, Bree and Gracie aren't that little anymore. And I hate to admit it, but the ranch was always about more than cows. This land is the place people come to when they need to escape. It was that for Nate after his deployments and divorce. It was that for Ray after his accident. It was that for Christian after Gretchen passed. It's always been the place you hide. It's been our haven for generations. It might be hard to get used to, but I don't think sharing our refuge is a bad thing."

Dottie eased over, putting us within arm's reach of each other. Dad patted me on the back. "Don't be selfish with your peace. Other people need it too. You won't run out."

I watched as he turned and rode back to the house, taking it slow and steady with Dottie.

There was something about talking to my dad that always left me with more questions than answers. Christian was the same. More than once, Cassandra had bitched him out for speaking like a "cowboy fortune cookie."

It was fitting.

Winter wildflowers floated in waves as the breeze warmed with the rising sun. I loved the shift of colors in the foliage as the seasons changed. I loved watching the land come alive with each passing week and month.

There were a million reasons I never wanted to leave this land. That I never wanted it to change. I found them in the billions of stars. The endless sea of green underfoot. The steadiness of the sunrise. The peaceful sound of rain. The heat of summer. The battle against the land to make it productive and hospitable. The fruitful years that yielded after the work we put in. The partnership of man and animal for survival and success.

I loved the fight. And I wasn't done yet.

17

LENNON

The restaurant kitchen had been eerily quiet since the moment I set foot in it this morning. I would have given anything for Julian to complain about my leadership or for a guest to gripe about their meal. Apparently, things were just too good.

I blamed it on the storm.

The lodge was nearly empty until the weekend, which meant the restaurant had been slow. Usually, I would have enjoyed the reprieve. It was always a chance to work out friction points in the kitchen or test out new menu items.

But the silence today made me uneasy.

No one had brought up the incident with CJ when he came barreling in with my employee file. On the bright side, my vitriolic reaction seemed to make everyone think twice about crossing me.

"Chef, the Griffith table would like to send compliments," a server said.

Of course they did.

I nodded. "I'll go right up. Thank you."

I did my best to keep my face neutral in front of the

cooks as I untied my apron and uncuffed the sleeves of my chef's coat.

At least I wouldn't have to face CJ again. I'd sneak to the bunkhouse, hop in my car, and leave when I was done.

I didn't want to think about the conversation that CJ had forced me into this morning. How I had bared my wounds. But I couldn't shake it. And as much as I wanted to, I couldn't forget how safe I'd felt sitting beside him or the feeling of his arms wrapped around me.

I couldn't shake the way I had wanted to fall into them and never leave.

But I had to ignore it. I had already slipped up somewhere, enough for the redhead to find me. I couldn't make another mistake.

The restaurant was nearly empty as I made my way up. The last reservation of the night was enjoying coffee and dessert. We'd be out of here soon.

I hurried up the stairs and crossed my fingers, hoping that the Griffith family wouldn't linger too long, and we could close up.

The glow of the standing heaters met me as I rounded the corner on the landing. The rooftop dining room was empty, save for a single seat at the Griffith family's table.

I paused in my tracks.

CJ, the man who refused to set foot in the restaurant, sat at the head of the table. The sharp angles of his face glowed in the dancing candlelight as he wiped his mouth with his napkin.

This had to be a joke, right? I was being pranked. I had to be. But if I called him out on it, he'd deny it, so I played along.

"How was your meal?"

CJ pushed away from the table and laid his napkin beside his spotless plate. "Excellent."

I eyed the spread. "You got the corn chowder again. I hope it was a better experience for you than it was the first time."

CJ's lips twitched with amusement, but he held it together. "It was significantly easier to eat this time since my mouth wasn't on fire." He paused. "But I think it's my favorite thing on the menu."

"Noted."

"Lennon—"

"We don't need to talk about it," I blurted out, cutting him off. "Thank you for pulling my car out. It won't happen again."

"Come back to the bunkhouse." It was an order masked as a request.

"I'll be fine."

"I have no doubt," he said as he stood and pulled a few bills out of his wallet to leave a tip for the server. "But I also know you didn't find somewhere to live in the last twelve hours."

"But I—"

I stammered as CJ rounded the table and stopped in front of me. His lips brushed the corner of my mouth as he leaned in. My breathing stopped when he reached out and traced the Griffith Brothers Ranch logo that was embroidered over my heart.

"You're wearing my last name on your uniform." Green and gold swirled in his eyes as they met mine. "Pretty sure that makes me your boss."

I tipped my chin up. "That's not what you called yourself that night at the bar."

A slow smile hitched at the corner of his mouth. "Do what I say, trouble. Come to the bunkhouse."

"Or what, *daddy*?"

He chuckled softly. "What's that old saying?"

"Play stupid games, win stupid prizes?"

CJ chuckled. "I was thinking more along the lines of 'fuck around and find out.'"

His palm was warm against mine as he brushed past me. As his boots thudded down the stairs, I looked down at the place where our hands had touched and found a daisy between my fingers.

The flower had wilted by the time I turned the lights off in the kitchen. Everyone had gone home after the staff meal, but I had found every excuse in the book to keep piddling around in the kitchen.

We needed to reorganize the walk-in cooler. The Cambros came out of the dishwasher a little greasy and needed to be hand-scrubbed. The hood over the grill needed wiping down. I needed to organize and file the invoices on my desk.

Finally, all I had left to do was leave.

It crossed my mind that I could sleep in my office. I could probably sneak out before the opening shift came in tomorrow morning, but I knew he would come for me.

Something impassable burned in CJ's eyes when he summoned me to the rooftop. Something that I knew I couldn't escape.

Either I had to go back to town and find somewhere to sleep, or I had to go to him.

My choice was made the moment I locked up and walked to the parking space where I had left my car after I left the bunkhouse this morning.

It was gone.

Shadows danced over the empty spot from the restaurant's buzzing exterior light, But it wasn't completely empty.

I walked closer and bent at the knees, taking in the bouquet of wildflowers tied off with a piece of twine around the stems. A bronze key dangled from the bow.

The walk to the bunkhouse wasn't nearly as long as I needed it to be to work through the warring thoughts racing through my mind.

My car had been parked beside an obnoxious-looking truck. I skipped attempting to get into it and headed for the door. A shadow watched from the window of the upstairs bedroom.

I untied the key from the bouquet and tried the lock. It slid in easily and turned without so much as a hitch. The door cracked open, and I peered inside.

The living room was dark. A light glowed from the kitchen, but it appeared that the house was deserted.

I stepped inside and shut the door as quietly as I could. The subtle click of the lock might as well have been a gunshot. I floated up the stairs on silent feet, cutting through the darkness like a wraith.

The strip at the bottom of CJ's door glowed like the neon lights at the bar the night we had met. I held my breath as I turned the knob and slipped inside.

CJ lay stretched out on his bed with his ankles crossed. He was shirtless and wearing sweatpants. A book rested upside down on his thigh, saving the page he was on.

"You stole my car." I pulled my keys from the pocket of my uniform pants. "Do I even want to know how you did it?"

He laced his hands together behind his head, hazel eyes flicking up and down my body. "Hot-wiring a car isn't that hard."

"I wouldn't know."

He smirked. "Then you're not the criminal I thought you were."

"Found this in the parking lot." I tossed him the spare key that he had tied to the flowers. "Better be careful. Someone might find it and break in."

CJ picked it up from where it had landed on the mattress and set it on the nightstand. "It's yours."

"I don't need a key to the bunkhouse."

"You do since you're going to be sleeping here," he said.

"In one of the empty rooms your guys told me about this morning while I was making them breakfast," I countered.

I thought that little bit of bacon-bribed information would be enough to throw him off, but CJ wasn't fazed.

"Those rooms aren't available," he said calmly as he picked up the book he had been reading, dog-eared a page, and set it on the nightstand.

"Really? Because they look pretty available to me."

"Keep your voice down, trouble." His feet hit the floor. "Everyone's sleeping."

"CJ—"

"You want somewhere to sleep? You'll sleep right here."

"And where are you going to sleep?"

"I usually stay on the left side, but I don't mind sleeping on the right."

I rolled my eyes, swore under my breath, and turned for the door. I'd go find somewhere discreet to park on the ranch and figure out a new spot tomorrow.

Heat pressed against my back, and pressure pinned me to the door.

"Lennon." His voice was complex and full like fine wine.

"What?" I hissed.

"Take your clothes off."

I guffawed at his brashness. "Wanna try that again, cowboy? I will—"

His hand wrapped around mine, gently tugging the flowers from my grasp. "Get in bed."

"First you try to get me fired, then you steal my car, and now you think I'm going to spend the night beside you and not kill you in your sleep? Get fucked."

Something long and thick pressed against my ass.

"To be honest, I hoped you'd be there for that last thing," he said. He raked a hand up the back of my scalp.

It sent pinpricks of heat dancing across my head and down my spine.

"Put your claws away. You don't need them with me."

A larger part of me than I wanted to recognize wanted to crawl between those covers. I wanted to curl up to him and close my eyes. I wanted to wake up without my neck killing me. I wanted to sleep through the night and not jolt awake at every ambient sound.

"I'm not so sure about that," I said as my head tipped back onto his shoulder.

"That's fine. I don't mind getting scratched up."

"Why are you being nice to me?"

He chuckled. "Because I may have realized that I have a lot of groveling to do, and groveling while also being an ass usually doesn't work."

"I don't like you." I turned and faced him. "You and I? We're not anywhere near good."

"That's fine. At least I know where I'm starting. Do you need a shower?"

The speed at which he dismissed my concern was, frankly, irritating.

"Yeah."

CJ stepped back and tipped his head toward his bathroom. "Go on, then."

I probably looked a little manic as I rushed into the bathroom and locked the door behind me. When I flipped the light on, I paused.

My toiletry bags were arranged neatly on the right side of the sink. I pulled the shower curtain back and clapped my hand over my mouth.

Bottles of color-safe shampoo and conditioner—a very expensive brand—were perched on the ledge of the shower beside CJ's soap. That hadn't been there yesterday.

A daisy rested on the lids.

It had been so long since I had indulged in an 'everything' shower. But with the door locked, the house asleep, and no one but CJ waiting for me, maybe I could break that one little rule...

A fancy shower steamer puck was arranged on top of a folded washcloth and towel. I turned the water on as high as it would go before dropping the steamer into the bottom of the shower. The rising tendrils of eucalyptus and lavender leached the stress from my muscles.

I took my time, partially to indulge and relax, but also to give myself space to grapple with CJ's posturing.

By the time the water turned cold, I wasn't any closer to figuring out what his angle was than when I had gotten in.

I showered, shaved, moisturized, and applied a hair mask, but my heart still felt muddy.

CJ was back to reading on his side of the bed when I

tiptoed out with a towel wrapped around my body. "I'm assuming you also brought my clothes in since you went through my bags to get my toiletries? Or was this just your master plan to get me naked?"

He chuckled and pointed to the chestnut dresser against the wall. "Top two drawers."

Warily, I crossed the room and peeked inside. The clothes I had kept in my duffel bag were neatly folded and arranged beside his.

"And the uniforms I had on coat hangers?" I asked.

"They're in the closet."

I held the towel a little tighter. "You just decided to move me into your room?"

Shadows eclipsed the warmth of his daylight gaze. "Time to cut a fire line, right?"

So that's what this was. Penance for his petulant antics. It wasn't anything more.

"I don't think cohabitating is what your brother meant."

"I know exactly what he meant," CJ said as he stood. "Sharing my space with you isn't a sacrifice, trouble. Far from it."

I tilted my chin up to meet his gaze as he stood toe-to-toe with me. "Then what's your fire line?"

"My pride." His eyes lowered to my mouth. "Admitting that maybe I was wrong. And maybe we need to go back to the beginning and try again. And that I have a lot of work to do to make up for the way I treated you."

18

LENNON

Pride. We were two peas in a pod.

"Wanna know something, trouble?" He slid his hand through the open edge of my towel and curled his fingers around my hip. "I hadn't stopped thinking about you when I came home from the bar." He tipped his head to the side. "Hadn't stopped thinking about how much I liked your fire. The way you talked back to me. The way we fit. That push and pull."

Our lips brushed.

"Are you ready to go to sleep?" he murmured.

I knew what he was asking, and I knew what my answer was the moment he asked.

I swallowed and let go of the towel. "No."

CJ caught it before it fell away from my body, holding it in place. "You sure?" He pressed a kiss to the corner of my mouth. "No harm, no foul if you want to take your side. I'll take mine, and I won't touch you. But if you're not going to sleep, we're going back to the beginning for a do-over."

Instead of words, I reached between us and squeezed the thick outline of his erection.

"You're so fucking sexy," he growled as his mouth crashed against mine. CJ ripped the towel away and wrapped me up in his arms. "Get on the bed."

I gasped as he sucked my lip between his teeth. "Pretty sure our quickie was up against the wall back at the bar."

His smile was feral. "We have to be quiet. Not quick. On your back."

"Demanding," I grumbled as I scooted backward on the mattress.

He was on top of me, kissing and nipping my neck before I could get another word out. Hands shackled my wrists above my head as he straddled my hips.

"Goddamn . . ." His voice was reverent as his eyes turned midnight black. He shifted his grip on my wrists, holding them together with one hand as he cupped my breast. "Not one night has gone by that I haven't thought about your tits." He rolled his thumb over my piercing. "Do you know how much I've been fucking my hand, thinking about you?"

I squeezed my eyes shut and bit my lip, trying to hold in my reaction.

"Look at me."

I focused on breathing through the ache that throbbed between my legs. I was desperate, but I didn't want to beg.

CJ pinched my nipple. "Look."

I squealed at the sensation. Heat flashed across my chest, melting into sumptuous mountains of pleasure.

He let go of my wrists and clapped his hand over my mouth. "I'm not opposed to waking this whole damn house up from the sound of me fucking you. But if you don't want that to happen, you have to stay quiet."

His thumb returned to my nipple, rolling over the tightened point and turning me back into a writhing mess.

"Hush," he soothed, but didn't let up. "Breathe through it."

"Easier said than done," I gasped.

"You can do it," he whispered against my mouth. "But you will keep your eyes on me." He eased off my hips and moved between my legs. "As much fun as our little bar tryst was, I never got to make sure you were wet enough." He shoved my thighs apart without warning. "Now lay back."

"Please." One pathetic syllable was the only thing I could get out.

His responding chuckle was warm against my inner thigh. "That's my girl."

I clasped my hands over my mouth at the first slide of his tongue along my slit. Droplets of water from the shower still clung to my skin. He drank up each one with warm, sloppy kisses.

"See how good you get to feel when you work with me?" he mumbled. "Play with your tits."

I didn't have to be told twice.

His hands kneaded my hips and thighs as he sucked and licked my pussy. CJ teased my clit with his tongue, prodding and massaging the sensitive bundle of nerves. I whispered pleas and phantom prayers as he used his tongue to spell out endless apologies.

"You want a little bit more?" he asked.

I nodded.

"So nice when you're desperate." He pressed an open-mouthed kiss to my clit. "Maybe I should get you on your back more often. You're much more compliant."

"Don't get used to it. I can still smother you with my thighs."

He smirked. "You know, I think I'd enjoy that. Breathe for me." With that brief warning, he slid two fingers inside me and pressed the heel of his palm to my clit. "Ride my hand. Give me a show."

"Give me your cock."

CJ chuckled. "All in due time, trouble." He pushed harder against my clit, rocking his hand back and forth. "Give me a little show, and I'll let you come."

"I can make myself come," I snapped in a whisper.

"I'm sure you can, but this will feel so much better, won't it? I can feel your tight little cunt squeezing my fingers. You want it just like this, don't you?"

I couldn't help the way I dug my heels into the bed, nor the way I rocked my hips back and forth, chasing that elusive end.

"My God, you're a fucking dream," he whispered as I tipped my head back and gasped. "Come for me."

Waves rocked my body as I crashed through wall after wall of ecstasy. CJ curled his fingers inside me, stroking and easing me down from the high.

I melted into the soft bedding as he stretched out over me, cupping my cheeks in his hands. His lips were soft and warm and tasted just a little bit like me.

I didn't mind.

CJ slid his tongue along mine, lapping in gentle strokes as he wrapped me up in those sinuous muscles. "You good?"

I nodded.

"Want more?"

I sank my teeth into his lower lip. "Yes."

"Good girl."

I giggled lazily. "I'm not."

He pecked my lips as he grabbed a condom. "We've all gotta have goals."

I traced the lines of his chest as he kicked off his sweatpants and tore into the condom packet with his teeth. "Both hands on my cock."

"Bossy much?" I muttered.

CJ's thick erection bobbed in front of me as he sat back on his haunches. "Don't know if anyone's ever told you this, but you're pretty stubborn." He handed me the open condom packet. "Put it on me."

His cock was warm and hard beneath my palm as I rolled the rubber on him. The gentle throb of arousal was hypnotizing.

CJ took my hands in his and wrapped them around his neck. "I'll be gentle this time, but I still want you to hold on."

"You don't have to be gentle with me. I like a good, hard fuck."

He chuckled. "I know you do."

I gasped as he slid inside me, stretching and filling me to my limit.

"But hard fucks are for when we're on even ground. And I hope we get there. But for now—" he wrapped his arms behind my back and held me flush to his chest "—just let me hold you and say I'm sorry."

The tears that pricked my eyes caught me by surprise. I buried my face in the crook of his neck, breathing through each rhythmic, pulsating thrust.

We crashed as one, cresting each surge and swell as we held onto each other.

CJ gently laid me back against the pillows, cupped my cheek, and pressed a gentle kiss to my forehead.

The placement was shocking.

He was so tender. So gentle. It was a stark contrast to the handsome playboy from the bar and the angry cowboy who had tormented me for weeks.

We did the awkward dance of waiting for each other to use the bathroom and get ready for bed.

I needed some space. Some time to process everything alone.

I was in the middle of putting on a pair of sweats and a hoodie so I could go out to my car when thick arms banded around me.

"What do you think you're doing?" he murmured as he pressed a kiss into my hair.

"Just running out to my car real quick."

"Don't lie to me."

"I'm not," I bristled.

"All your things are up here. You were about to run away."

"Was not."

"Lennon."

"Carson."

He froze, his hands softening on my waist. "What did you just call me?"

"That's your name, right? Carson James."

He threw me over his shoulder, turning my world upside down, and then tossed me onto the bed like a hay bale.

"That's it," he said as he yanked the covers back. "You're not going anywhere."

19

CARSON JAMES

I awoke with my arm around a nuclear warhead. She was terrifyingly still, beautifully delicate, and deadly if I jostled her the wrong way.

Lennon's black and white hair splayed across my chest. Her soft breaths warmed my skin with each gentle rise and fall of her chest. The sheets were draped over each curve, ridge, and valley of her body. They gave me another undeserved chance to admire her as she slept.

A million depraved desires raced through my mind. I wanted to wake her up with my mouth on her tits, my hand on her clit, and my name on her lips. There were worse ways to be woken from a deep sleep.

But I didn't move. I barely breathed.

Lennon had occupied the far-right edge of the bed, tossing and turning for the first hour in an attempt to get to sleep. Getting used to a new place always sucked. There were different sounds. Different flashes of light. Different ways the bed creaked and molded to a body.

She settled when I crossed the invisible line we had drawn between us and pulled her to my chest.

"I have questions." Lennon's sharp, accusatory tone startled me out of the morning haze.

I chuckled and brushed her hair away from her face. "What happened to *good morning? How'd you sleep?*"

She peered up at me. "Where did the hair stuff come from?"

"What hair stuff?"

"The shampoo and conditioner you put in your shower. It wasn't mine."

"Do you always wake up like this?"

"Like what?"

"One second you're dead asleep and the next you're firing off questions." I smoothed my hand over her ass and gave it a squeeze. "I'm a slow riser, trouble."

"I thought you cowboys were all the 'up and at 'em' type."

"Must've skipped me." I sifted my fingers through her hair and cupped her cheek. "How'd you sleep?"

"Fine. Whose shampoo was that?"

"Yours."

Lennon rolled her eyes and tugged the comforter up to her chin. "It's not mine."

"I got it for you."

"From *where*?" Lennon didn't return her hand to where it had been resting on my stomach, but she hadn't jumped out of bed and run away yet either. I'd say we were making progress, even though we were back to suspicious fire and mistrustful brimstone.

"I went into town and picked it up before I had dinner at the restaurant last night." I looped her hair around my finger. "I'm pretty sure you weren't born with the hair of a movie villain who has a hundred Dalmatians, so I figured you'd want something that doesn't fuck up your hair color if you came back here."

Her brows knitted together. "How'd you know I'd need a special shampoo? And where the hell did you find that kind in this little town?"

I chuckled. "I've listened to Cassandra bitch about the upkeep of her hair for years now. I asked her where she bought her shampoo. Since she orders so much of it, the little shop in town started keeping a stock of it."

I swear Lennon relaxed a little at that.

"Now. Hit me with it."

"With what?" she asked.

"The rest of the inquisition."

"What makes you think I have an inquisition?"

"You woke up with one. Now do you want to interrogate me more, or can we get back to waking up?"

"Why aren't you already gone?" she peered at the bedside clock. "It's almost ten in the morning."

"I'm on night shift tonight," I said as I reached over to the bedside table and plucked a daisy out of the bouquet I had left in the parking lot for her last night. "We've got a bunch of heifers about to give birth, so we take shifts, making sure someone's always out there keeping an eye on 'em."

Her eyes softened as I tucked the daisy behind her ear.

"What else you got?"

"Don't think I'm rolling over and playing dead." She yawned. "I'm still mad at you."

I took a chance and kissed her forehead, hoping that she was sleepy enough to opt out of strangling me. "I don't expect you to. I like when you fight me. It makes the yielding so much sweeter. I like working for it. Earning it." I kissed down her throat, softly massaging her thighs apart. "I like that you don't give me this side of you freely."

"We can chalk this up to a momentary lapse in—" Lennon's voice disappeared as I dipped my head below the covers and pulled her nipple between my teeth.

"In what?" I asked as I teased her with my tongue until she was squirming.

"A lapse in ... in ..."

"Spit it out, trouble." I grazed the entrance to her pussy with a phantom touch.

"Judgment," she choked out.

I chuckled. "If that's what helps you sleep at night."

Lennon whimpered as I rubbed her clit in steady circles. "I'll leave the spare key on the dresser."

"It's not a spare key," I growled.

Lennon gasped at the pressure against her clit as I eased her closer and closer to orgasm. "Then what—"

"It's *my* key," I said as I pushed two fingers inside her and curled them against her tight inner muscles. "So think twice before you go do something stupid with it to get back at me."

Her hands slammed into the mattress, twisting and fisting the sheets as her toes curled.

"Don't stop fighting me, trouble," I whispered against her lips. "Yield, but don't cease."

Lennon's head tipped back as she careened into a crushing end. I bit down on her lower lip, drinking down each gasp. Her breasts pressed against my chest. Her entire body sought mine like she was drowning, but clinging to driftwood to try to stay afloat.

I cradled her head in the crook of my shoulder as I eased my fingers out of her pussy. Slowly, she relaxed, curling into me and closing her eyes. I listened as her breathing steadied into a predictable, lazy rhythm.

"You working today?" I mumbled as I flopped back on my pillows, pulling her with me.

"I work every day." Lennon yawned, then sighed contentedly. "But I need to get up and get going."

"You and me, trouble. Peas in a pod." I brushed her hair away from where her cheek was pressed against my chest so I could study the lines of her eyelashes and the slope of her nose. "Sleep here tonight. You'll have the bed to yourself until morning. I'll tell the guys to leave you be."

"I can take care of myself just fine," she groused.

"I have no doubt."

Her eyes opened, lifting to meet mine. I adjusted the daisy that had nearly fallen out from behind her ear in the heat of her orgasm.

"You know, if I had gotten my way that night, this is how the next morning would have gone."

Lennon's gaze drifted away from mine. "I knew you'd be sweet to me if I would've had that second drink." Her index finger traced abstract shapes in my chest hair. "There was something about you. You smiled at my attitude." The corner of her mouth lifted. "I was up shit's creek without a paddle the moment I saw you, cowboy. I had to walk away."

I found her hand and tangled our fingers together. "What about now?"

"I'm still up that creek, but I'm floating instead of flailing."

I hummed under my breath. "I'll float with you."

We drifted in and out of lazy sleep and shared hushed notes of pleasure as our hands wandered. After a while, Lennon peeled away from my arms and got ready for work.

She pulled the daisy from her hair and ran a brush

through it. From the bed, I watched as she dressed in a crisp chef's uniform, then braided her hair into a neat plait down her back. She didn't say anything about it, but I noticed when she slid the daisy into the pocket on her bicep where she usually kept a pen and a permanent marker.

I cracked a smile at the sight, because I knew I had a chance.

∼

"Chef, can you taste this?"

Shouts, questions, and a cacophony of clattering dishes met me in a wall of sound as I slipped in the back door to the restaurant. It was propped open as the semi-truck that made weekly deliveries to the lodge and restaurant was being unloaded.

I gave the two guys who were shuffling boxes a nod and pretended like I belonged.

I didn't. That much was clear as day.

Chefs, cooks, servers, and support staff danced around in shades of black and white. Everyone was in crisp, pressed perfection.

I spotted Lennon in the middle of the chaos, commanding the kitchen with militaristic precision.

A strange energy radiated off of her as she shuffled along the front line, hurrying to get plates out to hungry diners.

Julian—the punk who had run his mouth when I was fixing the tilt skillet—caught sight of me and gave me a chin tip. There was a wariness in his eyes as he tracked my every move.

I couldn't blame him either. The last time I had been in

the kitchen, Lennon and I were taking literal and metaphorical jabs at each other.

They probably thought I was coming back for round two.

I lifted the bouquet in my hand and tipped my head toward Lennon, hoping he'd get the message that I was coming in peace.

Another body stood out among the sea of black and white. A man in a sage green suit that was far too tailored to be off the rack.

So that explained Lennon's nervous energy.

Chef DeRossi stood at his post, arranging dishes and releasing them to tables. He saw me before Lennon did.

"Mr. Griffith," he said, flashing a Hollywood smile. "To what do I owe the pleasure?"

Lennon stiffened and glanced over her shoulder, peeling her eyes away from the sauté pan in her hands.

As I stood in front of reality TV royalty, I felt a little stupid holding the handful of yellow and pink primroses that I had pulled from the field closest to the bunkhouse.

I cleared my throat. "I—uh—I was hoping I could speak with Chef Maddox for a moment."

Lennon's cheeks turned as red as the raw steak she had dropped into her pan.

It was mid-afternoon. I hadn't expected the kitchen to be this busy. I especially hadn't expected Lennon's boss to be here.

I thought I would be able to slip in, flirt a little, then head out.

She hadn't said it in so many words, but I knew she had been struggling to earn everyone's respect.

Why had I come here again?

"Absolutely. Is this about her car?" Chef DeRossi asked

as he tipped his head to Lennon. "If there's anything we can do for you and your family, just ask." It sounded like a warning to Lennon more than a blank-check offer to me.

"Chef Simmons," Lennon said as she handed off her task to the guy on her left.

"Covering," he said.

Lennon's eyes finally flicked up to meet mine. "Two minutes."

I followed her out of the kitchen and down the hall to the office. I didn't hear her breath until the door closed behind us.

"What are you doing here?" she clipped as she peeled off her tall chef's hat and knotted her hand in the top of her spilling braid.

I held out the pathetic bunch of flowers that had roots still hanging from the stems. "Just dropping by. What's wrong with your car?"

"Why are you dropping by?" she asked.

"Tell me what's wrong with your car."

"CJ—"

She had that fight-or-flight look in her eye. With Lennon, I never knew which one she would choose.

Today looked like it would be a flight response. She would run back to the kitchen and ignore me under the guise of work.

I dropped the flowers on the desk and pushed forward until I had her backed against the wall. "What's the matter with your car?"

Her eyes dropped to the floor.

"Save us both the time and just tell me. Either you tell what the matter is, or I'll go find out for myself. I stole your car once. I'll do it again."

She sighed and closed her eyes as she rested the back of

her head on the wall. "Someone slashed my tires, and I have neither the time nor the money to fix them. So, I hope you don't mind me crashing at the bunkhouse for a few more nights. I can't walk to work from town."

I saw red.

"*Who* did it?" I hissed as I braced my hands on the wall behind her head, caging her in. "Give me a fucking name."

Her eyes flashed with rage. "You think I wouldn't take care of it myself if I knew?"

"You called the cops, right?"

She cut her eyes away from me.

"*Right*?" I pressed.

Lennon crossed her arms over her chest. "The cops and I don't exactly have the greatest track record. So, no. I won't be calling the cops, thank you very much. And if you break my trust and get them involved, you'll have hell to pay, cowboy."

I froze. "You trust me?"

"I let you fuck me, didn't I?"

Those brash words and her sharp tone were nothing but a defense mechanism. She could be as prickly as she wanted, but I had gotten a peek beneath that façade.

"Give me your keys. I'll take care of it."

She bristled. "Drop it. I'll handle it when I have a day off."

I snaked my hand up the back of her neck, cupping the base of her skull as our lips brushed. "Let me take care of it. I owe you, remember?"

"Carson . . ."

My name on her lips was the shackle. Her exhausted whisper was the iron ball that dragged me to my damnation.

"Just give me your keys, Len."

She reluctantly fished them out of the pocket on her

thigh and dropped them in my hand. "Whoever did it knows the difference between three and four tires."

I cupped her cheek. "Let me take care of it."

"Save your receipts."

"Get those tally marks out of your head. We're not keeping score here. I'll see you in the morning."

I left her with a soft kiss that shook her to her core.

Lennon lifted her fingers and pressed them to the pout of her lips as I backed out of the office, twirling her keys around my fingertip.

20

LENNON

"Should've known I'd find you here." Arms banded around my waist as I stared out of CJ's bedroom window. "You can go out there, you know."

There was something poetic about watching the horses being fed into the circular horse walker for a cool down or to get a little exercise.

I felt a little bit like those horses—running under the guise of freedom, but still trapped.

It had been a week since that night I ran through the rain to the bunkhouse.

A week of sleeping in CJ's bed—sometimes beside him, sometimes alone.

A week of waiting until every restaurant employee had left before sneaking over to the bunkhouse.

A week of his hands on my body, worshiping and pleasing me, but not himself.

A week of wildflowers at every turn. He'd leave them on the bed. By my toothbrush. On top of my work shoes. In the pocket of my chef's coat.

"You have a good spot for keeping an eye on the ranch," I

said as I pushed off of the window and peeled away from him.

"It used to be the best view," he admitted as he grabbed the back of his t-shirt and pulled it over his head. "I used to sleep with the curtains open so I could watch the sunrise every morning." He tossed it into the hamper. "Now I have to sleep with them closed so the headlights don't wake me up."

"That sucks," I mumbled. Guilt sank like a stone in my stomach. I couldn't imagine growing up here, having free rein of the land, only for it to completely change in the blink of an eye.

I felt his body against mine again as he pressed a kiss to my shoulder. "It used to."

My curiosity got the best of me. "It used to suck?"

CJ chuckled. "You'd like to know, wouldn't you?"

He sat on the edge of the bed and snagged the hem of the shirt I was in as I passed by to get to the closet. CJ reeled me in, keeping one hand knotted in cotton and one hand on the back of my thigh.

"This is a good look on you."

"You're just saying that because I'm in your shirt and you can see my nipples." The outlines of my piercings were rather prominent.

He chuckled. "I'm not arguing."

"Tell me why it used to suck and why it doesn't currently suck."

Gold eyes glinted with mischief as he licked his lips. "Tell me why you'll lock yourself up here like a princess in a tower instead of watching the horses against the fence like everyone else? Brooke doesn't bite. In fact, she's probably the nicest one out of all of us."

I didn't particularly like being called out like that. "I'm not locking myself in a tower."

"You never leave on your days off. I didn't put those shiny new tires on your car for nothing. All you do is walk to the restaurant and run back here when you think no one's looking."

"No one likes a know-it-all," I snapped as I pulled away from his grip.

I should have known CJ wouldn't let me go. He yanked me down until I collapsed on top of him. Right when I got my bearings, he trapped my legs in a death roll.

CJ grabbed my hands and pinned them to my sides as he straddled my hips. "Just so we're clear, I can rope a calf faster than that. So, either you can cooperate, or I can tie you up."

"I'm cautious. That's the only answer you're getting," I snapped with a little more vitriol than I meant to. "And you're filthy. Get off me."

CJ had been working through the night again, leaving me to sleep alone, snuggled up to his pillow so I could smell him.

His thumbs stroked my wrists with a tenderness I had only seen in movies. "You're safe here. No one will touch you."

"And how do you know that?" I grumbled as I tried to wrench free.

I should have known better. It only made him hold me down tighter. He used his knee to pin my thigh down.

"Because they know you're mine."

I let out a laugh that was loud, long, and wholly insulting to the seriousness of the moment.

"Don't believe me?"

I rolled my head across the mattress. "I think you want me to think you're serious."

"Ever wonder why the guys don't make a move on you? I told them not to."

My teeth sounded like sandpaper on gravel, but CJ never bluffed. Not once.

"Ask me again."

"Ask you what?"

"Ask me why the view doesn't suck as much as it used to."

Pressure pricked at the back of my eyes, and I shook my head. "I don't think I want to know that answer," I whispered.

"Ask me, Len."

My whisper was broken. "Why?"

CJ eased off of me and helped me off the bed. The niceness of the gesture was gone when he marched me up to the window and pressed me against the glass.

"Because I stay up late and watch you." He took my hand and laced our fingers, then pointed, trailing my finger along the glass pane. "I watch you get out of your car there and walk inside the restaurant. I watch you all night long when you stay overnight to keep the smoker going so I know you're safe. I watch you walk from the restaurant to your car when you're done for the night. *You* are my favorite view."

He pulled a wilted flower from his pocket and slipped it into my hand, then turned away to finish getting undressed.

I reeled from his confession and desperately needed to get hold of my sanity. Feelings were the quickest way to let my guard down, and I couldn't risk that. "Did you have a chance to look at the security cameras to see who slashed my tires?"

His expression grew solemn. "Whoever did it avoided them. We have a lot of cameras, but it's a big property. There are a lot of blind spots."

"Oh..." My heart sank.

CJ had insisted on changing my tires, my oil, and fixing a few other things that were overdue. It took him some time, but he finally stopped trying to convince me to go to the police. I didn't need their help. I just wanted to know who had done it so I could be careful.

"That's fine. I was curio—"

"The new cameras have shipped. They should be here by the weekend, and I'll get them installed right away when they come in."

That had me freezing in place. "You ordered more cameras?"

CJ had stripped down to nothing but his boxers. He stood toe-to-toe with me and crossed his arms over his chest. "I told you. I made it clear that no one fucks with you. And I take it personally that someone ignored that order. It won't happen again."

I pressed my hands to his chest and pushed him away. I needed space. I needed to breathe, and it was impossible when he was near.

"We're even. You can stop being my knight in cowboy boots now. I need to get to work."

"We're not even," CJ said as he watched me get dressed.

If I was being honest, I didn't like the days when our schedules were opposite. Even though I was used to being alone, I never felt lonely. Not until I had a taste of what companionship felt like.

Maybe that's what we were.

Not friends, but not enemies. We understood each other, and that was enough.

While I slipped on my tread-safe shoes, his shadow appeared in front of me. "Put this on. It's cold out today."

"I guarantee it's not the kind of cold I'm used to," I said

as I stretched up and looked at the heavy tan coat in his hands. "Winter in Texas is basically spring in New York. I'd wear shorts in this weather."

"Humor me," he said without a hint of it in his voice.

"It's a two-minute walk."

"Put the fucking jacket on, Lennon." There was a tiredness in his words. It bled into his eyes, drawing them down with the weight of the world.

I didn't feel like arguing and being late. "Fine," I clipped as I slid my arms into the sherpa-lined jacket and adjusted it over my chef's coat. A logo was embroidered on the breast, mostly matching the one on my uniform.

"It's the original ranch logo. Before Cassandra had it redesigned to include the lodge and restaurant, too."

"It's nice," I said as I grabbed my phone and shoved it into my pocket.

One of those weighty thoughts floated across his face, but he didn't bring it to the tip of his tongue.

Instead, he said, "Keep it. It looks better on you anyway."

I shoved my hands in the jacket pockets to keep them warm on the walk, only to find a handful of little flowers.

I laughed as I pulled them out and set them on top of the dresser. "What is with you and picking wildflowers?" I asked as I wiped the dirt out of the bottom of the pockets.

CJ smoothed his hands over my shoulders and arms. "They remind me of you. Wildflowers grow where they want. Soil. Sand. Cracks in the sidewalk. Cities and open fields. They thrive in the worst conditions. And just when you think you've cut them down, they spring back up. They're always the first thing to grow back after a wildfire as a reminder of hope and a little audacity."

I stood still as a statue while he kissed me on the cheek and wished me a good day at work as he caught up on sleep.

The walk over to the restaurant was a blur. The weight of CJ's coat pulled me down. Instead of warming me, it was a cinder block dragging me to inescapable depths. I wanted to relax into the softness and comfort, but I couldn't. Unease gnawed at my gut.

I needed to leave.

If my brother or the person he was working with knew where I was, I couldn't stay. I couldn't put these people at risk.

"Lennon."

I looked up at the sound of my name. Cassandra and Brooke were walking down the pebble path that led to and from the lodge. Brooke's jaw was on the ground. Cassandra's surprise was much more restrained, but still palpable.

I balled up my fists in the pockets of the jacket, digging my nails into my palms. "Good morning."

Cassandra cut her eyes in the direction I had come from, then turned her full attention to me. "Nice jacket. Where'd you get it?"

Ah, there was the cutting tone everyone at the restaurant had come to fear. There was no sense in lying. She'd sniff out the truth.

"CJ loaned it to me." *That sounded amicable, right?*

Brooke choked. "I'm sorry. I think this pregnancy affected my hearing. *What?*"

I lifted my chin and turned to Cassandra. "You told us to get along. We're getting along."

"A little too well, apparently," Cassandra clipped. "Heading to work?"

"I'm sorry," Brooke said as she wrapped an arm around her baby belly and leaned on Cassandra for support. "He gave you *his jacket?* But that's—"

Cassandra clapped her hand over Brooke's mouth, muffling whatever else she had to say.

"Okay..." I said, stepping back cautiously. "This is weird, and I have to get to work."

Brooke squirmed and shouted against Cassandra's hand, but I ignored it and headed into the restaurant.

"Yo, Chef. What's good?" Zach gave me a chin tip from the prep station where he was busy peeling potatoes and dropping them into the water.

I cut through the kitchen and dumped my things and CJ's jacket in the office. The warm aroma of brisket corn chowder filled the kitchen today as aromatics were sautéed and giant batches of soup were simmering in the tilt kettles.

"Good morning," I said as I grabbed my apron and tied it around my waist. "How are things going?"

"Good," Julian said with a yawn as he sauntered in, smelling like a bonfire. "We're out of mop sauce."

I let out a quiet laugh under my breath. The poor guy had drawn the short straw of babysitting the smoker all night long.

"How was your night?"

"Boring," he grumbled as he beelined for the staff coffee maker and filled a paper cup to the brim. "Those briskets are looking sexy, though."

He shotgunned the caffeine, then went to work. He mixed water, minced onion, salted butter, Worcestershire sauce, and vinegar in a giant pot until it was steaming.

"Cut the heat and leave it there," I said as I finished my rounds, checking in on everyone before settling in for the day. "Wrap up your side work. I'll keep an eye on the smoker so you can get out of here and get some sleep."

"Say, I didn't see you leave last night," Julian said as he

went to work, sorting through our vegetable discard to make a mirepoix for beef stock.

I liked that very little went to waste. Chef DeRossi and I crafted a menu that honored the cattle raised on the ranch by using almost every part of the animal.

"Late night," I clipped. "I had business with the family."

That was enough to stop him from asking more questions. From day one of everyone's onboarding, Chef DeRossi had made it clear that we were guests at the ranch, and that the Griffith family held more sway than he did.

"Right," Julian said as he ran his knife through a few pounds of carrots, onion, and celery, topping off what the vegetable discard lacked. "So, what's the deal with you and the Griffith who came storming in here the other day and called you Eleanor?"

I bristled, but tamped it down. "Mr. Griffith and I had a misunderstanding. That's all. It doesn't pertain to this kitchen, and we resolved it."

"Sounded pretty serious," Julian said without any heat behind the comment.

It wasn't uncommon for us to make small talk throughout the day. I just didn't particularly enjoy being the center of that small talk.

"Did you guys know each other before working here or something?" he asked.

"Or something," I clipped.

The steady rhythms of knives on cutting boards and the clank of dishes filled the silence. There was a certain peace in it. A safety in it. Those sounds were music to my ears.

I didn't want to leave this kitchen.

I didn't want to leave the ranch.

But I didn't have a choice.

21

CARSON JAMES

"Brooke!" I shouted as I stormed through the stables. "Why are the horses rainbow?"

My sister-in-law had the good sense to look guilty as she clutched the hose in her hand. "We just finished horse therapy camp. The kids loved it."

I pinched the bridge of my nose as Anarchy glared at me from her stall. "You painted my horse pink!"

"The pink paint showed up better on a black horse," Brooke said with a smile. "And it's safe for animals. I even ran it by the doc when she was out here last time."

Pink, yellow, blue, green, and purple smears and handprints coated my horse.

"I don't even know what I'm the most pissed off about: you bringing Anny around children, or the fact that you fucking painted her."

Brooke shrugged. "They painted Dottie too."

I huffed. "Dottie is basically a lap dog. She wouldn't hurt a fly. She's also not *my* horse."

Brooke trapped her lip between her teeth. The innocent look made me feel like shit for yelling at a pregnant woman.

"You made the mess. You clean it up," I groused.

"Sure thing," Brooke said as she rested her hand on her belly and took a deep breath. "As soon as I can catch my breath."

I pinched the bridge of my nose. "Leave the hose. I'll take care of it. Go sit down or something."

Brooke didn't hesitate to drop the hose and beamed. "Ten out of ten. My favorite brother-in-law. You're the best!"

"I promise I'm not."

Brooke sat on a bench pushed against the wall. "So, you and Chef Maddox, huh?"

"What are you talking about?" I asked as I started to hose down Anny, watching as the paint melted off in a pool of color.

She beamed from ear to ear as she flipped open the lid of a water bottle and took a long drink. "She was wearing your ranch jacket this morning."

"So?"

"So!" Brooke squealed. "She's the one, right? You get a jacket when you're part of the ranch for good."

I grunted as I scrubbed Anny down. "It was cold out this morning. That's all."

She rolled her eyes. "Please. You know as well as I do what those jackets mean."

"You, Becks, and Cass don't need to be getting any ideas."

"Oh really? Is that why I've seen her sneaking out of the bunkhouse every morning?"

"It's not what you think."

"I think you should stop fighting whatever is going on between you two."

I had stopped fighting it. I was trying to gain back the

ground I had lost in the battles. There was something to be said for diplomacy over brute force.

Lennon had put her sword down and taken her armor off, but she was still gun-shy around me.

Brooke left me to finish cleaning off the horses and waddled back to her house for the evening.

I debated slipping into the restaurant for dinner, but I didn't want to. The most face time I'd get with Lennon would be a minute if she came over to the table.

But when I left the barn and spotted her working outside at the smokers, I seized the opportunity.

Lennon jumped when I came up behind her and slid my hands around her hips. She was wearing my ranch jacket again, and it did something funny to my gut.

I needed to take an antacid.

"Geez. Don't do that," she gasped as she clutched the basting mop like a weapon. "You scared me."

I pressed a kiss to the side of her neck. "Who else would come up behind you like this?"

Lennon stiffened. "Someone sneaking up behind me is generally a bad thing."

"Smells good," I said as I took in the black bark of the brisket.

She shrugged me off and went back to work, covering the briskets with the sauce in her pot before closing up the smoker again.

"How's your day going?"

"Fine," she clipped with no hint of emotion.

"Just fine, huh?"

I took the liberty of sitting in the lawn chair positioned beside the smoker and stretched out.

"Restaurant's been busy."

I let out a lazy laugh. "I don't give two shits about the restaurant, Len. If I cared about the restaurant, I would've asked about the restaurant."

The sun was setting, casting warm rays across us as the glow dimmed from daylight to twilight.

She huffed and crossed her arms. "What do you want from me?"

I scoffed. What did I want from her? How about for her to stop being so fucking hot and cold with me?

"I want you to be human for thirty seconds instead of a kitchen robot. How about that?"

Lennon's features twitched the same way Anarchy's did when she was pissed off, so I stayed right where I was.

"It's been a long day, and I'm trying to finish work."

"How much longer do you have?"

Her eyes returned to the pot as she mechanically stirred the sauce.

"Lennon."

"I clocked out an hour ago."

"Then why are you still out here?"

I knew the answer before I had even asked the question. She was hiding in plain sight. Pretending like everything was fine. But she was still in my jacket.

And that fucking meant something.

Lennon's phone rang, cutting the tension between us. She fished it out of her pocket and tensed at the number on the screen. She swallowed and steeled herself, summoning her courage.

"Hello?" she answered, flexing her hand. "Yeah, I can talk. Why are you calling?"

I snapped a blade of grass out of the ground, wrapping it around my finger over and over again as her tone turned more and more serious.

"How much time do I have until . . ." she rasped as her breathing picked up. Lennon swallowed and licked her lips. "Okay. I'll figure it out."

She hung up without saying goodbye.

"Len—"

I barely caught her arm as she grabbed the pot off the metal work table beside the smoker and spun. Sauce sloshed over the rim as we collided.

"I have to go," she begged as she glanced all around, descending into a manic spiral. "Please, let me go."

"What the fuck happened?"

"Let me go," she whispered in desperation. Her eyes were pleading and terrified. "Please, Carson."

It was my name on her lips that did me in, twisting and pulling at my heartstrings. "No."

She jerked away, stumbling backward and looking at the sky. "I should've known."

"Should have known *what*?" I was growing more and more irritated by the second. If people didn't start looping me in, I was going to lose it. "Lennon, you have to talk to me. I'm not a mind reader. What the hell is going on?"

Lennon's eyes were glassy. "That you . . ." She let out a laugh of despair. "That this place . . . It was all too good to be true."

The swish of a horse's tail could have knocked me over.

"Come on. I'm not going to let you run off like a tattooed Cinderella."

I dragged Lennon through the kitchen, not caring that anyone saw me holding her hand. I stood guard as she dumped her utensils and got everything squared away for the next day.

There was no way I was letting her go.

I kept a tight hold on her, lacing our hands together as I

walked her to the bunkhouse and made her change out of her chef's whites. While she shimmied into jeans and a long-sleeved shirt, I loaded up a pack.

Lennon hadn't said a word since I dragged her off, but she broke when I took her to the stables.

"What are we doing?" she said as she eyed the horses warily.

"Getting out of here."

She let out a soft laugh. "Let me guess. You were always the kid who ran away from home?"

I grinned as I dropped the pack on the ground and started tacking up Anny. "Yep. My folks would even let me camp out all night until I tucked tail and came back the next morning. They didn't get worried until I started liking it." I grunted as I hoisted the saddle onto her back. "I guess that was the beauty of us being the only people out here when I was a youngin'. It was safe. We were raised with the understanding that this land was here before we were, and will exist long after we're gone. We're visitors. I was taught to respect the wild. I think I became one with it. Any mistakes I made that led to me getting hurt were my fault. Not the land's."

Lennon kept a safe distance but didn't seem scared. She wasn't as skittish as Cassandra or as reckless as Brooke when they were first introduced to the horses.

"This is Anarchy," I said as I checked her over. "She's mine."

Anny made a little snap at Lennon when she reached out to touch her nose, but Lennon didn't flinch.

It was like living a fever dream as Lennon held her palm out for Anny to sniff it, then pressed it to Anny's nose. Lennon looked her in the eye as she warned her. "If you bite me, there's no coming back from that. Understood?"

Anny seemed to agree to that and went back to ignoring Lennon.

I moved to the next stall and went through the motions of getting Indy ready to ride. "This is Independence. She belongs to Ray and Brooke, but I work with her since neither of them ride much these days."

Lennon snorted. "Anarchy and Independence. How poetic."

She was coping with humor. I could smell it a mile away. Whatever had been said to her on the phone had rattled her.

I grabbed her hand. "Up you go."

"Whoa, whoa, whoa." Lennon stumbled back. "You expect me to ride that thing?"

"Yes." It was as simple as that.

She argued a little as I braced my hand on her ass to boost her into Indy's saddle. Frankly, I just wanted to grab her ass.

We moseyed out of the stables and headed into the field. I had put Lennon on Indy since she typically deferred to following Anny around when they were out together.

"My jacket looks good on you," I said as we dodged the beams of light flooding out of the bunkhouse and the lodge and headed deep into the pasture.

Lennon bobbed back and forth beside me as she tried to get used to the sway of the saddle. "Cassandra and Brooke saw me in it this morning. They made it seem like it was a thing. What did you rope me into, cowboy?"

I found her eyes in the moonlight. "As long as you wanna be here, you wear that jacket. You put it on, and you're not alone anymore. You get me?"

She was silent. The only sounds floating between us in the night air were the grunts of the horses.

When the lodge and houses had disappeared behind us, I asked, "Who was on the phone?"

I watched as she stared at Indy's mane.

"I can't fix it if you don't tell me, Len."

"You can't fix it," she croaked. I realized that I had never heard her get emotional before. She always kept her true emotions carefully locked up behind bars of strength and self-reliance.

"You don't know that unless you tell me what it is."

Lennon took a deep breath. "My brother is being released early." She swallowed. "My old parole officer called to tell me since I don't qualify for victim services. Apparently, there's an overcrowding problem. He's been recommended for parole based on good behavior."

I swore at the sky, trusting the stars above us to hold our secrets. The breath I exhaled clouded around us. "And you want to pack up and hit the road to hide."

She had that thousand-yard stare as we trotted along. "Someone slashed my tires. Chances are, he already knows I'm here."

"Or maybe that punk from the kitchen thought he'd slash your tires instead of going up against you in a dick-measuring contest. Yours is bigger by a long shot."

Lennon let out a quiet laugh.

The shadow of my favorite tree loomed ahead. Anny knew where to go. She and I had come out here thousands of times.

My boots hit the ground before Anny had come to a complete stop. "Give me your hand."

Lennon slid her palm into mine and dismounted.

"What are we doing out here?"

I grabbed the pack I had strapped onto Anny and shouldered it. "If you're going to run away, I'm going to give you a good reason to stay."

While Lennon and Anarchy had a staring contest, I unfurled the thick quilt I had snagged from the house and spread it on the ground.

"Come here," I said as I toed my boots off and stretched out on the blanket.

Lennon followed, but kept a watchful eye on Indy and Anny. "You're not going to leash them up or something?"

I laughed. "Leash them up?"

"You know. So, they don't run away."

I patted the spot beside me. "They're not going anywhere."

She didn't seem too convinced. "How are you so sure?"

"Because they're loyal. They've been on the ranch for a long time. They know they're safe and cared for here. They weren't before."

Lennon sat beside me and hugged her knees. "You rescued them?"

I nodded. "Dottie was abandoned. Now she's spoiled to shit and gets painted with fucking rainbows for horse therapy camps. Independence and Liberty came from a hoarding situation. We agreed to foster them while Animal Control looked for a permanent home, then we didn't want to let them go. And Anny—" I looked over at my girl "—she was abused. Getting her in the trailer to bring her out here was a pain in the ass. We couldn't keep her with the other horses because she'd act up. It took a lot of gentle pressure to get her to trust me. The new horses we got in for the equine program are retired racehorses. They have a pretty good life out here."

"I think everyone has a pretty good life out here," Lennon said. Sadness and regret danced along each word.

"Then stay." I shuffled behind her and bracketed her body between my knees.

"I can't. I have to go."

"Len—" I brushed her hair over one shoulder and pressed a kiss to the side of her neck.

That was when I noticed the tears.

"C'mon, slugger," I soothed as I wiped her tears away.

Lennon curled into my arms and closed her eyes.

"Ain't nothing that serious," I said as I cradled her head to my chest. "He'll be on parole, right? He can't come here."

She let out a caustic laugh. "That won't stop him in the slightest. I sold him out to try to avoid being charged."

"How much money was it?"

"One and a half million. Apparently, you can fit it in a backpack when it's in hundreds."

I let out a slow whistle. "Jesus."

"Yeah." Lennon's voice was raspy. "And he thinks I have it."

"Tell me something," I said as I stretched out on my back and pulled her down with me so we could stare at the stars together. "Are you happy here?"

A lazy laugh slipped free. Lennon exhaled at the sky. "Yeah, I am. Especially now that a certain asshole cowboy stopped fucking with my job."

I grinned against her mouth as I turned and cupped her cheek. "I like fucking you better than fucking with you."

"I'm happy here," she admitted as she rested her forehead on mine. "It's safe. Quiet. I get to run The Kitchen. It seems like it's too good to be true. I guess it is."

"What if I promised that you'd be safe here?" My eyes met hers. "Would you stay?"

"You can't promise that."

"I can."

"Carson..."

"Nothing happens on this ranch without my say-so." I cracked a smile at the anomaly in my arms. "Well, except you."

22

LENNON

"I would stay," I whispered. "But—"

"No buts. Just stay." CJ rolled over, pinning me beneath him.

I had been looking at the stars, mesmerized by the way they coated the sky like glitter spilled across the heavens. Now, I saw the way they reflected from my eyes into his.

"What changed?" I asked as my eyes fluttered closed, and I melted into his roaming hands. "One day you're on a warpath to get me out, and the next I'm in your bed."

Contrition blanketed his face. "I started thinking about what I could gain instead of what I lost." His lips were soft against mine as he kissed away my fears. "I kept thinking about the woman at the bar who stole my breath and emptied my wallet. I kept thinking about how I'd give her every penny I had to my name, just to spend a few more minutes with her around a pool table. I kept thinking about how I hate the lights from the restaurant. But if it means I get to watch her walk to work and walk back home at the end of the night, I'd want them to be a million times brighter. I kept thinking about how I'd give up all the stars in the sky if it meant I got to hold the one that fell into my arms."

I wrapped my arms around his neck and slanted my mouth over his. "So, that's your fire line?"

"I thought I could dig a fire line to keep us from going up in flames, but I can't." His eyes bore into mine with undeniable heat. "I'd burn it all down for you."

I clawed at his belt buckle before he could get another word out.

No one had shown up for me the way CJ had. No one had defended me the way he had. No one had protected me the way he had.

"Fuck me," I begged and unbuckled his belt, fumbling with the zipper of his pants. "Please, please, please—"

His smile was devilish, but his eyes were kind. "Since you asked so nicely."

CJ worked my jeans and panties off my hips and balled his shirt and hoodie under my head like a pillow.

"I've had enough sweetness for the night," I whispered as I raked my nails down his chest. "You won't break me." Cold air flooded my chest as he lifted my shirt and bra over my head.

"Hello, beautiful."

Heat flooded my cheeks as he gazed at my body in the moonlight. CJ sifted a hand through my charcoal hair and used the other to gently trace the black and white tattoos on my arm as he straddled my hips. "I should have known the first night we met what lay beneath. Embers always hide under ash, but they're still as hot as the flames."

Heat and pressure tugged at my breast as he sucked on my nipple. Flashes of ecstasy bolted through my extremities and settled deep in my core.

"Touch me," I pleaded.

He released my nipple with a pop. "I am touching you."

I grabbed his hand, forcing him to cup my sex. "There."

CJ chuckled. "You want my fingers inside you?"

"Yes."

"How bad?" he mused as he circled my nipple piercing with his tongue. "Goddamn, I love these. You're so fucking sexy."

I pinched his nipple, making him hiss in excruciating delight. "Get the show on the road."

"Bad girl," he said with a grunt. He flipped me over to my hands and knees with surprising ease. CJ grabbed my hips, forcing them up and making my back arch down. "Feel free to scream. There's no one out here to hear you."

That was the only warning before his hand came down on my ass. Heat seared my skin as he turned my ass bright pink. My breath came in gasps and pants, but I held in the sounds he was trying hard to pull from my body.

"You look incredible like this, Len." His palm flattened between my shoulder blades. "Stretch out for me. Knees wide. Ass up and arch your back. Chest on the blanket. Stretch those beautiful arms out in front of you."

The position pressed my piercings to the ground, teasing them with each jolt and shift. My pussy was open and dripping for him in a lewd display.

CJ growled as he gripped my ass, squeezing and spreading it as I lay prostrate in reverence to him.

"Is this where you want me, darling?" he teased as he curled his finger around the opening of my pussy.

"Yes," I begged as he moved his finger up to tease my clit.

"It doesn't sound like you want it badly enough." CJ rubbed my clit in steady strokes. "But goddamn, you sure are wet. It's practically dripping down your leg. This pussy is begging for me, so why aren't you?"

With each teasing jab, I grew more and more desperate. I craved him. I ached for him. I needed to feel him inside me, stretching me to the brim.

"CJ, please!" I cried out into the night air.

Fingers scraped up my scalp, grabbing my ashen hair and yanking back to expose the burning coals beneath. "Louder," he barked. "Every time I've been in this pussy we've had to be quiet. I want to hear you, Lennon. I want to hear how badly you want me to fuck your cunt and fill you up. Scream for me, trouble. The stars will keep our little secret."

I gasped as he knocked my knees farther apart. Three quick spanks against the sensitive folds of my pussy had every scream he demanded ripping free from my chest. I clawed at the grass, digging into the dirt for purchase as he cupped and squeezed my cunt, teasing me.

I heard the rip and tear of a condom packet, then felt the blunt head of his cock nudging at my entrance. Wide hands spanned the crease where my hips met my thighs as he pushed into my pussy and sheathed himself inside me.

I cried out at the stretch and sting of being filled.

"You sound so pretty when you scream for me." He slammed his hips against my ass, driving into me again and again and again.

I ached for him. I craved him. I couldn't breathe without him.

"Yes, yes, yes!" I screamed to the stars that were listening.

"That's my girl. Tell me how good it feels."

"S-so fucking g-good," I gasped.

"Please let me come," I said with a pathetic squeak. "I need to come. I need it. Need you."

He slowed his strokes and bent over me, placing a gentle kiss on my spine. "Yes, ma'am. Since you asked so nicely."

CJ grabbed my hips and levered up, stroking my G-spot with the head of his dick as he set a steady pace that allowed him to tease my clit. "Come when you're ready. I'm right behind you."

It wouldn't last ten more seconds. I gasped and groaned as my body seized around him. The rush of blood in my ears blocked out the sound of him grunting as he came.

It was dirty and animalistic and primal and so, so depraved.

And my God, I loved it.

We righted ourselves and caught our breath. While CJ handled the condom, I started pawing around for my clothes.

"Hey." Safe arms banded around me, pulling me back into his chest. He pressed soft kisses against my neck. "You okay, love?"

Something warm broke inside me, crashing around in churning waves.

"Just fine."

"Len . . ." Concern filled his eyes. "Tell me if I took it too far."

The emotion that was strangling me turned into a laugh. "It was everything."

It wasn't the act that broke me. It was him calling me "love."

There was a distinct difference in being loved and being *love*. One was received. I felt CJ's love when he stood up for me. But him calling me "love" meant that he saw something in me that no one else ever had.

He saw the ability for me to be love for others.

People had always expected me to be the screw-up.

To be the abrasive one.

To be the bad girl.

To be the hustler.

No one had ever expected love from me or seen it in me. But he did.

We rode back to the stables in silence. My ass ached and stung with each rock of the saddle beneath me. I had never been so grateful to be back on my feet in my life.

CJ did most of the work. He got the equipment off the horses and settled them for the night, but he talked me through it like this wasn't a one-time thing.

We walked back to the bunkhouse with his jacket on my shoulders and his hand in mine.

"Will you take me out there again sometime?" I asked.

CJ looked at me, a little surprised. "You liked it?"

"I don't think I've seen stars like that before. There were so many." I looked up at the sky the closer we got to the bunkhouse. Endless galaxies still hung above us, but light pollution blurred them.

He paused in the shadow of the bunkhouse and pressed a soft kiss to my temple, lingering for a moment as the crickets sang us a serenade. The tenderness of the moment was a knife to the heart.

"I'll take you out there anytime you want, as long as you stay." There was sincerity in his words and conviction in his eyes. "You and me, trouble. Every night under the stars. I'll build you a house with a glass roof so you never have to go far to find them."

I couldn't help myself. I crashed into his chest, tucking myself between his arms and soaking in the safety he promised.

"Come on," he said as he dropped a kiss on top of my head and guided me to the door.

We snuck through the darkened bunkhouse, avoiding the curious glances from the ranch hands who were still awake. They all knew CJ and I had been cohabiting, but no one said a damn thing about it. Probably because I usually made breakfast for everyone before work.

Bacon was an excellent bribe.

There was an ease between the two of us as we went through our routine and got ready for bed. We shared little touches as we danced around each other, swapping positions at the sink and getting undressed. Gliding hands and gentle squeezes connected us with each pass.

"What's this?" I asked as I crawled into bed and picked up the charred piece of wood from the nightstand on his side.

CJ paused as he flicked the bathroom lights off. His body tensed, every muscle rippling and flexing as he looked at the wood chip in my hand.

I placed it back slowly and shifted to my side of bed. "Okay . . . Sorry. I won't bring up the mysterious piece of burned wood again."

He climbed into bed without a word and picked it up. "This . . . this is my anger." A sigh escaped his lips. "Brooke came to the ranch back when the restaurant and lodge were being built. She had some trouble follow her out here. Some guys she used to live with thought the ranch would be an easy target to make some quick cash. They stole tools from the construction site. They broke into Ray's house and stole some drugs."

He worked his finger over the charred edge that had been worn smooth from the motion.

"We were having a bonfire when they decided to fuck around the construction site where the restaurant was being built. Some of the guys and I went in after them. I ended up tackling one of them." His voice turned hoarse. "He pulled a gun on me and fired. Didn't get me, but the bullet hit a welding tank and it exploded. Caught the restaurant and part of the lodge on fire."

"Oh my God," I whispered. "Were you hurt?"

He shrugged. "No. I kicked his ass."

"Carson..."

I knew how it felt to have that kind of near-death experience. I'd never forget the moment my brother pulled a gun on me. It haunted me at night when I closed my eyes.

"It's fine. The fire pushed the construction back about nine months. Fuckin' red tape and all that shit. The investors were pissed, but they ponied up to get it done."

I rested my head on his shoulder and curled into his side. "I'm glad you're okay."

"Why's that?"

"Who else would have given me such a warm welcome to the ranch?"

CJ chuckled. "Smartass."

"It's better than being a jackass."

"I'm sorry I took my anger out on you." He cupped my cheek, cradling my jaw as he pressed another kiss to my temple. "But man, I'm glad you were tough as nails and didn't run. I'd have regretted it every day if I didn't get a chance to win you back. And if giving up my land for that eyesore was the price I had to pay for you, it was worth it."

My spine stiffened. "You gave up your land?"

"I guess 'give up' wasn't the right phrase for it." He dug his fingernail into the wood. "I sold it. The spot where the lodge is... That used to be mine. My parents, my brothers, and I—we all had a plot of land that belonged to each of us. My brothers had already built on their pieces. I had started thinking about it, but didn't see the need to pull the trigger yet. I was happy living here with the guys. So, when Cassandra offered me money from the investors, I took it."

My heart broke for him. Regret marred every piece of him.

"It was the only logical place to put the lodge and restaurant. Building them farther out would have cost a fortune to extend the water and electric. Plus, it would've messed with the herd rotation. There was no right choice," he said as he stared at the wood. "If I kept the land that was rightfully mine, the ranch might have gone under. I would never have forgiven myself. But if I sold my land, I'd lose something I could never get back."

"So, you chose the ranch and kept your family safe."

"Yeah," he said as he set the wood aside and cut off the light. "And dammit, it hurt."

23

CARSON JAMES

"Fancy meeting you here," I said as I came up behind Lennon where she was stationed in front of my bedroom window. "How many times have I told you that you can go down there instead of watching from your tower?"

Lennon was watching a girl who had us boarding her horse as she galloped in the riding ring. The two of them looked good out there. She was a confident rider and had a great animal to work with.

"Brooke's down there," I said as I peppered Lennon's neck with kisses. "Pretty sure I saw Becks heading over there to watch."

She stiffened.

Lennon had tentatively agreed to stay, but I wasn't convinced I wouldn't find her trying to run away in the middle of the night.

I had never been this far gone for a woman. Sure, I had short-lived flings and hookups when the mood struck, but I had never wanted what my brothers had settled on early in life. The ring. The partner. The family. I had never cared about settling down because I hadn't found someone like Lennon.

Screw that. I just hadn't found Lennon yet.

And now that I had, I wasn't letting her go. If she was running away, I'd pack a bag and follow her to the ends of the earth.

I wanted that sharp mouth and that quick-tempered wit. I wanted that body I spent the entirety of my days thinking about. I wanted her disciplined, organized, and methodical mind. I wanted her soft side. The stolen moments when she trusted me enough to take her armor off and hide in my arms.

Maybe I was crazy for thinking that far ahead, but no one ever succeeded by being cautious.

"I'm fine up here," she said, her eyes tracking the horse as it jumped over fences and weaved around obstacles.

"You can go wherever you want, you know." I pulled her into my chest. "Just don't go wandering off the paths in the middle of summer like Brooke did. Heatstroke is a bitch."

"Staff aren't supposed to interfere with the guest areas or the ranching operations."

"You're not just staff."

Her eyes were shrewd and mistrusting. "Then what am I?" Her palms flattened against my chest. "I'm not a cowboy."

"You're mine. And that's all that matters." I wrapped Lennon up in my arms and buried my nose in the crook of her neck, dotting her skin with kisses. "How are you not going stir crazy? You've been in here for a day and a half."

There was a sad sort of smile on her lips. "I like being alone. Sleeping in peace and quiet in a bed still feels like a luxury. There's not a whole cell block making noise at all hours of the night. I'm not cramped up in my car." She let out a slow breath. "It's peaceful."

I held her a little tighter. "Thank you for trusting me."

Warm brown eyes met mine with overwhelming sincerity. "Thank you for working for it."

I chuckled. "Best advice I ever got was, 'When you're in a hole, the easiest way to get out is to stop digging and start scooping the dirt back inside.' Saying you're sorry goes a long way. People don't do it enough these days. They're too worried about what will happen if they admit they're wrong. So, for what it's worth, I'm still sorry."

"Thank you," she said into my chest.

I rubbed her back as we stood at the window and watched the horses. My sisters-in-law had convened along the fence, and it looked like they were laughing about something.

I swore then and there that Lennon would join them someday.

She had Cassandra's tenacity, Brooke's heart, and Becks's intuition. But more than that, she had a strength that I had only seen in one other person.

My mom.

I had heard my parents' tale of how my dad won over my mom damn near a million times. Few men would fake a job offer and pay her salary out of his pocket to keep her near. Few people would willingly endure rejection for an entire year. But my dad always swore up and down that my mom was the only woman he wanted to live this life with.

I never understood it until now.

"Want me to go down there with you?" I asked, hoping I could tempt her into leaving the bunkhouse.

"I'm fine up here, babe."

Our eyes locked as her mouth dropped open in surprise. My heart ricocheted in my chest.

Lennon stammered as she pulled away. "I—I didn't mean to say—I shouldn't have—"

I grabbed her wrists and put her palms back on my chest. "Say it again."

She shook her head. "It was a slip of the tongue. I wasn't thinking, and I—"

"Len," I whispered as I cupped her chin and drew her lips to mine. "Say it again."

"I'm fine up here," she murmured.

I shook my head. "You know better than that, trouble. Say the other thing."

I watched the graceful lines of her throat constrict as she swallowed. Her voice was barely audible as she closed her eyes and rested her forehead on mine. "I'm fine up here, babe."

Our lips met like soft whispers of wind dancing with each other across the plains. The taste of coffee on her tongue as it slid along mine was the strongest fix. I soaked up her soft moans and gentle whimpers as she took some of the weight off her body and put it on me.

We stood there, lingering in the morning light. She relaxed in my arms, sharing sampled kisses like a wine tasting.

"Thank you for letting me hold you," I said as I pressed a kiss to her forehead.

She let out a soft laugh. "You are the most polite troublemaker I've ever met."

"I've heard that a time or two. Don't get my mom started, or she'll tell stories about me for a week."

Lennon's smile tugged at my heart as she burrowed into me and closed her eyes.

I rocked between my feet, making her sway with me. "I know it's self-sabotage to take a world-class chef out to dinner, but can I take you on a date?"

She laughed. "I'm far from world class. Chef DeRossi is world class, but I'm not."

"Well." I kissed her again. "Considering the ranch is my world, I'd say that makes you world class to me."

She kicked me out of my own damn house.

I paced the swatch of grass beside my truck as I waited for Lennon to come out. I decided that if she didn't come down to the truck in the next ninety seconds, I'd go up there, break down the door, throw her over my shoulder, and walk her out my damn self.

She was down to five seconds when the door to the bunkhouse finally opened and closed.

I lifted my cowboy hat from my head and pressed it to my chest.

My God, that woman was going to give me a heart attack.

A skin-tight dress wrapped around Lennon, stopping mid-thigh. Her long legs, thick thighs, and *that ass* nearly made me swallow my tongue. The straps that crisscrossed her back left her sleeves of tattoos on full display.

Her hair was down in soft curls, toning the edge that she sported day and night.

"Sorry," she grumbled as she tugged at the hem of the dress. "Apparently, I don't own anything that isn't black, and I haven't worn this in forever and—"

"Len." I pushed away from the hood of my truck and stalked toward her. "Shut up. You look beautiful."

Her eyebrows lifted.

"Don't believe me?" I said as I slid my hands up and down, digging my fingers into her waist, hips, and the soft curve of her lower stomach. "Turn around."

Eyes peered through every window shade in the bunkhouse. Lennon's lips parted in shock when she saw what I saw.

"They can't stop staring at you, and I can't blame 'em."

It was a warm day, but Lennon still had my ranch jacket draped in the crook of her arm. I took it from her and held it up so she could slip her arms in.

"You take my breath away," I murmured as she shimmied into the jacket and stuffed her hands in the pockets.

She let me open the door for her and held my hand as I helped her up onto the truck's running board. We drove into town in silence, hands laced together, with Bruce Springsteen on the radio.

"I figured you've probably had enough steak and potatoes at the restaurant," I said as I parked in a space at the edge of the downtown district.

All the traffic brought in by the ranch guests had begun to revitalize the area. New specialty shops and boutiques catered to tourists who wanted to shop for unique, local finds during their stay.

Lennon laughed as she unbuckled her seat belt. "You're not wrong. I love steak, but the smell has gotten a little old."

"How do you feel about food trucks?" I asked as I opened her door and helped her down. "I know it's not fancy, but the food is solid."

She closed her eyes and sucked in a deep breath, giving

the wafting aroma of street tacos, barbecue, and Thai food a tentative sniff.

"Yes, please," she groaned. "I want one of everything."

I laced our hands together and we walked to a vacant lot. Food trucks had parked in a circle, leaving the middle for picnic tables, cornhole, and horseshoes.

"Do you come out here often?" Lennon asked as she gave my hand a little squeeze.

I laughed. "No. I'm a homebody. I don't leave the ranch unless I have to."

She looked at the sidewalk, watching her steps. "I wouldn't either."

Then don't, I thought to myself.

"If you never leave the ranch, you'd at least have to leave the bunkhouse."

She huffed. "I know what you're getting at."

"You don't have to be a stranger. My family already loves you. Why do you think they started having family dinners at the restaurant instead of up at my folks' place? We used to have family dinners at their house at least once a week. Usually more."

"Probably so no one has to cook?" Lennon guessed.

"Fair, but no." I nudged her shoulder with mine. "One of these days you'll stop and realize that the only person who doesn't love you is you. And when you have that realization, I hope it makes you want to stay where you're celebrated." I lifted our clasped hands to my mouth and kissed her knuckles. "Because I adore you."

"You must've been kicked in the head by a horse," she sassed.

It felt like I had been. Everything about Lennon threw me off. I had never been in love before. I didn't even know what it felt like, just that it had completely fucked up my brothers in every conceivable way.

But now, I understood it.

I stopped Lennon dead in her tracks. "I fell for you the moment you punched a guy in a bar and pushed me out of the way so you could get some ice. Because you're tough, but you're human. I like watching you kick ass. But more than that, I like it when you feel safe enough to be hurt around me."

Lashes fluttered as she tried to blink away the glassiness in her eyes. "Stop fucking talking. I don't know how to handle it when you're all sweet." Her lip quivered, warping her words. "It's giving me a cavity."

"Eleanor."

We both froze at the sound of her government name. But neither of us had uttered it.

Lennon's eyes widened in terror. "I'm not going to look," she whispered. Her hand tightened around mine as she gritted out, "Keep walking. Not too fast."

I followed her lead, walking down the sidewalk, not too fast and not too slow.

"Eleanor!" the woman shouted again from behind us.

Out of the corner of my eye, I saw Lennon watching the storefront windows to try to get a glimpse of the person attached to the voice.

"WF-372891!"

Lennon stumbled, but didn't look back. "Take me back to the truck," she clipped. "*Right now*."

We rounded the block, slipping into stores and narrow alleys, trying to lose whomever it was so they wouldn't follow us back to the truck.

By the time we made it back to the parking space and climbed in, Lennon was nearly in tears.

So much for a first date.

"You're safe with me," I said as I pulled out of the spot and headed back to the ranch. "You hear me? I'm not going to let anything happen to you."

Lennon's head pressed against the back of the seat as she struggled to keep her breathing under control.

"Did she have red hair, or did I hallucinate that?"

The truck rumbled beneath us as we bumped and bobbed over the pothole-riddled street.

"I think so," I said as I glanced in the mirrors to make sure no one was following us. "What was that she shouted at you? That number."

Lennon sucked in a deep breath. "An inmate ID." She swallowed. "It wasn't mine."

"Do you think it was hers? Whoever she is?"

Lennon shrugged. "Could be."

There was only one other person who it could have belonged to. "Do you think it was your brother's?"

"No. WF means it was from a women's federal prison. I think that was the same person who followed me at the gym. You know—the night of the storm."

"The one that showed up at your car?"

She nodded.

"Okay," I said as I held her hand against my thigh. I didn't know if I was trying to convince her or myself that things were going to be alright. "I'll tell you one thing. You look too damn good for us to let this night go to waste."

I put my backup plan into action the moment we got back to the ranch. By the time Lennon walked into the ranch office, I was lighting the candles and finishing touches on our dinner spread.

"If you tell me you cooked that, you're going to put me

out of a job," Lennon said with a laugh as she navigated the filing cabinets and neared Cassandra's desk.

I had done a damn good job if I said so myself.

I didn't think Cassandra would mind if I moved her files, and if she did, I didn't really care.

I had thrown a tablecloth over the desk, picked some flowers outside, and stuffed them in a vase. I'd also stolen some wine glasses, silverware, and candles from the restaurant.

"I did not cook," I said as I took her hand and pulled the rolling chair out for her. "But I did ask the cooks at the restaurant to make something that isn't steak. Julian came through for me."

Lennon laughed as she peered at the professionally plated dinners. "Pasta is my love language. I love carbs."

"Good. Sit, and I'll pour the wine."

"You know there's a perfectly good table at the bunkhouse," she said as she picked up her fork. "Why are we eating in Cassandra's office?"

"Dinner at home is easy." I took the office chair across the desk from her. "I told you I play for keeps, trouble. And once upon a time, this was how a Griffith brother got his girl."

24

LENNON

"Mail's here!" Reed, one of the ranch hands, shouted up the stairs.

I groaned and burrowed into CJ's chest. "It's too fucking early."

The chest beneath me rumbled with laughter. "It's nine in the morning."

The yawn was inevitable. "And I was at work until two in the morning."

The lodge had held a wedding that lasted until midnight. Of course, the restaurant was the exclusive caterer. So, we had to stay to break down the dinner setup and wash the dishes so they'd be ready for a corporate dinner tonight.

"Sleep," CJ said as he pressed a kiss to my forehead and stroked my hair.

When I was in CJ's arms, any worries I had about sleeping in the same bed as another person vanished. They were safe and soothing. His chest was my favorite place in the world.

We held each other in a tangle of limbs and bedding,

soaking in the quiet morning since we had both worked overnight. His fingers traced gentle lines up and down my hip as our breathing steadied to match each other.

A fist pounded on the door, shattering the sweetness of the moment. "Chef! You got mail!"

"I got it," CJ murmured as he nibbled on my earlobe.

"I can get up," I said as I peeled the covers back.

"Absolutely not." CJ grabbed a pair of sweatpants and stepped into them. "Do you see what you're wearing? No way in hell I'm letting the guys look at you." He bent over the bed and pecked my lips. "You're all mine."

"Neanderthal," I snickered as I tugged the covers up to my chin and rolled onto my side.

CJ opened the door and grabbed the mail from Reed, then slammed it in his face.

"That's enough interruptions," CJ said as he climbed back into bed.

I stretched against him, curling my fingers and toes like a cat basking in the sun. "Well, now I'm awake. How was your night?"

He sighed. "A calf was born early and the momma rejected it. We've got him in the barn. Looks like he'll be bottle-fed for a while."

"And that's it? He'll live in the barn for the rest of his life?"

"Nah, we can usually reintroduce them to the herd. It's just a slow process." CJ sifted through the mail. He put his aside on the nightstand and handed me an envelope. "You wanna go check him out in a little bit? I'll teach you how to feed him."

"You're trying to bribe me into hanging out somewhere outside of this room and the restaurant."

"Is it working?" he murmured against the back of my neck. "Calves are pretty cute."

"We'll see," I grumbled as I turned the envelope over in my hands. The letter had no return address, but the postmark came from New York.

"What's that?" CJ asked as he settled behind me.

"Dunno." I wedged my thumb into the fold and tore it open. "Probably my tax forms from my old job."

But the familiar sight of obnoxious IRS forms wasn't what I pulled out of the envelope. A chicken-scratch scrawl made every molecule of oxygen in my body vanish.

I couldn't breathe as I read the words that had only been said once before.

Blood is thicker than water. I have eyes everywhere.
See you soon, Sis.

"The hell?" CJ eased up and peered over my shoulder. He grabbed the page out of my hand and scanned it as I fought to breathe.

I expected him to storm out and threaten to kill someone. I expected him to call in the cavalry and go to war.

But he dropped the letter.

My vision went sparkly as it fluttered to the wood floor. CJ set the envelope aside, rolled me over, and pulled me into his chest.

"Breathe for me," he said as he cradled the back of my head. "I've got you, Len."

His palm sliding up and down my back in gentle rhythms was calming. He held me like I deserved to be protected. Like I was valuable.

"We dug the fire line, remember? That doesn't mean the

fire won't happen. But it means that you don't have to face it alone. I'm right here with you. I'm on your side."

"I knew this was too good to be true," I said in choked out syllables between ragged breaths.

"It's not too good to be true." CJ pressed a kiss to the top of my head as my world came crumbling down. "You know why?" He tipped my chin up. "Because he's wrong."

I pressed my forehead to his chest to keep my tears from showing.

I knew this day would come. It had always been inevitable. I had just been hoping I could buy a little more time with CJ before I had to disappear.

"He got the saying wrong." CJ's calloused thumb worked across my cheeks as he wiped the tears away. "It's not 'blood is thicker than water.' It's 'the blood of the covenant is thicker than the water of the womb.'"

Slowly, my lashes raised until I met hazel eyes staring down at me with inexplicable love.

"It's not where you're born or who you're related to, Len. It's who you choose." His lips met mine in a kiss so soft it rivaled the heavens. "And I choose you."

CJ held me for the longest time. After a while, he dozed off, exhausted from his night of work. But I couldn't sleep.

Anxiety and adrenaline crawled up my skin like centipedes, making me uncomfortable in my own body.

I wanted to run.

I wanted to hide.

I wanted to keep him safe from my chaos. From my ugliness. From my darkness.

CJ was out like a light when I slipped out of his bed. I dressed for the outdoors and toed on a pair of sneakers.

The bunkhouse was empty as I snuck out into the late

afternoon sun. I would have given anything to be able to clock in at the restaurant. But, of course, it was my day off.

I wanted to bury myself in work. Hell, I would have been perfectly happy going in and deep-cleaning the walk-in cooler and freezer.

Instead, I found myself walking away from the restaurant and toward the barn. The smell of hay and feed warmed me as dust danced in the beams of light that poured inside.

At the sound of unfamiliar shoes, Independence and Anarchy peered out of their stalls.

Indy sniffed around my shoulder while Anarchy glared at me for waking her from her beauty sleep.

"Are we going to be friends or are you going to be an asshole?" I asked Anny as I carefully approached her stall. I held my hand out flat, the way CJ had taught me, and waited to see if she was going to give it a sniff.

Maybe it was because she could still smell CJ on my skin, but she dropped her head right into my hand and nuzzled against me.

"You know, I've always believed that animals are good judges of character."

I jumped back as Ray Griffith wheeled into the barn with a toddler on his lap.

"I was just passing through," I clipped.

Ray's eyes fell on the jacket I had slipped into.

I yanked it off and tied it around my waist. I really needed to stop wearing it. CJ's jacket was like playing dress-up—an ill-fitting dream that I had no business prancing around in.

"Hi!" the little boy squeaked. "Color you?"

"What?"

Ray grinned. "It's kind of a thing around here. If you

have tattoos, the youngins think you're a human coloring book." He reached out and showed off his own sleeves of messily scribbled-over tattoos. "Welcome to the club."

I looked down at my arms, then back at the kid, laughing nervously as I stepped to the side so I could bolt.

"Since you're here, do you mind giving me a hand?" Ray asked. "Seth wanted to see the new calf."

"I—I don't do the live cows," I stammered as I looked around. "I cook them."

He let out a loud laugh and pointed to the wooden door that was two spaces down from Anarchy. "I meant, could you open the stall?"

"Oh." I hurried over and slid back the latch. Sure enough, there was an adorable little rust-colored calf curled up in the stall.

"I'm a little surprised CJ isn't down here."

"He worked last night," I said without thinking.

Great. Now everyone would know I was somehow privy to CJ's work schedule.

Ray positioned his wheelchair in the stall door and held his son's hand as he wiggled down to get a better look at the calf. He kept the little boy at a safe distance from the animal, but the excitement was written on both of their faces.

"I'd usually find CJ spending the night in the stall," Ray said as he popped his son back up on his lap. "I was surprised he went back to the bunkhouse."

"Len."

I whirled around and found CJ standing behind me.

"And speak of the devil," Ray said with an amused smirk.

"EeeeeeeJ!" Seth squealed.

CJ laughed and reached out for his nephew, propping

him up on his hip. CJ tipped his head to me. "Seth can't say 'CJ' yet. Eeeeeej is the best we can do."

"Eeeeeeej! Cow!"

CJ smiled from ear to ear. "I know. He's just a baby. Did your dad and Len give you a look?"

"Len! Cow!" he shrieked.

"Shhhhh," CJ said. "You'll wake him up. Wanna help Len and me feed him?"

Seth nodded.

"Alright, but you gotta be real quiet so you don't scare him," CJ said. "Can Lennon hold you while I fix his bottle?"

Two little hands reached for me.

My eyes widened. "I've never held a kid."

I expected Ray to take his son back after my little confession, but he just laughed. "If Cassandra can hold him, so can you."

"Aunt?" Seth said.

"Cassandra is your aunt," I said as I awkwardly took him from CJ and mimicked the hip-holding position.

Seth shook his head and stabbed me in the forehead with his finger. "Aunt."

"I'm not your aunt," I said, then pointed to myself. "My name is Lennon."

"Aunt," Seth declared.

Ray choked on a laugh.

"Good job, buddy," CJ said as he filled a bottle and carried it over. "That's your Aunt Lennon."

I glared at him, and that motherfucker smiled.

CJ slipped into the stall. After checking over the calf, he motioned for me to come in.

The little calf was standing in the hay, wary of all the newcomers. CJ stood over him, straddling the animal. I watched as he braced his hand under the calf's head to lift it and eased the bottle's nipple into its mouth.

Seth gasped as the calf freaked out and shuffled back in the corner of the stall. But CJ was calm. He moved with the calf until it had nowhere to run.

Slowly, the little guy started chewing and sucking on the nipple.

"Seth, you wanna come give him a pat?"

Seth wiggled until I set him down. He grabbed my hand and tugged. "Aunt. Pat cow."

I walked over with Seth and knelt as he placed a chubby toddler's hand on the calf's rust-colored coat.

"Gentle," I said softly when Seth got a little grabby.

CJ's crinkle-cornered eyes met mine with a smile.

Since we were already down there, I gave the calf a gentle pat. CJ manipulated the animal with gentle hands, making sure it focused on eating and not the strange environment or weird people staring as it ate.

Seth's attention span waned quickly, and he waddled out to his dad.

"See y'all at family dinner," Ray called as he wheeled out with Seth.

I raised an eyebrow at CJ. "You're supposed to be asleep."

"You think I slept at all?" he said, keeping his voice gentle. "Honey, I didn't sleep a wink. I wanted to hold you. And when I felt you get up, I knew you needed your space. So, I watched out the window to make sure you were okay."

"Anarchy didn't bite me, so that's good," I clipped, trying to hide the tears that pricked at my eyes.

CJ chuckled. "I think it's because she knows you bite back." When the bottle was empty, he set it on the top ledge of the stall wall. "I'm glad you came out here."

"Why?" I asked as I watched the little calf curl up in the hay.

CJ pulled me into his chest. "Because it's always been my safe place. I want it to be yours too." He cupped my cheeks, wiped my tears, and kissed me. "I got in trouble a lot as a kid," he said as he sat down and tugged me into his lap. "I'd come out here and sit with the animals. When my brother, Nate, got hurt overseas, I came out here after my parents told me. When Christian's first wife died, this was where I grieved. When Ray got hurt, this place was my altar. The animals will never tell how much you cry." He pressed a soft kiss to my temple. "And neither will I."

25

CARSON JAMES

"You're not running away, are you?" I asked as I slipped into the bedroom and closed the door behind me.

Lennon looked down at where she was buttoning her chef's coat. "Do I look like I'm running away? A runaway chef doesn't have the same pizzazz as a runaway bride."

Her ass looked delectable in those black pants.

I slid my hand up her hip, standing behind her as she twisted her hair back into a low bun. When Lennon dropped her hands, I slid the daisy I had picked behind her ear.

"Don't think I can wear that at work," she said with a coy smile.

I dropped a little purple bloom that had sprung up by a fence post into the sleeve pocket of her chef's coat.

"Wear flowers on your sleeve rather than your heart. You've bled enough, darling. Let yourself bloom."

"You have a way with words, cowboy." A soft smile painted her lips as she reached for the hairspray. "You make me feel delicate."

"Glass is always delicate, even if it's sharp and shattered." I pressed a kiss to the side of her neck. "It just takes someone picking up the pieces and forging them back together to make cathedrals." I cupped her chin, craned my neck, and kissed her. "I'd worship you every day of my life if you let me."

Her eyes squeezed in happiness in the corners. "You don't have to do this, you know?"

"Do what?" I murmured as I peppered the side of her neck with kisses.

"Drop into the bunkhouse in the middle of your workday to make sure I'm still here."

That woman had me pegged. I knew she was scared. I could feel it in her body every time I was near her. A tension. An unease.

"I want you to stay," I said, skating my hands up and down her arms.

Her eyes lowered to the cuffs of her sleeves. "I'm here, aren't I? You don't have to babysit me. How's the calf?"

Lennon had taken a liking to the little bottle-fed calf we were keeping in the barn. I'd find her checking on him on her days off and after her shift. As the weather crept out of the chilly winter temperatures and prepared for spring, she spent more and more of her time outside the bunkhouse.

Her responsibilities at the restaurant had only grown as events and reservations packed the schedule. The difference was that when she was off, she'd take walks. Once, I had even found her talking to Becks outside the restaurant.

That was a damn good day.

If I hadn't experienced this song and dance before, it would have thrown me off. But Lennon came to me the same way Anarchy had—untrusting and prone to bolting.

It was that hole my dad had been talking about. Just

because you stopped digging didn't mean you were out of the darkness. You had to put all the dirt back in and climb out. That was a lot more work.

"You can't distract me by talking about the calf," I said. "He's fine. One of the guys has him out in a little fenced-off area today. It's out behind the ranch office if you wanna go visit him."

"He needs a name," Lennon declared.

I laughed. "Hate to break it to you, but we don't name the cows."

"Mickey has a name," she argued as she pocketed her phone and my key to the bunkhouse.

"Mickey is a pet. He's not going to end up on someone's plate."

Lennon pressed her hands to my chest. "He needs a name."

My gaze lowered to her mouth. "Yes, ma'am."

She smirked. "I've gotta go to work. I'll see you tonight?"

I bit the inside of my cheek. She'd be seeing me tonight, she was just under the impression it would be when she clocked out and crawled back into my bed.

"Yes, ma'am," I said softly as I kissed her lips, soaking in the softness—the tenderness of the moment.

Despite her protests, I walked my girl to the restaurant, holding her hand the entire way.

The day flew by. I was sweat-soaked and panting by the time I hurried back to the bunkhouse to rinse off for family dinner.

What had once been a ranch institution had changed when we became more than a generational cattle ranch. We used to gather at my parents' house for dinner at least once or twice a week. The tradition had begun out of necessity. Even though my parents, brothers, and I all lived on the same land, we could go a week without seeing each other.

As my brothers went through the life changes of divorce, injuries and accidents, death, birth, and love, it was more than an institution. It was survival.

There was someone else in survival mode, and I knew that getting her to join family dinner was going to be worse than pulling teeth.

I garnered a handful of strange looks as I plodded up the path to the restaurant and dipped inside.

Jessica looked up from the host stand. "She's in a mood. Consider yourself warned."

"Probably my fault," I clipped as I dipped through the dining room and into the kitchen. The smell of searing steaks and roasted vegetables made my stomach growl.

Julian looked up from the grill and tipped his head down the hall. "She's yelling in the office."

"Good luck," Javi the pastry cook said as I passed him.

I followed the sound of shouts until I pushed open the office door and found Lennon in a screaming match with Chef DeRossi.

Well, Lennon was screaming. Chef DeRossi was sitting in the desk chair in one of his fancy suits.

The moment the door creaked open, she whirled around, wielding a takeout container of soup as a weapon.

"Out," she snarled.

I crossed my ankles and rested my shoulder against the doorframe. "Why? It's dinner time."

Lennon pinched the bridge of her nose. "I will deal with you later. Get out."

I glanced at my watch. "We're gonna be late."

"*We* are not going anywhere. I have to work," she shouted.

Chef DeRossi pressed his fist to his mouth and tried to hide his amused smile. "Lennon, have I ever told you that you remind me a lot of my wife?"

She cut him a sharp glare. "Does Maddie want to kill you regularly for messing with her work schedule?"

He chuckled. "Actually, she does. So I'm going to tell you what I have to remind her of all the time. Having a life outside of your job does not make you bad at your job or less respected in it. You need a break. You need people outside of the ones who report to you."

"I take it you told her she was off the clock?"

"*She* has a name," Lennon snapped.

I glanced down at the takeout container in her hand. "Oh good. You got Brooke's soup ready to go. Apparently, it's the only thing she wants to eat during this pregnancy."

"I'm about to dump it on your head," she hissed. I watched as Lennon huffed, then put on the façade of a professional. "I do not appreciate my schedule being messed with. I'm on the schedule tonight. Ergo, I will work tonight."

I may have heard from Cassandra that Chef DeRossi would be dropping in for a visit for the next few days. And I may have put a bug in her ear that Lennon needed a night off.

And that night might have happened to land on the day I'd head up to my parents' house for family dinner.

The only way I could convince her to go was by forcing her.

"Len. Take the night off. Come up to the house," I said.

She gave me a searing look filled with fear and tears.

Chef DeRossi hunched over the desk and laced his hands together. "You wanna have this job long-term? Be a whole person outside of the kitchen. And if I see another schedule like the one you made for the last two weeks, you and I will have a different conversation. You can't do good work if you're dead. I'm not here because you're not doing well. I came out here because I want you to continue to do good work."

Lennon huffed and stormed out. Her tantrum was accompanied by the sound of stomping feet and slamming doors.

"Word of advice," he began, clicking through the schedule on the screen. He erased the back-to-back work weeks Lennon had signed up for, with no days off.

"I'm all ears."

Luca glanced up. "Keep at it. Lennon gets angry at people she trusts because she doesn't want to risk that anger getting her in trouble again if she lets it out around the wrong people. Be honored that she gives you her emotions." Mindlessly, he worked his finger over his wedding band. "I'm happy to see that you two worked things out."

I rubbed the back of my neck. "Yeah ... Sorry about all that shit before."

"Trust me, I get it," he said with a laugh as he stood and buttoned his jacket. "I need to get behind the line. You two have a good night."

I found Lennon out behind the ranch office, watching the little calf in its pen.

"Let me have it," I said as I rested my arms on the fence post beside her. "I can handle it."

She didn't say a word.

"Talk to me." When she didn't, I took her hand and laced our fingers together.

Surprisingly, she walked with me instead of having to be dragged along.

"Len, I—"

"Don't ever fuck with my job again," she clipped, staring hard at the horizon. "I thought you were past doing that. I don't care if it was well intended. You wanna know my line? That's it. Don't fuck with my livelihood."

"Noted, and I'm sorry," I said as we hit the dirt path that connected the ranch office to Christian and Cassandra's house. "But I knew—"

"No buts. I don't care what your reasoning is. Don't do it."

I nodded. "Yes, ma'am."

We paused at a leaning fence post halfway between Christian's house and Nate's house. I picked a primrose and tucked it behind her ear. "If I had a flower for every time I thought of you, I could walk through my garden forever."

Her brows lifted in surprise. "That's . . . beautiful."

"Should be. Tennyson said it." I cupped her cheeks. "For the millionth time, I'm sorry. I know we haven't exactly put this thing between us in definable terms, so let me clarify a few things for you. I wanted you the night we fucked in that bar, and the moment you showed up at my door, you were mine. We can fill in the gaps at any pace you need, but the beginning was us, and the end will be us."

"You make it sound like you'll never let me leave the ranch," she said. Her body language relaxed as she faced me, uncrossing her arms.

"If I had it my way, you'd never leave my bed, but we both have work to do."

She tossed her head to the side, causing her black and white hair to spill out of her bun. "And what if I want to work at another restaurant?"

"Then I will build it right here with my own two hands. Every inch of my land is yours. It was yours long before you ever came through the gates."

Lennon let out a long breath and rested her head on my shoulder as I wrapped my arms around her. "It feels like home." She rested a little more of her weight in my arms. "I'm sorry you have to say all those things."

"Hey," I said as I tugged her hair free from the elastic and combed my fingers through it. "Wanting affirmation isn't a bad thing, and I'm sorry you never got it before this." I pressed a kiss to her temple. "Now, can we have a good night off and head up to my folks' house to have dinner so neither of us has to cook?"

"I'd rather not."

I knew she was going to say that.

"Len—"

"Staff doesn't fraternize with the family or mess with the ranch operations. Remember?"

I tugged on my jacket that she was still wearing. "This makes you family, Len. And you look damn good with my name on your chest."

She looked down at the embroidered ranch logo. "I thought you said your name would never be mine."

The memory hit me like a shot to the heart. "I was wrong."

A self-satisfied smirk winked at the corner of her mouth. "I think those are the three sexiest words a man can say."

"Well, there y'all are!" Momma said as she whipped her front door open. "I was about to send out a search party." She beamed at Lennon. "Hey there, sweetie. Take your shoes off and come on in."

"Your mom did know that you were dragging me here against my will, right?" Lennon hissed as she toed off her work shoes.

I set my boots beside hers. "Nah, I didn't mention it."

"What?" she shrieked.

"Don't worry. She's been setting a place for you for a few weeks now. I think she might be psychic. This is just the first time I could get you up here."

The dining room was packed with my brothers and their families, but to my surprise, Lennon peeled away from my side and dipped into the kitchen.

"This smells great, Mrs. Griffith," she said as she peered over the stovetop.

Nate sidled up to me as I watched Lennon from the dining room.

Momma chuckled. "None of this *Mrs. Griffith* business. We're not at the restaurant, are we? It's Claire or Momma. You choose."

Across the room, Brooke, Becks, and Cassandra waited with bated breath for Lennon's answer.

"Yes, ma'am," Lennon said, throwing everyone off with the evasive answer. "Can I help with anything?"

"I'm always happy to have a hand," Momma said. "Mind carving that ham for me? If I don't get food on the table soon, I fear the boys will riot."

"They can wait," Lennon said as she wielded a knife and glanced up at me to punctuate the point.

Nate chuckled and elbowed me in the side. "About time."

Seth, Ray's son, bolted into the kitchen. "Aunt!"

Lennon lifted her eyebrows as she started to slice through the ham. "What's up, little man?"

"Cow?"

"Yeah, I saw the cow," she said. "Did your dad take you down there again?"

Seth nodded.

Lennon cocked her head in my direction. "Tell your Uncle CJ the cow needs a name."

Ray crowded in beside Nate and me, catching Seth as he bolted for us.

Christian joined us in the doorway and crossed his arms, watching Lennon help my mom put the finishing touches on the meal. "She fits."

I couldn't take my eyes off her.

Lennon in this place. Lennon in my jacket. Lennon in my family.

"Yeah," I said as Seth climbed up onto my hip. "She fits."

26

LENNON

"Thank you, Chef," Reed said with a tip of his chin as he moved through the buffet line I had set up at the bunkhouse. His plate was piled high with the summer menu items I had been playing around with.

I needed to plan the seasonal menu changes in the next few weeks so that my staff had time to learn them before we introduced them to the restaurant guests.

"Chef, you can stay here as long as you want," Jackson said with a grin as he piled heaping scoops of summer corn salad on his plate.

I had turned everyone's favorite soup into a cold salad for the summer and it was killer.

There were a few crisscrossing hours in the day when the bunkhouse was full. Morning, when everyone was going out to the fields or returning from a long night. And lunch, when the night crew woke up for a bite and the day crew stopped in for a break.

I smelled CJ before I saw him. "There's my girl." Hands slipped around my waist as he craned around and kissed my cheek.

"You reek," I said with a laugh. I flicked my wrist. "Out of my kitchen."

CJ chuckled as he took stock of the buffet covering the island. "Your kitchen?"

"That's right. I cooked. Therefore, it's my kitchen."

His smile was playful as he grabbed a plate and started filling it up. "I like the sound of that. What's this?"

I glanced over my shoulder as I washed my hands. "Smoked watermelon and feta on skewers."

He took three.

"Thank you, Chef," one of the older men said as he passed by.

"Are they treating you right?" CJ murmured in my ear as he slid behind me.

"Of course."

"Any problems or attitudes I need to take care of?"

I pecked his cheek. "Nope. You know what they say. The way to a man's heart is through his stomach. I'm pretty sure if I keep feeding them, they'll let me hang around."

CJ's smile split wide across his face. "You don't have to cook for them, you know. This is supposed to be your morning off."

"They're good test subjects, and the upside is that they don't mind doing the dishes after."

"That's right, Miss Chef," Cody said. "You cook, we clean."

I snickered under my breath. "You'd better watch out. I might steal your guys to come over and work at the restaurant."

The front door opened, ricocheting off the wall. "Well, there you are," Cassandra said as she stood with her hands on her hips.

The ranch hands scattered, taking their plates with them.

I looked around at the empty kitchen and living room. "What just happened?"

CJ shrugged with a mouthful of food. "They're scared of her."

"Don't know why," Cassandra grumbled. "I've never been anything but nice."

I snorted.

CJ laughed. "What are you doing, Cass?"

"Kidnapping your girlfriend, obviously," she said as she perused the buffet and picked up one of the watermelon kebabs. "What's this?"

"Fuckin' delicious," CJ said around his bite. "Try it."

Cassandra stole a skewer and took the most ladylike bite I had ever seen. "Put it on the menu."

I cackled. "We'll see."

Cassandra cut me an exacting glare. "I believe the proper response is 'yes, Mrs. Griffith.'"

I lifted an eyebrow. "I'd recommend changing the tone you're using with me, *Cassandra*," I clipped as I crossed my arms and rested my hip on the countertop. "What you actually mean is, 'That was delicious, Chef Maddox. I'd love to see that on the summer menu of *your* restaurant.' Shall we try that again?"

Cassandra paled, silently fuming.

Becks and Brooke had piled up at the door with their jaws on the floor.

"Holy shit," CJ muttered as he abandoned his plate on the couch and crossed the room, planting a hard kiss squarely on my mouth.

I squealed and stumbled backward, catching the counter to stay upright.

"I had you pegged from day one, didn't I, trouble?" CJ snickered.

I tipped my head back and laughed. "I may have just gotten myself fired."

"You guys coming or what?" Brooke said. "I'm starving."

"That jacket he gave you is the only reason you're not fired," Cassandra glowered. "But Brooke might kill you if she doesn't get fed within the next half-hour. Let's go." She glanced at CJ. "You can grope your woman when you're off work."

I lifted an eyebrow as I stole a bite off CJ's plate. "I'm not going anywhere."

"Come on," Brooke whined. "It's a rite of passage. Let us kidnap you."

"We'll have you back before you have to be at the restaurant," Becks said.

"Did you know about this?" I asked CJ.

He shook his head. "I'm innocent. But I've gotta get back to work." CJ pecked my lips. "I appreciate you."

"Wha—" I watched as he waved to his sisters-in-law and walked right out the door. "You're going to leave me with them?" I called after him.

"Getting kidnapped is fun," Becks said. "There's margaritas."

"Sold," I said as I grabbed CJ's key to the bunkhouse and locked up.

I was unceremoniously stuffed into Brooke's minivan and told to buckle up. Before I knew it, I was heading off of the ranch with the Griffith sisters.

"So, what's this all about?" I asked as we bumped and bobbled over the dirt path that headed out to the service road. "Why am I being kidnapped? And I don't think you're supposed to tell someone when you're kidnapping them. It kind of spoils the surprise."

"It's what we do," Brooke chirped as she popped a curb. "Oops! Sorry!"

"I should have driven," Cassandra muttered from the front seat.

Becks laughed from her spot beside me. "None of us want you driving, Miss Passenger Princess."

"Someone wanna fill me in?" I asked as I watched the scenery fly by.

"We're just getting lunch," Becks said. "It's what we do on Saturdays, so make sure you leave it open on your schedule."

"I made lunch at the bunkhouse. You could've eaten there."

"But then we wouldn't get to interrogate you," Brooke said like the cheeriest secret agent known to man. "Not with CJ around, anyway."

"Interrogate me about what?" I groaned as she went full force over a speed bump. The startling jolt rattled my bones.

"CJ," Cassandra said. "You finally showed up to a family dinner. That means you're finally eligible to be interrogated."

We came to a screeching halt in front of a Mexican restaurant, and I let out a terrified breath.

"Brooke, you're parked on the line."

Brooke peered out the window. "It's close enough."

"Close only counts in horseshoes and hand grenades," Becks said.

"Whatever," Cassandra said as she hopped out. "I'm starving and far too sober. It's been a damn week."

I followed the parade of Griffith women into the restaurant and stole the spot in the booth that put my back to the wall and faced the front door. Becks squeezed in beside me, while Brooke and Cassandra slipped into the restroom.

"Best spot in the restaurant," Becks said before thanking the server who dropped off a basket of chips and a dish of salsa. "Let me guess—you've already scoped out the exits, too."

I had, but I didn't think I was that obvious.

She let out a soft laugh. "Nate had you clocked the second you came up to the rooftop during the grand opening. Were you in the military?"

I took a chip from the basket and tried not to let my poker face slip. "Prison, actually."

If she was fazed, she didn't show it. Not in the slightest. "Not that big of a difference."

Cassandra and Brooke weaved through the tables to get to us.

"It's not a secret," I said, trying to maintain the high ground. "Cassandra knows."

"If Cassandra knows, then it's still a secret. She's a steel vault."

"Christian and CJ know," I clarified.

She smiled. "The boys are less reliable when it comes to secret keeping."

I shrugged. "It's public record."

"How are you liking the ranch?" she asked as Cassandra and Brooke slid into the booth.

The server swung back by, taking our orders before disappearing again.

"It's great. Chef DeRossi does a great job with his restaurant concepts," I said evasively.

The ladies shared knowing looks, like they knew I was trying to get out of giving them a direct answer.

"Cool. So are you and CJ serious?" Brooke said as she munched on a tortilla chip.

"CJ and I aren't anything," I said with a cool neutrality in my voice.

It was the truth, whether I wanted it to be that way or not. We were . . . I didn't know what we were. Fuck buddies? Frenemies with benefits? Accidental roommates?

I had never been in a place where I could allow myself to fall in love. Where I could slow down, stick around, and let myself breathe.

Stay.

Don't run away.

Don't go.

Every pleading word CJ had ever begged rang in my mind.

But those words didn't mean a damn thing in the long run.

"Ooh, she's quiet," Cassandra said as her eyes flicked up and down, studying my body language.

"You have a jacket, don't you?" Brooke said. "That's a hop, skip, and a jump away from a ring."

I also had a psycho brother and the boogeyman out to get me, but that wasn't exactly proper lunch conversation.

"A jacket?" I snapped a tortilla chip in half so I wouldn't double dip.

"Yeah, the ones with the ranch logo on them," Brooke said.

"I have a chef's coat with the ranch logo."

Cassandra rolled her eyes. "Lennon's been wearing CJ's jacket, you adorable little moonbeam. But I have hers ordered so she can give his back. It should get here next week."

Becks beamed. "I figured. Once she came to family

dinner, I knew that was that. When did he ask you to order it?"

"I'm sorry," I said as I snatched a margarita off the server's tray. "You all realize I'm sitting right here, right?"

Brooke squeezed a lime wedge into her water and stirred it around with the straw. "You get used to it after a while. The first time I got kidnapped, it was awkward, too."

I pinched the bridge of my nose. "Look, I have no problem hitchhiking back to the ranch. So, if someone doesn't fill me in on why I've been abducted for lunch, I'll go wait on the side of the road."

Becks shifted on our side of the booth and smiled. "CJ gave you his ranch jacket."

"It was cold," I said. "Isn't that the southern gentleman thing to do? Or did the movies lie and oversell chivalry? I think it might be a scam."

Cassandra snickered as she sipped on her margarita. "Sweet, innocent Lennon."

I snorted.

"CJ didn't tell you?" Brooke asked. "When you get a jacket, it means you're part of the ranch. We all have one. They're only for the family. Ranch hands have different jackets. The lodge and restaurant staff have their uniforms. Wearing the ranch jacket tells everyone you're part of the family." Her eyes softened. "I thought you knew. You've been wearing one forever."

The server came and doled out sizzling plates of tacos and fajitas, but all I could taste was the bile in my mouth.

"Now that we've terrified her—" Cassandra reached in her bag and pulled out a giant three-ring binder "—let's tell her how to handle a Griffith brother. Fun fact, cowboys are stubborn. But we've basically discovered the cheat code, so listen up. You're going to want to hear this."

They delivered me back to the bunkhouse like a pizza. My head swam, and it had nothing to do with the tequila I had imbibed to survive that lunch.

The Griffith sisters were nice. After I had been inundated with Griffith Brother management tactics, the conversation quickly shifted to Brooke's baby. She and Ray had decided to name their little girl "Olivia."

CJ was waiting for me in our bedroom—*his* bedroom—when I ran up to change into my uniform before work.

"Geez." I clutched my hand to my chest when I opened the door and found him sitting on the edge of the mattress. "You scared the shit out of me. Why are you here? Aren't you supposed to be at work?"

His brows lifted in a kind sort of way. "Brooke texted me and said you might be in a mental spiral after lunch."

"So that's who she was texting while driving," I grumbled as I pawed through the closet. "She almost hit an old lady trying to cross the street."

He laughed. "I don't know why the hell they let Brooke drive." His hands slid up my hips as I dumped my chef's coat off the hanger. "Talk to me, slugger. I can see the wheels turning in your mind."

The bile returned, stinging my throat and tongue as acid ate away at everything good I had gleaned since I showed up on his doorstep. "You can have your jacket back."

"I don't want it," CJ said with an unflappable calm. It was infuriating. "I gave it to you. It's yours."

I let out a caustic laugh. "Apparently, one has been ordered for me. Wanna fill me in on that?"

"Not until you look at me." He pressed a kiss to the back of my head. "It's too easy for you to put up walls when you're not looking me in the eye while you build them. So turn around and look at me and I'll tell you."

I couldn't look at him. Not with the tears that were already rolling down my cheeks.

Gentle hands turned me until I had no choice but to face him.

"Len," he said with a smile as he cupped my cheeks and wiped my tears away. "Why are you crying, darling? This is a good thing."

Every gut-wrenching thought and disparaging emotion I had silently worked through at lunch came crashing through all at once.

"No one's ever wanted me before," I admitted in a whimper.

CJ pressed his lips to the crown of my head. "That's because you were always meant to be here, Len. It just took you a long time to find us."

I wrapped my arms around him and held on for dear life. "You say that like it's supposed to mean something to me, but it doesn't. And I feel like shit over it because I know I'm supposed to have butterflies and fireworks, but I don't. It makes me feel sick inside. Everything's always been temporary for me. I don't . . . I don't know what staying looks like and that scares me. Uncertainty has always been my constant."

"Can I tell you a story?" he murmured as he rocked between his feet, gently swaying with me. "My mom came to the ranch because my dad had asked her out over and over. She always rejected him because she didn't want to date a cowboy. So, he sent her a job offer to be the ranch's accountant. The ranch didn't need a full-time accountant, so my granddad told my dad that her salary would have to come out of his. So, for a whole year, he lived on next to nothing, just so my mom would work at the ranch. He spent that year making her fall in love with him. Showing her around. Teaching her how to ride horses. Talking to her. Bringing her flowers he found in the fields."

Something delicate tickled my palm. I looked down and saw that CJ had slipped a violet into my hand. Dirt and pollen still streaked the stem.

"When did your mom figure it out?" I asked as I fingered the soft petals.

He smiled. "When she asked my granddad for a raise. He told her to talk to my dad. The way he tells it, she was mad. But she had already fallen for him and the land, so she stayed. Since my dad had been giving her most of his salary, he didn't have any money for an engagement ring. So, he gave her his ranch jacket. It was the best way he could think of to let everyone know that she was his. And ever since then, a woman getting a ranch jacket has been our way of bringing them in. Making it known that they carry the weight of the Griffith name, even before there's a ring."

His thumb ghosted over my bare ring finger. "My jacket's yours, Len. I wasn't waiting for Cass to order a new one for you. What's mine is yours. That jacket. This land. My family. My name. I'm a prideful man, but I will lay it all down for you. Because you have me, too."

27

CARSON JAMES

"You look beautiful," I said as I took Lennon's hand and helped her out of the truck.

The March warmth was a welcome reprieve from the cold snap we had suffered through.

Things had somewhat settled down. The two of us had fallen into a predictable routine, and I couldn't remember ever feeling this . . . this at peace.

Certainly not since we had broken ground for the lodge. Even before then, I couldn't remember being this content.

Lennon's pale-yellow dress floated in the breeze as we walked hand in hand down the sidewalk that snaked through the revitalized downtown district. Her hair was in long, soft curls, brushing across her bare back with each step.

A new restaurant had opened last week, and she was insistent on needing to check out the competition. I was more than happy to take advantage of the impromptu date night. But Lennon, in that dress, was a cock tease.

It was going to be a long night.

"You're sure you don't mind coming with me?" Lennon

said as she pulled on my hand, trying to wiggle out of my grasp.

I held on tighter, stroking the back of her hand with my thumb. "Len, I've told you a million times. I don't mind. Not in the least bit. It's kind of the point of dating."

She turned a little green at the label of dating.

"I'm sorry that it blew a hole in your day. I could have gotten someone from the staff to come with me. Or Cassandra."

I stopped her dead in her tracks and had her backed up against a brick storefront before she could blink. "I left work early because I can, and because I wanted to. You're not an imposition."

Her long lashes softly closed as she looked down. "I'm sorry."

"Stop apologizing," I said with a chuckle.

The bashful blush on her cheeks was so fucking adorable. "I know you and your guys are busy."

I pressed a kiss to her forehead. "My guys would light themselves on fire for you, if you so much as hinted that you were cold. And that doesn't even begin to cover what I'd do for you."

Lennon had become beloved in the bunkhouse. Whether it was because she kept the kitchen stocked with leftovers, regularly used us as test subjects for new menu items, or because she could kick everyone's ass at cards— they would have gone to battle for her.

A pink flower I had picked right before we left the ranch was tucked behind her ear, softening her rough edges. It contrasted the dark color she had swiped over her lips.

"You gave me a chance to take you out to dinner, and we don't get to do that often."

Lennon cupped my cheek and initiated the kiss. "Thank you."

"Now, let's get going, pretty girl," I said as I slid my hand down her spine and rested it on the curve of her ass. "I'm starving."

She bumped her shoulder into mine as we headed down the sidewalk. As soon as we rounded the corner, Lennon stopped dead in her tracks.

"Oh my God," she whispered in what I could only describe as sheer terror.

The red-headed woman was stepping out of a shop, clutching a piece of paper to her chest.

Lennon stumbled backward as their eyes met.

"It *is* you," the redhead said with pure shock in her voice. "Elean—"

"Who are you?" I snapped as I stepped between the women, keeping Lennon's hand in mine as I blocked her with my body.

I was done with this bullshit. If Lennon was right and this woman was some kind of snitch for her brother, I was going to make it clear that she needed to get the hell out of our town.

The woman paused, her eyes going wide. "I—I don't want any trouble."

"That didn't answer my question," I growled. "Who are you, and why are you harassing my girlfriend?"

"What?" she blinked and shook her head. "No, no. I didn't know if I was going crazy or if it was actually you."

Lennon peeked over my shoulder. "I don't know who you are. Leave me alone."

The woman looked a little hurt. "You didn't have tattoos back then. Your hair was a little different—mostly blonde with some black streaks. But I guess it has been, what—a decade?"

"Len," I said under my breath as I felt her hand squeeze my arm.

"We were transferred to Danbury at the same time. You were that kid who got shanked. I felt real bad for you."

Lennon stiffened.

The woman put her hands up. "It wasn't me. But everyone was talking about you. Trying to figure out if you really stole all that money or not. You kept swearing up and down that you didn't do it."

Lennon's grip softened, and I heard her breath catch.

"I couldn't believe my eyes when I saw you around town. I saw you going in and out of the gym a lot. Tried to talk to you. Didn't know if you were passing through. You're a long way from home. New York, right?"

Slowly, Lennon peeled away from my back and sided up to me, keeping her hand in mine.

"I don't go by Eleanor anymore."

The woman cracked a smile. "Good for you. It's a shitty name."

"Why don't I remember you?" Lennon said.

I could tell she was trying to get a little more information about the woman without asking for it, or offering up any of her own. As much as I wanted to jump in, I stood quietly by her side and let her navigate the intricacies of post-prison etiquette.

"Name's Victoria. My hair used to be black. I went red after I got out." She brushed her ruby hair over her shoulder. "Looks like we both changed things up. Looking for that fresh start?" She lifted the paper in her hand. "Just want to leave it all behind. Job hunting sucks ass."

I saw the change in Lennon. As if I could read her mind,

she let out a relieved breath at the realization that it wasn't the redhead who had attacked her a decade earlier.

"Yeah, it sucks."

"You live around here now?" Victoria asked.

Lennon stayed quiet.

"No worries. I get it," Victoria said as she rolled the edge of the job application repeatedly. "I finished my time in Oklahoma. Struck out in Dallas. Figured I'd keep heading south until I found somewhere to settle. Moving on is hard when no one will let you."

Lennon cut her eyes at me. The silent question was so quick, but undeniably clear. I gave her a subtle nod.

"You got a phone number?" I asked.

Victoria's eyes widened. "Yes."

I pulled my phone out and put in her contact information as she rattled it off. "Might be a couple of days, but you'll get a call from a lady named Cassandra Griffith. If you keep your nose clean, she'll have a job for you."

"Really?" she said as something akin to hope filled her face.

"Really," Lennon said.

"Thank you," she stammered. "Oh my god. Thank you." She looked at Lennon. "Thank you. And I—I'm sorry I scared you, Elean—"

"It's Lennon," she said kindly, tugging on my hand as she picked up her pace again. "Look out for a call from Cassandra." She paused when she was shoulder to shoulder with Victoria. "And good luck."

As soon as we stepped into the restaurant, Lennon dipped into the restroom. I waited outside the door, keeping watch until she came out.

"You alright?"

Lennon nodded, swallowing tightly. "I'm sorry. I needed a minute."

"Hey," I said as I smoothed her hair down and cupped her cheek. "Take all the time you need. If you want to head back to the ranch, we can."

She shook her head and tipped her chin up for a kiss. "I'm good." Our noses brushed as she rested her forehead on mine. "Is it weird that I'm kind of relieved? It doesn't explain the letter that was sent to the ranch, but maybe that's who kept calling the restaurant."

The hairs on the back of my neck stood up. "What phone calls?"

Lennon sighed. "Someone kept calling the restaurant yesterday, asking for Eleanor." Her eyes turned weary. "I kept playing dumb since I go by Lennon there. The calls finally stopped before dinner service."

"Why didn't you tell me?"

"Griffith, party of two!" the host called out.

Lennon waited to answer until we were sitting at a candlelit table. "Because it was weird. There was nothing you could do about it."

I huffed. "You should've told me."

"Why?" she sneered. "I can handle it."

"But you shouldn't *have to*," I countered. "Len, that's the whole purpose of having a person who loves you. I'm on your side. I want to know what's going on, even if you have it handled."

Lennon blinked over the glow of the candles. "What did you just—"

"Good evening," the server said as he came up to the table and laid the menus in front of us.

"Shush," Lennon snapped, then looked back at me. "What did you say?"

I glanced up at the server. "Can you give us a minute?"

Lennon blinked. "Say that one more time."

"What? That I know you have it handled? That I'm on your side? Lennon, if you haven't figured that out by now, then I've done a shit job of making it up to you."

"The other thing." Her voice tightened. "Did you just say the 'L' word?"

"Why do you look so surprised?" I asked. Truth be told, I was trying my best to keep my cool, but I was a goddamn wreck inside.

Her lip quivered. "Will you say it again?"

If Lennon Maddox wanted to break me, she leveled me with those five words. I reached across the table and laid my hand over hers. "I love you, trouble. I love all your sweetness, and the sass and spite you use to protect it."

"You sure?" she whimpered as tears welled up in those pretty brown eyes.

Brown like the earth I worked day in and day out. Brown like the soil that had coated her when she showed up, rain-drenched on my doorstep. Brown like the dust that found its way into every part of me no matter how hard I tried to keep it out. Brown like the jacket that carried a storied legacy I would die for.

"I'm sure, Len," I said softly. "I'm sure."

Throughout dinner, Lennon gave her exacting assessment of each dish, cutlery piece, and the flow of the restaurant. I valued peace and quiet, but if my days were filled with the sound of Lennon humming around each bite and telling me the pros and cons of the floor plan, I'd die a happy man.

We skipped dessert and stole away to an ice cream shop before heading back to the ranch.

There was beauty in the mundane. I didn't much care

for activity-packed dates or the fast-paced nature of life outside the ranch. Little things with her were my favorite.

It was the way she lit up when I slipped a wildflower into her hand. The way she made a point to stop by and see the little bottle-fed calf who had yet to be named. It was finding takeout containers in the bunkhouse fridge with my name and reheating instructions on them when she came up with a new dish she wanted me to try.

I pulled back into the ranch under the cover of darkness. Lennon was half asleep on my shoulder, but jolted awake when we hit a pothole.

She blinked, taking in the chaos down the dirt road. "Oh my God," she whispered, eyes widening as we rounded the bend at my parents' house.

Blue lights flashed across the night sky in neon strobes.

"Maybe something happened at the lodge," I said as I squeezed her hand.

Lennon was stiff as a board. "They're at the bunkhouse," she whispered when she spotted the trio of cop cars.

My phone lit up with Christian's name. I grabbed it out of the cup holder and pressed it to my ear. "What's going on at the bunkhouse?" I asked, skipping the hellos and pleasantries.

"Where's Lennon?" he countered.

Lennon's eyes widened, and she shook her head.

"Not what I asked," I clipped. "Why are there cops at the bunkhouse?"

Christian sighed. "I was making sure she was okay. I figured since she wasn't at the restaurant, she was with you. Someone broke in and tossed the bunkhouse. Reed and Jackson were there, asleep. Everyone else was either working or out in town."

Lennon's face turned ghostly white. "What?"

Latent memories of the night someone broke into Ray and Brooke's house ate at me. I pulled off into the pasture and cut my headlights. "Did the guys catch who broke in?"

"No. Whoever it was bolted as soon as they heard the guys getting up. Looks like they were going through your room."

"I'm gonna be sick," Lennon said, gasping for each shoddy breath.

"Can you pack a bag for us while you're over there?" I asked as I kept a hand on the back of Lennon's neck, gently stroking her scalp.

"Y'all wanna crash in my guest room?" Christian asked. "Or y'all could stay up at Nate's."

Lennon shook her head.

"Nah. Bring it over to the lodge," I said. "Let's keep this between you and me."

"Understood," he said before ending the call.

"I want to get off this rollercoaster. I want it to stop. I want it to be over," she gritted out in frustration and anger. "Victoria was right. Moving on is hard when they won't let you."

"It's gonna be okay," I said as I let her cry into my chest. "You didn't have people on your side before, but you do now. A whole lot of us."

I loved her. I knew it in my bones. But when I found the bastard who had wrecked her life and haunted her mind, I couldn't guarantee that we would have a happily ever after.

The hatred and pure contempt were back. Because trouble had returned to the ranch. And this time, it wasn't her.

28

LENNON

The hotel room door opened and closed with a click as CJ let himself in. Crusts of sleep clung to the corners of my eyes, even though I hadn't gotten much rest. Tossing and turning was all I had done for the last seven hours.

"Len?" CJ's voice called out.

I cut the water to the sink and grabbed a hand towel to pat my face dry. "In the bathroom."

Knuckles rapped on the door. "Can I come in?"

I yanked it open and found him on the other side of the door with a cup of coffee in his hand.

CJ had been up all night, bouncing between the mess at the bunkhouse and the room we had crashed in at the lodge. Apparently, being attached to a Griffith had its perks. Namely, fancy hotel stays whenever we wanted.

"How bad is it?" I asked, swallowing the emotion and wearing the poker face I thought I had finally cashed in.

The idea of cops crawling all over the ranch made me sick, but CJ never once made me feel vulnerable. We stole away to the lodge and slipped into a room. When things seemed to settle down, he went out to see what had happened.

CJ sighed and swiped through his phone, showing me pictures of the room that had become my safe haven. "It's not good."

Someone had pulled every piece of furniture away from the walls. The dresser drawers were open and spilling over. Clothing cascaded from wire shelves in our shared closet, creating a tangled heap on the floor.

The bathroom door was open, giving a look at the ransacked state of it all. Bottles and sprays were scattered across the floor. The under-sink cabinet was wide open, having been cleared out so the person could pull the plywood base out of it. Floor planks had been yanked up in a haphazard pattern.

The scene painted a picture of rage. It wasn't methodically searched. It was impulsive and chaotic. No wonder Reed and Jackson had woken up.

The cowboys who lived in the bunkhouse could sleep through a nuclear explosion and barely stir.

"I'm sorry," I said as I turned the light off and slipped back into the luxurious suite.

If the circumstances hadn't been so dire, I would have soaked up every moment in the room. It was, by far, the swankiest place I had ever slept. The thought of how much one of these rooms would cost for a night made me slightly nauseous.

Beautiful wood beams with a rich brown stain planked the ceiling. Crisp white sheets and clouds of comforters and pillows were piled high on the beds. Thoughtful amenities like fresh-cut flowers and pillow chocolates dotted the room. A stocked mini-fridge and coffee bar were up against the wall. Pastries and breakfast bites had been delivered this morning in case we didn't want to eat on the patio with the other guests.

I wanted to devour them, but I couldn't stomach the thought.

French doors swung wide, opening onto an ornate balcony with two lounge chairs. Snaking vines danced along the wrought-iron bars.

The view was incomparable. Endless plains stretched as far as the eye could see. Clusters of cattle dotted the horizon. Ranch hands on horseback raced across the fields as the sun lifted higher and higher into the sky.

"Where's your head at, Len?" CJ asked as he came up behind me and wrapped his arms around me.

I had wandered onto the balcony and stared out at the cattle. "It's all my fault."

"Baby, it's not," he said softly as he braced his hands on the railing and rested his forehead on the back of my shoulder. "You didn't do a damn thing to deserve this, so get that bullshit out of your head."

"Don't patronize me."

CJ sighed. "The cops are gone, but you should lay low today. They're out looking for your brother, but I don't want to take any chances."

"I'll stay here until I have to go into the restaurant."

His body stiffened behind me. I knew he wasn't going to like that answer, but I didn't have another choice.

"Besides—" I turned and walked back into the suite "—you have to work today. Life doesn't stop just because we want it to."

"Len—"

A pounding fist on the door cut off his plea. I froze midstride and glanced back at him.

CJ looked equally startled. The weary expression he had

been wearing since he walked in the door morphed into stone. "Get in the bathroom."

"What?"

He reached into the back waistband of his jeans, grabbing hold of a pistol.

"Oh my God! Are you for real right now? Do you know how much trouble I could get in because you have a—"

"Get in the bathroom. Lock the door," he snapped. "You do realize I carry a gun for work, right? We're on a cattle ranch in the middle of fucking nowhere, and the police response time sucks."

The person on the other side of the door pounded again.

"I don't think bad guys usually knock," I hissed as I slipped into the bathroom. "Get rid of whoever it is, and then I'm going to bitch you out."

"Understood," he said. "Lights off."

My heart was in my throat as I stood against the locked door and listened to the conversation on the other side.

CJ yelled for someone to get lost, but Christian's voice cut in. What was he doing here?

A woman's voice broke through the chorus of men. Probably Cassandra.

Someone knocked on the bathroom door, and I jumped, smacking my elbow on the sink. I bit my lip, whimpering to stave off this skittering pain that lanced through my funny bone.

Sweet fuck, that hurt.

"Len, come out for a sec," CJ said.

My heart raced and my head spun. Beads of sweat broke out all over my neck.

CJ tapped on the door. "Len."

I swallowed the anxiety, cracked the door open, and

peered out. CJ, Christian, Cassandra, and two grim-looking police officers crowded the room.

Cassandra looked like a guard dog, standing with her arms crossed as she filled the space between the entryway and the bedroom. Christian sat on the edge of the bed. The cops stood next to the TV, handcuffs gleaming on their belts.

CJ slipped his arm around my waist, holding me back against his chest.

"Miss Maddox, I'm Officer Tate," the older looking cop said. He gestured to his partner. "This is Officer Strickland. We're with the Bell County Sheriff's Department."

I said nothing.

"Maybe get on with it and skip the formalities," Cassandra said.

Christian sighed. "Cass . . ."

"Ma'am, are you aware that your brother, Justin Maddox, was recently released from prison?"

I wasn't talking. Not without an attorney present.

Cassandra pinched the bridge of her nose. "Get to the point already."

The older officer removed his hat and tucked it under his arm. "Ma'am, we believe your brother was the one who broke into the house here last night."

Not a surprise. There were only two possible suspects.

"This morning, he was found deceased in a vehicle about thirty miles from here, just outside of the town limits. Investigators found evidence of the burglary inside the vehicle."

The room spun and tilted sideways.

"Whoa—hey, hey, hey." CJ caught me as my knees buckled. "I've got you."

"I need to sit down," I stammered as I pawed at the bed.

CJ brought me down with him, sitting far enough back on the mattress to keep me secure between his legs.

"Miss Maddox, we have reason to believe foul play was involved," the other officer said. "He was a long way from where he was supposed to be. Do you know of anyone who would want to kill him?"

I shook my head. "I'd tell you if I knew," I croaked.

"Why do you think it was murder and not suicide or an accident?" Cassandra asked.

The officer was frank. "Most people don't slit their own throats. But given that there were no signs of a struggle, it seems he trusted the person enough to let them into his vehicle."

"My stars," Claire Griffith said as she opened her front door and shooed me in. "Come on in, child."

I walked aimlessly inside after being delivered to her porch.

CJ was busy fixing the damage in the bunkhouse and didn't want me anywhere near it, but also didn't want me to be alone.

His mom wrapped me up in a tight hug and squeezed with all her might. "I'm so sorry, Lennon. Christian stopped by and told me what happened. Come on in the kitchen and sit a spell. Ray's at physical therapy and Brooke's working, so I've got Seth here with me this morning."

The wind tunnel that had whipped up inside my ears when the cops broke the news hadn't died down in the slightest. It felt like a fever dream.

"I've got sweet tea, hot tea, and coffee. What's your poison?" she asked.

"Sweet tea, please," I mumbled from where I sat on a barstool that was pushed up against the kitchen island.

Seth was busy scribbling in a coloring book. He spotted me and slid down two seats, grabbing my arm and filling in my tattoos with washable markers.

He did a terrible job.

Claire slid a glass in front of me. "Wanna talk about it?"

I trailed my finger up and down the beads of condensation on the side of the glass. "I don't even know why I care that he's dead." Tears welled up in my eyes, and I focused on the blunt pressure of the marker moving around my wrist. "It's not like he cared about me. It's not like he ever loved me. He ruined my life."

"But he was your family, even if he was only family in your mind," Claire said gently. "It's okay to grieve the idea of something. It's okay to admit that we hold on to the hope of things being different. It's okay to be hurt when things don't end the way we want them to."

Tears dropped onto the speckled stone countertop, one by one. "He was the only family I had left."

Her smile was soft. "Brooke knows something about that. She lost her parents. So does Becks. Her brother died and she searched for answers for a long time. That's what brought her to the ranch. Christian lost his first wife. You're in good company here, honey." Claire laid her weathered hand on top of mine. "You've had to be strong for so long. It's time to lay your burdens down."

Seth laid his little head against my bicep. I hung my head and let silent tears drip onto the kitchen island while Claire held my hand.

She was right. The greatest heartbreak wasn't that I had

lost someone who had done nothing but hurt me. It was that I lost the figment of what should have been.

It was the acute realization that I didn't know where I belonged now. I guess that's why people cared about their families, even when the family did nothing to deserve it.

We're all just looking for a place where we belong.

Slowly but surely, the house filled up. Cassandra cut out of work early and headed up to the ranch house. We convened on the couch when Brooke joined after a few hours of paperwork, now that she was on maternity leave before the baby was born.

Becks and her daughter, Charlie, joined us when they wrapped up their homeschooling. She took over the tattoo coloring and did a far better job than Seth.

Christian's daughters, Bree and Gracie, rounded out the bunch when they came home from school and crowded in.

There was an acute sadness that permeated the house. A morose tone whenever one of CJ's brothers dropped in to see their spouse and kids and give me a hug.

But the women remained unfazed.

Hell, they were strong—none of them strayed away from hard topics. Even Christian's teenagers asked thoughtful questions. Cassandra blamed therapy on their extreme emotional intelligence.

Night fell, and the doorbell rang.

"I'll get it," Cassandra said. "I called down to the restaurant and asked them to send some food up so no one had to cook."

"I can get it," I said as I jumped out of my spot on the couch. I needed a breather from spontaneous group therapy. I opened the door and found Julian on the other side, holding stacks of aluminum catering trays.

"Heard the news," he said with a sad sort of smile. "Sorry

about your brother, Len. Shit, I mean Chef. Sorry, Chef Maddox."

"Don't worry about it. Thanks for bringing this up."

He followed me into the kitchen and stood still as I unloaded everything from his arms onto the counter. "You know the rule. When Cassandra calls, you don't say no."

I let out a soft laugh. "That's the damn truth."

"Holler if you need anything."

"Do I smell brisket corn chowder?" Brooke squealed as she struggled to get up from the recliner she was parked in. "If I weren't already married, I'd kiss you on the mouth."

Julian laughed and gave a salute as he slipped out the door.

"What are you gonna do if the craving passes when the baby's born?" I asked.

Brooke shrugged and tore into the soup container. "That will be future Brooke's problem. I'm sure you'll dream up something for the restaurant that will make the postpartum phase suck a little less."

"You know where to find me when you want food." I grabbed a handful of cutlery and piled it on the end of the counter to start the buffet.

Becks looked a little misty-eyed as she watched from the doorway with CJ's mom.

"The boys did good, didn't they?" Claire said.

Becks's smile was soft. "It was a lot quieter when it was just you and me. But this is so much better."

29

CARSON JAMES

"You should call it a day," Nate said, appearing in my bedroom doorway.

I looked up from the mountain of laundry I was sorting and raised an eyebrow. "What are you talking about?"

He sighed and loped over, then grabbed one of my shirts and an unused hanger. "The girls are up at Momma's. Chris and I are heading down to Ray's. Let's go."

"I need to finish up," I mumbled as I moved to the next stack of clothes.

It had taken me all day, but I had put the door to the under-sink cabinet back on its hinges. I replaced the ripped-up floor planks. All the shit Lennon's brother had scattered had been organized and put away. I'd even washed the sheets for good measure.

Putting away the clothes that had been ripped out of the closet was the last item on my list, and it was taking fucking forever to finish.

"You need to walk away," Nate said.

I cut my eyes over at him. "You can go. I have shit to do. And if you mean to walk away from Lennon, you can fuck off."

He sighed. "I didn't mean it like that."

"Don't know how you could have meant it any other way," I said as I jammed the hanger back on the rail.

"Take it from someone who has a long track record of avoidance tactics. You aren't gonna be able to distract yourself out of this shit. But given the fact that you banished your girl to the ranch house, it's clear that you're not ready to work through it yet. So, walk away from it and come eat at Ray's. The mess will be here when you come back."

He was right, but I wasn't ready to admit it out loud.

"I want to get this shit cleaned up before Lennon comes back down here. I don't want her to see the mess."

Nate watched me for a moment as I worked through getting Lennon's and my clothes back in the closet, but I didn't care. He could fucking stare all he wanted.

After a long stretch of silence, he wandered over and picked up a shirt and a coat hanger.

"You love her, don't you?"

"I thought that was obvious," I said.

Nate chuckled. "I've never seen you with a woman. You don't date a lot. You've never brought anyone around."

"Pretty wild guess considering you were rarely around to know whether I was dating or not."

Nate's shoulders stiffened. "I kept tabs."

"Keeping tabs isn't the same as being here." I shoved a flannel button-up onto a hanger. "You were deployed. I get it. But don't pretend like it changes anything. It was what it was."

"We're still brothers," Nate said with an irritated edge to

his voice. That was him—Mr. Army Captain. He was used to giving orders and having people hop to it immediately.

I scoffed. "So are Lennon and her brother. Saying we're brothers doesn't mean shit if you don't act like it."

"You're angry."

"No shit, I'm angry!" I shouted as I pitched a coat hanger at the wall. "Some psychopath broke into my bunkhouse, and then got his throat slit. And now I'm having to deal with this and you while she's up at Momma's house."

I pressed my fist to the closet door frame. Goddamn, I was in deep shit with this woman.

Nate picked up a pair of pants. "Come on. I'll help you finish up."

We worked in silence until we reduced the piles of tossed clothes to nothing.

"I'm sorry I wasn't here," Nate said as he hung the last piece on his side of the closet. "Truth be told, I was dealing with my own demons. The divorce. Getting hurt over there. I wasn't the brother you needed."

"You don't get to make that decision."

"We're all out here trying to rewrite the script that was given to us. I didn't want to become Dad, so I went off and joined the Army. Christian watched me leave and felt like he had to stay. Ray saw Christian settling down with Gretchen to start a family, so he went out and joined the rodeo circuit. And you didn't want to become any of us, so you dug your heels into the land. Nothing wrong with that. It's damn admirable. But you have to realize that we're all doing the best we can. Making choices that affect the trajectory of your life is hard. Trying to avoid becoming someone else doesn't make you become better or worse. There's no right answer, Carson."

Nate stopped me with a hand on the back of my shoulder. "I couldn't be prouder of the man you've become, even if I wasn't around to see it."

I worked my tongue over my teeth, again and again, trying to keep the stinging in my eyes from getting the better of me.

"I've made my fair share of mistakes, Carson. Ask Becks. I bet she keeps a list on hand for reference when we fight. Hell, Becks, Cass, and Brooke are probably initiating Lennon into the council of Griffith women so she can consult them if she doesn't think you're groveling hard enough when you fuck up." He chuckled. "I don't know her that well yet, but I hope she sticks around so I can. I think she's good for you. You need a woman who's not afraid to tell you when you're wrong."

That made me crack a smile. Lennon pulled no punches.

"She's a lot like Becks."

Nate cracked a grin. "Mouthy as hell?"

I snickered. "Maybe more than Becks."

"Then she's good for you."

I closed the closet and started picking up my tools, stuffing them back in the bag. "Sorry I was a dick. You still heading to Ray's for dinner?"

Nate shrugged. "Pretty sure that's what brothers do. I'd be worried if you weren't."

I took the long way to Ray's house, letting my arm hang out of the truck window and float in the breeze.

Nate and Christian parked in the driveway beside Ray's wheelchair ramp. I found a spot around back, headed up the ramp, and let myself in through the sliding door.

Christian looked up from the kitchen island where he

was opening pizza boxes. Several packs of beer were stacked in rows beside them.

I remembered times when Christian and Nate would get together, drink beers, and shoot the shit. I had always been too young to join them. By the time I could partake, their lives had turned upside down.

"I tell you what—the girls learning how to drive used to scare the shit out of me," Christian said. "Then I realized I could call 'em up when they're in town and ask them to bring pizzas back to the ranch."

Ray laughed as he pulled clean laundry out of the dryer and dropped it into the basket on his lap. "Your own personal gophers?"

"Just wait until Seth is driving," Christian said. "It'll change your life."

"I'll take him out with me," I said as I snagged a beer from the cardboard pack. "Get him driving around the ranch before he's tall enough to reach the pedals like Dad did with us."

Ray grinned. "That's the beauty of my truck. No pedals. All hand controls."

Nate clapped his hands together and grabbed a plate. "I'm starving."

"Aren't we waiting for the girls to come down?" Ray asked.

"Nah. Becks texted and said they got food from the restaurant. They're already eating," Nate said.

"How's Lennon holding up?" Christian asked as he loaded his plate.

I rested my shoulder on the wall. Honestly, I had no idea. She was a steel vault.

"Shocked is an understatement," I said.

Ray slammed the dryer shut, spun his wheelchair

around, and rolled into his room to set the laundry basket on the bed. "You gonna put a ring on it?"

The thought of proposing to Lennon was a given. It wasn't that I had sat down and thought about the event of it—the ring, the location, and the words I would say. It was simply that I knew deep in my soul that I was at peace with her.

Maybe that's where I had gotten it wrong before. For most of my adult life, I had been waiting for the fire to die down, when I should have been looking for the person I wanted to walk through it with. I should have known she was the one the minute I saw that phoenix tattooed on her arm.

Fire fears what it cannot consume.

"Thinking about it," I said as I snagged a slice of pepperoni.

"Gonna move out of the bunkhouse?" Christian asked.

A definitive "yes" was on the tip of my tongue, but I wanted to hold my cards close to the vest. Besides, there were a few loose ends I needed to tie up to make that possible.

"If you're hesitating, you're fucking up," Ray said as he shuffled a slice out of the box and onto a plate. "Don't be a jackass and make her wait because you don't want to seem too eager."

"If you don't treat her right, I'll kick your ass," Christian said.

I scoffed. "If I don't treat her right, Lennon will kick my ass. Or are you forgetting about the little family reunion we had in the office when she clocked me in the face?"

Christian laughed. "And look how well it turned out for you. You deserved that, by the way."

"I know I did."

Fire Line

"Lennon punched you in the face?" Nate asked.

Ray grinned. "I knew I liked her."

"What's the deal with the dead brother?" Ray asked.

"Geez," Christian muttered as he cracked into another beer and settled on the couch. "You don't bury the lede, do you?"

"I lost all my spare fucks when I was in the hospital," Ray said. "No sense in dicking around."

"I don't know. The cops don't know. Lennon doesn't know," I said. "We haven't talked about it since this morning. She's been up at Momma's, and I've been trying to clean up shit so we can sleep in the bunkhouse."

Ray smirked. "Cass has been texting me updates. She hasn't said much, but she's been letting Seth color her tattoos. That practically makes her family. Once you get your tattoos colored, there's no going back."

"Wait," Christian said. "You and my wife text?"

"Yeah," Ray said as he looked at his phone. "And I kick her ass in our crossword puzzle game."

Nate looked at Christian. "Becks used to play it with them, but she won too much, so they kicked her out."

I loved the women my brothers had married.

Becks had filled a role none of us knew was missing when she joined the ranch. Her presence strengthened my mom and gave everyone a reason to get together.

Brooke and I worked together as she learned about horses and took over the equine program with Cassandra. Cassandra and I had bonded over her hatred of riding horses. Slowly, I changed that.

For some reason, knowing Ray had bonded with them in different ways than I had brought a smile to my face.

Even with the distance I felt from Nate, the four of us

had always been brothers. But with the girls joining the ranch, they felt more like family than ever.

Part of me wondered how Lennon fit into that equation. The thought of my nephew coloring her tattoos with markers, like my nieces used to do to Ray, made me want to rush to the house and get down on one knee right then and there.

But would she stay for the long haul? She was so fucking talented. She could be working in any one of DeRossi's restaurants all over the country. I had looked them up—New York, Chicago, North Carolina, California, Vegas . . .

I couldn't ask her to give up a career she had fought for tooth and nail.

"What's Lennon's number? I need to get her in on it," Ray said. "She's quiet, which means she'll probably wipe the floor with Cass and me. Always gotta watch out for the quiet ones."

"Yeah," I said as my beer soured in my stomach. "She'd probably be good at it."

Christian was staring at me from across the room. He tipped his head in Nate's direction. "He's got that look."

Nate nodded. "Yep. He's got it bad."

"The fuck are you talking about?" I muttered as I took another sip to wash down the nervous acid in my mouth.

"Cards on the table," Ray said. "You wanna marry her?"

"Yeah." It slipped out before I could stop it.

"Good," Nate said. "At least he can admit it. That's a start."

I scrubbed my palm down my face. "What are y'all getting at?"

Christian wiped his hands clean. "Consider us at your disposal for planning your proposal. Nate and I have each done it twice."

"I learned what *not* to do the first time," Nate said.

"Ray's done it once," Christian said as he hopped up and grabbed a bag that was beside the pizzas and beers. He dropped it at my feet.

I opened it up and lifted out Lennon's ranch jacket.

"We know she's going through shit," Ray said. "And we've all been there. So don't rush it. You do this 'lone cowboy' thing, but it doesn't have to be that way. If you need advice on how to handle things, you don't have to go at it alone."

It doesn't have to be that way—alone.

I didn't know who needed to hear that more: me or Lennon.

The lights in my parents' house shone brightly as I drove up to get Lennon. She met me on the porch, easing out of one of the rocking chairs and heading down the stairs.

"Hey, trouble," I said as I pulled her into my arms and held her tight. "Sorry I was gone so long."

"It's fine," she said as she closed her eyes. "Cass told me you were with your brothers. I figured you needed that."

"Why do you say that?"

She shrugged. "You don't spend a lot of time with them."

I pressed a kiss to her temple. "You might be right. I need to get better at that."

"I'm sorry if you stopped hanging out with them because of me."

I shook my head. "Nah. You're the reason I see them more now. You're good for me." I swayed in the porch light, keeping her close. "How are you holding up?"

Her eyelids fluttered closed. "I've been fed and had my tattoos colored. And I'm now part of a crossword puzzle game with Ray and Cassandra, which is kind of weird."

I chuckled. "That's not what I meant, love."

Lennon was quiet for a moment before finally piping up again. "I feel numb."

"It's a complicated situation," I said. A tear streaked down the corner of her eye, and I wiped it away. "It's okay to grieve, Len. He was still your brother."

"I want things to go back to the way they were two days ago." She sucked in a shaky breath. "We were happy."

"I'm still happy with you. Just because there are clouds doesn't mean the sun doesn't exist. You don't have to put up a front and pretend like it doesn't hurt. Let it hurt. Let it heal. You don't have to have all the answers right now."

Lennon nodded against my chest. "I like your family," she admitted. "A lot."

"Good," I said as I softly kissed her lips. "Because I'm pretty sure they love you too. And Len?"

"Hmm?" She looked up with diamond-covered lashes.

I wiped her tear-stained cheeks again. "I love you too."

Lennon looked down at her feet. "I . . . I don't know how to take that. I mean, I know you've said it before, but I . . . It's weird saying it. I feel it. But it's like, if I admit that I love you too, then I'm risking getting hurt and I . . . I don't know if I'll survive that."

It stung, given the conversation about my intentions that I had with my brothers.

"You don't have to say it back," I reassured her. "But I want you to know where I stand. I love you, and I will not hurt you."

She let out a nervous laugh. "Can't you just push me against the wall and fuck my mouth or something? I know how to handle that. I'm good at that. I've never thought about what it would be like to fall in love, and it scares me."

"It's okay to be scared, Len." I rested my forehead on hers.

"It's not," she whispered as the words choked her.

I pressed a long kiss to her forehead. "It is. You know why?" I cupped her cheeks. "Because you scare me."

30

LENNON

"Morning, Chef," Zach said as he pushed a cart chock-full of ingredients from the storeroom.

I greeted him with a nod and slipped into the office, grabbing the inventory clipboard off the desk so I could make my rounds.

Jessica strolled down the hallway with a pile of linens in her arms. "Hey, Lennon. How are you holding up?"

I paused in the entrance to the storeroom. Things had been fine. They were neither good nor bad. I still hung in the numbness that I chalked up to shock.

I didn't know how to work through everything that had happened over the last week. Physically, I was fine. Mentally, I was a wreck.

Security at the bunkhouse had been beefed up with an electronically locking door. It required a numerical code to enter. The system logged a different code for each person, so we knew exactly who was coming and going, or who had shared their code.

CJ had kept me close, taking me out with him to check on the herd. We barely spent a minute apart. If he had to work, one of the other Griffith brothers escorted me to and from the restaurant each day.

It was annoyingly sweet.

"I'm fine," I said, finally responding to Jessica. "I'm ready for everything to get back to normal."

"Zach did a great job leading things for the few days you took off. You trained him well."

I offered a weak smile. "Thanks."

I waited until Jessica dipped back into the dining room to let out a breath. Inventory was a reprieve. It gave me a chance to clear my head. The methodical documentation of stock was calming. I liked the reset. I needed it.

"Morning, Chef," Julian said as he slipped in the back door and headed to clock in.

"Morning," I called back as I counted the cases of granulated sugar and headed for the liquor cage. I pulled my keys out of my pocket and unlocked the padlock.

"Yo, Chef!" Javi yelled.

"In here!"

Javi poked his head inside. "You doing inventory?"

"Yes, sir," I said as I found the column for whiskey and ticked the box to order more.

"Cool. Can you throw in an extra bottle of orange liqueur?"

I smiled down at the clipboard and made a note in the margin. "Only if you tell me what you've got up your sleeve."

He smiled from ear to ear. The simple joy of creating something new for the guests lifted my spirits.

"Ice cream truck treats, but fancy."

I lifted my eyebrows. "Like the orange sherbet popsicles you push up with a stick?"

He nodded. "Layered with mousse and a sponge soaked in an orange-basil reduction."

I made another note to ask our paper product supplier about the push-pop containers. "If you make something like the strawberry shortcake popsicles, I'll love you forever, Javi."

He gave me a salute. "You've got it, Chef."

I crouched and ran my fingers over the boxes of salt and pepper, making sure we had enough to get through the week. When I stood to check the containers of cornmeal and cornstarch, hands dug into my waist, grabbing me from behind.

I opened my mind to scream, but a calloused palm clapped over my mouth, muffling the sound.

"Quiet, slugger. You don't want people coming in here to check on you if you scream."

I smiled against the hand and relaxed at the sound of CJ's voice. "What are you doing?" I whispered as he pinned me against the metal wire shelving with his chest to my spine.

"You wanted normal, so I'm giving you normal." He ripped the clipboard out of my hands and spun me to face him. "On your knees for me, beautiful."

My legs buckled, and I dropped like a sandbag. "We could get caught," I whispered as I pawed at his obnoxious belt buckle.

CJ cupped my jaw. "Whose name is on your uniform?"

"Yours," I whispered as I pulled his zipper down.

"Whose name is on the building you work at?"

"Yours," I said as I peeled down the elastic waist of his boxers.

A slow smile worked up his devilish face. "My last name. My ranch. My pretty mouth to fuck." He worked his thumb over my lower lip. "Be a good girl and open up."

I could smell the crisp freshness of his soap still clinging to his skin as I wrapped my hand around his cock and traced its thick head with my tongue. CJ was nothing if not considerate.

"Goddamn," he hissed as he grabbed the top shelf with one hand and held on as he leaned forward, pushing his dick closer to my mouth. With the other hand, he pulled off his cowboy hat and held it at his hip, shielding my face from view of the door. "Eyes on me while my cock is in your mouth, Lennon. You don't focus on anything but me."

Heat flooded my body, cascading down my shoulders. It pooled deep inside my core. I sucked the tip of his dick and gently pumped his shaft.

"That's so good, baby," he rasped. "But I know you can take more than that."

I closed my eyes and worked more and more of his cock into my mouth until I could barely take it.

Labored breaths escaped his chest as he let go of the shelf and tangled his fingers in the back of my hair, steadily fucking my mouth. "That's my good girl," he rasped, shuffling his boots wider.

I whimpered as he pulled my hair, tugging my head back as he pushed his cock in farther. My eyes watered and I gagged.

CJ didn't let up. "You feel so fucking good, Len. Give me a little more. I know you can do it. You're so good for me."

I gasped for air as he pulled back, offering a momentary reprieve. It was gone as fast as it came when CJ pushed back into my mouth with a snap of his hips.

The whispered praises mixed with the cocktail of fear of getting caught took me back to the night we met. The night we flirted and fucked without exchanging life stories.

The night that everything changed.

Because if it hadn't been for CJ hating me when I

showed up at the ranch, he probably would have ignored me.

I wouldn't have found the only person I could trust enough to be soft around.

We wouldn't have gotten to where we were.

Which was with me on my knees, sucking him off before the restaurant opened.

I had been in worse places. In fact, the wicked smile he had as I edged him closer and closer to orgasm was pretty damn good.

The hat in CJ's hand wobbled as he did his best to hold back. "Len—stop—" he gasped as I massaged his balls. "Fuck—"

I swirled my tongue around the head of his dick and sucked, holding the pressure for a long moment.

"Len, I'm gonna come. Stop."

I opened my eyes, lifted an eyebrow, and released his dick with a pop. "Well, don't be a pussy about it. Come in my mouth, cowboy."

CJ threw his head back and stifled his laugh. He pushed into my mouth again. "I fucking love you, Len."

I wrapped my hand low around his cock and pumped it eagerly as I sucked. A desperate, choked groan rumbled in his lungs. His knees buckled as I sealed my lips around the head of his cock and swallowed him down.

CJ looked down at me with dazed eyes. He cupped my cheek and swiped his thumb across the corner of my mouth. "You're something else, you know that?"

I couldn't help but smile up at him as he zipped up his jeans and buckled his belt.

"Get up here." He dropped his hat back on his head, helped me up, and leaned in for a kiss.

I pulled back. "I just had your cum in my mouth. You don't want to kiss me after that."

His brows furrowed. "Are you fucking with me? Come here."

The kiss he planted on my mouth was nearly pornographic. CJ held me close enough that we became one, his arms around my waist and mine around his neck.

I tucked my forehead into the crook of his shoulder. "Thank you for that."

CJ laughed. "Pretty sure I should be thanking you." He kissed my neck. "And I will. Over and over and over again tonight."

"Go to work," I said as I pushed him off with a laugh. "I'm on the clock, and I have things to do."

Footsteps echoed down the hallway, and Julian strolled in, grabbing a bag of clean side towels. He tipped his head toward CJ. "Morning, Mr. Griffith."

CJ reached into his pocket and slipped a violet into my hand. "Have a good day."

I pecked his cheek. "You too."

"Hey, Chef," Julian said. "Did someone tell you the tilt skillet is acting up again? Simmons is trying to get it to pull up, but it's full right now, so it's twice as heavy."

"I'll take a look," CJ said.

I grabbed my clipboard and pen. "You sure you have time?"

"We're on the same team, right? Same ranch."

Something warm bubbled inside me. I squeezed his hand. "Thank you."

"Be back in a sec," CJ said as he walked out of the storeroom.

Finding my place on the inventory spreadsheet was nearly impossible after what we'd just done. My body was on fire. I had never been one to cut out of work early, but I would have given my right tit to go back to the bunkhouse for a quick romp to cool down.

Today was going to be excruciating. CJ demanding a blowjob in the middle of the restaurant storeroom turned me on more than I had ever been.

He better have something spectacular up his sleeve for later if he's making me wait this long . . .

I squeezed my thighs together to ease a little of the ache inside.

Love. It had been on the tip of my tongue when he told me to have a good day.

You too. I love you.

It would have been so easy to say. It was right there.

I looked down at my pen and debated running out to catch him so I could tell him. But saying it in the middle of the kitchen didn't feel right either. I didn't want him to be distracted or think it was just a slip of the tongue.

I'd tell him tonight.

With that decided, I went back to the inventory list. The back door opened and closed, and I heard the jingle of CJ's tool bag and the heavy thud of his boots heading into the kitchen.

"Chef, we're almost out of oil for the fryer," Julian called through the door.

I glanced around the shelves. I knew I had seen an extra boxed jug somewhere. I spotted it shoved into the corner. "I've got another one in here," I hollered. "More will be on the truck tomorrow."

I dropped the clipboard on the shelf and tugged the enormous jug of oil out of the corner. "Here you go."

Our shadows met as I turned, but the man staring at me

wasn't the one I had been tirelessly working to gain respect from.

"Poor little Eleanor," he said with a disturbing mixture of malice and glee. "All you had to do was drive the car and keep your mouth shut." The blade of a freshly sharpened chef's knife gleamed in the fluorescent light. "Justin swore up and down you could do that."

I started to scream, but the tip of the blade pushing against my throat silenced me immediately.

"It was you?" I rasped as terror fogged my vision. "Wh- who are you?" I stammered.

Julian chuckled. "I gotta admit. Hunting you down wasn't easy. I didn't even know if I had the right person when I applied for the job listing down here. Prison changed you." He smirked. "Sorry about that. Pity you and your brother got out so soon. I was hoping someone on the inside would get tired of you both and take care of this for me, but no. I guess some loose ends have to be tied up by hand."

"Y-you killed him," I said as my head spun. "You s-slit his t-throat."

"A little messy, I'll admit. But it's like you and DeRossi always say. Presentation matters." Julian's gleaming smile was manic "You got his letter, right? I left enough bread-crumbs to lure him down here. Even got him to go through the bunkhouse for me to make sure you weren't holding onto anything incriminating. It would be a shame to have gone through all this effort only to get caught a decade later."

He shoved the point of the knife into my throat, piercing my skin enough that I knew he meant business. "As fun as this little immersive field trip has been, it's time for me to get rid of the only other person who was there so I can start spending all that money."

"Why?" I croaked as tears welled up in my eyes. The tip of the knife jammed a hair farther, and I bit my lip.

"Why, what? Why did I convince your brother he could get away with robbing a bank?" Julian cackled. "He was a shitty dealer. I had to repurpose him somehow." He yanked the knife back and traced it down the front of my pristine white coat, leaving a stream of blood trickling down my neck. "Or maybe you want to know why I called the cops as soon as he left the bank?"

His grin was sharp like a sickle, and just as deadly.

"To get you two out of the way, of course. It was only supposed to be him. Making one person disappear is far easier than two. But for some reason, he got you to drive the car I left for him. So I had to pivot. I'm nothing if not adaptable. I called the cops on you and your brother, and picked up the money before you two could use it as leverage. Controlling you in prison was a little more involved. All it took was me promising your brother I'd split the money with him when he got out to keep him quiet. But you . . . You kept running your mouth about how innocent you were. So, I had to scare you straight." The delight in his eyes was frenetic and unhinged. "Did it work, Eleanor?" he panted. "Did you get my message?"

Julian pushed the knife against my sternum to keep me in place and yanked my chef's coat up, revealing the scar I had gotten in prison.

Tears blurred my vision as they poured down my cheeks.

"Not her best work, but beggars can't be choosers. I told the bitch to kill you. You're like a fucking cat with nine lives, but you're about to run out. Hope that cowboy used you good. I'm sure he'll find another piece of ass soon enough."

The click of a recoiling pistol jolted me from the paralysis of fear.

"What did I tell you about disrespecting the women on this ranch?" CJ crept forward on smooth feet with his gun drawn.

"Ah, the cowboy rides in, just in time to save the day. How fucking poetic." Julian let out a demented cackle. "Too late!"

The sound of the gunshot rang out, and searing pain ripped through my chest.

CJ screamed my name, but I was already falling.

31

CARSON JAMES

Blood pooled on the storeroom floor as Lennon lay in my arms, gasping and groaning. The flurry of bodies swarming around blurred into a mass as people shouted orders and called 911.

So much blood.

"What the hell happened?" Nate roared as he barreled into the doorway. He stopped dead in his tracks, saw Lennon and Julian, and shoved a hand back through his hair. "Oh my God."

He bolted over and dropped to his knees.

Whether it was shock or sheer stupidity, all I could grit out was, "What are you doing here?"

Nate looked up at me like I was an idiot. "I know what gunshots sound like, and that I shouldn't be hearing them while I'm out for a run. Has someone called 911?"

I nodded.

"Okay. You're doing good. What'd the operator say?"

"Helicopter," slipped out of my mouth in a rasp.

Nate glanced over his shoulder and shouted, "Get me a

fucking first aid kit!" He turned back to me. "Who's the other guy?"

"Cook," I said as Lennon's eyes fluttered shut again. "He attacked her. Long story."

"She's gonna live to tell it to me, so I need you to hold it together. Copy?"

I nodded.

Nate grabbed a first aid kit and rummaged through it. He pulled out a small roll of gauze and packaged wound dressings. "Don't take the knife out. Hold it steady."

There was a fucking knife in Lennon's chest, and I couldn't do a damn thing but sit there and hold her, biting back tears.

Lennon whimpered as I kept the knife from moving while Nate wrapped gauze around the puncture to stem the leaking blood flow.

"You with me, slugger?" I bent and pressed a kiss to her clammy forehead.

"Hurts," she cried. "Can't . . . breathe."

"It probably collapsed her lung," Nate said. He pressed his palm on the right side of her sternum, around the knife's tip. "Help her sit up."

Lennon gasped, letting out a desperate cry as I eased her upright. "It hurts—hurts!"

"I know, sweetheart," he soothed. "Try to stay awake. Sitting up will help you breathe until the helo gets here."

Nate had spent his entire military career in and out of war zones, but he didn't talk about it much. I knew he had some training in combat medicine, but I had never seen him in action.

All my resentments and grudges vanished as he coached us through the minutes it took for the helicopter to land.

After what felt like an eternity, the flight nurses rushed into the restaurant and found us.

Cops swarmed the property as the medevac crew loaded Lennon onto a stretcher and pushed her into the back of a helicopter.

"Let's go," Nate said when the rotors started spinning. He clapped his hand on my shoulder, practically hauling me to his truck.

I tripped over my own feet as we crossed the grass. The bunkhouse shimmered through waves of tears. "I should—I should get—"

"She doesn't need stuff," Nate said. "The hospital will take care of that. But she needs you to be there as soon as she opens her eyes."

"Okay."

We didn't speak on the way to the hospital. Nate gripped the wheel in silence and sped twenty over the limit for the entire drive. The world on the other side of the windows became a blur.

What if she didn't wake up? Why had I walked away to fix that damn piece of equipment? Why didn't I check on her sooner?

Why did I leave her in the room with him?

"Get your head right," Nate said as he came to a screeching halt in a parking space. "I know where you're at. Trust me—I've been there. If you let yourself go down the rabbit hole of all the things that could have prevented it, you'll never climb out of it. Sometimes you get to cut the fire line to stop the blaze, and sometimes you have to walk through it to get out of the heat. Today you have to walk, because your girl is counting on you to carry her through it. So pull up your boots and get going."

Fire Line

The doors of the Baylor emergency department slid back, and a blast of frigid, recycled air rushed out.

"Lennon Maddox. She came in on a helicopter. I'm her—"

"Fiancé," the nurse behind the desk supplied as her fingers flew over the computer keys. "They told us you were coming."

It must have been a slip of the tongue, but I didn't care.

"She just went into surgery. Someone will call you when we have an update."

Nate had to physically pull me away from the desk and shove me down into a vinyl chair.

I braced my arms on my knees and dropped my head into my hands. "Thank you," I croaked as I cupped my palms over my mouth. The world hadn't stopped spinning, and I wasn't sure it would until I had Lennon back.

"It's gonna be alright," he said as he wrapped his arm around me and pulled me into a hug.

For the first time in a long time, it felt like I had my brother back. Now I needed my girl.

The door opened, and Ray wheeled in with Christian beside him. "How is she?" Ray asked when he spotted us.

"Just went into surgery," Nate said when I couldn't find the words. "It could be a while."

Ray parked his chair in front of us, and Christian pulled a seat over to complete the circle.

"Cass is handling things at the ranch. Brooke is helping her and watching all the kids. Becks and Momma are getting some stuff together for you and Lennon."

"I don't need anything," I said as I stared at the floor.

Ray looked around. "You'll be here a couple of days at least. Maybe more."

I sighed and raked my hands through my hair. "I have so much shit to do..."

Christian put his hand on my back. "All you have to do right now is be there for Lennon. Everything else is taken care of. I'll jump in and work with your guys like the old days. Cass said DeRossi and his wife, Maddie, are already on a plane to cover for Lennon."

I didn't know what to say because every version of "thank you" was wholly inadequate.

My brothers sat with me as the hands of the clock went around and around and around. My parents and Becks joined the cluster of chairs soon after, expanding the circle.

"Thanks for coming," I said like some kind of morose party host.

Mom reached across and squeezed my knee. "We'd do the same if it were one of you. You know that. She's ours as much as you are."

"Carson Griffith?"

I whipped around at the sound of the man's voice and nearly knocked my chair over with how fast I stood.

Nate gave me a little push. "Go get your girl. We'll be here."

I grabbed the bag that someone had thrown together for me and followed the nurse. He escorted me back through the maze of hospital corridors, and handed me off to a woman in green scrubs.

"Lennon is out of surgery," she said as we stood outside of a closed door. "The knife went through the space between her ribs over her lung and punctured it. Her care team and I decided that surgery would provide the best outcome. She's stable and improving. We'll probably keep her in the hospital for a few days so we can monitor her recovery." The surgeon cracked a smile. "For right now, I think she's ready to see you. She never stopped talking about her fiancé while she hung out in the PACU."

"Thank you," I said as I opened the door and slipped inside without asking for permission.

Lennon was resting upright in the bed. Her hospital gown was half-open, revealing bandages wrapped tightly around her chest. A tube snaked out of her body and down the side of the bed. IV lines and monitors dotted the rest of her body.

She peered at me through heavy eyes as the clomp of my boots echoed in the pristine room.

"They gave me drugs." A lazy smile painted her face as she closed her eyes. "They're really good. I think I told them we're getting married."

I chuckled as part of the knot inside my gut loosened. "I'm glad you're feeling good."

"Did you bring my jacket?" she asked through labored breaths. "It's cold."

I reached into our bag and pulled out my ranch jacket. "Momma and Becks threw it in here for you." I opened it up and draped it over her lap like a blanket. "Better?"

"Mhmm."

"What do you need?" I asked as I pulled a chair up to her bedside and wrapped her hand in mine. "Say it and it's yours."

"Marry me?" she mumbled as her head lulled to the side again.

I leaned over and pressed a kiss to her forehead. "I'm planning on it."

"Mmmkay," she said in a labored breath. "'Cause I think I love you."

Time was a myth in hospitals. There was no distinction between day and night. The fluorescent lights and relentless interruptions had completely fucked up my circadian rhythm.

It had only been three days, and I was about to start climbing the walls.

Lennon yawned as she rolled her head across the back of the bed and looked at me. "Hi."

I offered a weary smile. "Hey, trouble."

"You're still here?" She tried to shift to a more comfortable spot, but froze and groaned. "Everything hurts."

"I'm still here," I said softly as I readjusted her pillows. "Told you I wasn't going anywhere."

She stared at the wall in front of her and gave a vacant nod. "Sorry. I've been kinda out of it."

I pressed a kiss to her forehead. "Rest. That's all you have to do right now."

"I'm so tired of resting," she grumbled. "There's shit to do."

Lennon was perfect. A work-hard, play-hard force of nature. They say opposites attract, but I wasn't so sure about that. Lennon and I were more similar than I ever would have guessed.

"Everyone's covering for us. Chef DeRossi was here a little bit ago." I pointed to the flowers that were in a vase sitting on the windowsill. "He brought those and lunch from the restaurant for all the nurses on the floor." I pointed to the takeout containers on the rolling table. "And for us."

Something sad crossed her face, like clouds eclipsing the sun. "I'm *so* getting fired."

"No, you're not," I said as I settled onto the bed, carefully draping my arm around her. "You know why?"

Lennon tucked her head into the crook of my arm.

"Because when you're part of the Griffith family, you can't get fired by someone outside of it."

Cops and a few FBI agents had been in and out of the hospital room today. They were trying to sort out jurisdiction and what the hell had happened.

All I cared about was the fact that Julian was dead.

Even though the restaurant's security cameras recorded our—uh—tryst, we still had to recount everything to ensure it all added up. I'd probably never live that blowjob down.

A knock on the door startled us both.

"Hi, Lennon," the surgeon said as she slipped inside. "How are you feeling?"

"Like I got stabbed in the chest and then ripped open in the OR, and then someone stuck a tube inside me."

The surgeon hid a laugh behind a professional smile. "We're trying to lower your meds today to see if we can get you out of here. How does that sound?"

Lennon closed her eyes. "Awful, but I'll take it."

"You'll have some outpatient appointments to remove your chest tube and keep an eye on things." She looked at me. "Can Mr. Lennon drive you to those?"

"I've got it covered," I said.

Lennon glanced over at me. "You need to go back to work."

As much as I missed the peace and stability of my routine, I wasn't leaving her side until she could come home with me.

"What's home like?" the surgeon asked. "Stairs are not a good idea. We want you to rest as much as possible."

"I can sleep on the couch downstairs," Lennon said as she glanced up at me.

I shook my head. "I'll make arrangements. Don't worry about it."

"Babe," Lennon grumbled.

I didn't care that she was mad that I was handling things without her input. She called me "babe." That little bit of affection from her made me stand that much taller.

"Good. We'll continue to monitor things for the next twelve hours or so, and then revisit this conversation." The surgeon backed toward the door. "I'll let you rest. Don't be afraid to hit the call button if you need something."

"Thanks," I said as she slipped out the door.

"I can sleep on the couch," Lennon argued. "If it gets me out of here, I don't give a shit."

"Trust me?" It was both a question and a request.

Lennon tucked her head into my chest and tried to get a little more comfortable. "With my life."

Another knock at the door had us both annoyed.

"What?" I snapped as it opened.

Ray wheeled in, and I was a little bit confused.

"What are you doing here?"

The door opened again, and another wheelchair poked through. Brooke was wearing a hospital gown that matched Lennon's. She was being pushed by a nurse because she was holding a baby.

"Holy shit," I muttered as I sat up straight.

Lennon's eyes widened as she grabbed my arm for help sitting up.

Ray was smiling from ear to ear. I had never seen him so happy. "Thought we'd come down and see you guys before we get settled in a room."

Brooke looked exhausted but happy as she cuddled the little bundle in her arms.

"Oh, that baby is *fresh* fresh," Lennon said with a mix of shock and awe.

"Why didn't you tell us Brooke was in labor?" I asked as Ray came around to my side of the bed.

He shrugged. "It happened pretty fast."

The nurse pushing Brooke's wheelchair parked it beside Lennon.

Brooke tilted her arms, showing off the little baby. "Want to meet your niece? This is Olivia."

Olivia had little brown curls just like Brooke, but her features were all Griffith.

"You can hold her if you want," Brooke said.

Lennon reared back. "I've never held a baby."

"It's easy," I reassured her as I reached out and carefully scooped Olivia out of Brooke's arms.

I could feel Ray breathing down my neck as I brought the baby to my chest and settled back beside Lennon.

Olivia let out a displeased grunt as she was jostled around, but she quickly went to sleep.

"Hey, girlie," I soothed as I cradled her in the crook of my arm. "I'm your Uncle CJ. This is your Aunt Lennon."

Lennon looked at me with wide eyes as I eased the baby into her arms, careful of the IV lines still taped to her hands and arm. "Is it okay if I hold her, or would you prefer I don't?"

Brooke's eyes were kind. "Hold her if you feel up to it. It won't offend me if you don't. I know you're hurting, too."

Watching Lennon hold little Olivia did something funny inside me. She looked absolutely stunning like this.

The black and white strands of her hair blended into a

silver braid. *Shadows and light.* She embodied both beautifully. Ash coated what flames couldn't take down.

"Oh, you're very snuggly," Lennon said with lifted brows.

Olivia squirmed and started to cry.

"Shit," Lennon muttered in a panic. "I fucked it up. Someone fix it."

Ray chuckled as I passed Olivia back to Brooke. "Don't worry. She did that to me too. Apparently, my little princess was rather unhappy with her surprise birthday party today."

"Hope you feel better," Brooke said as the nurse carefully pulled the wheelchair away from the bed. "When do you think you'll get to go home?"

"Hopefully tomorrow," Lennon said. "Fingers crossed. I'm ready to go back to the ranch."

"Maybe we'll go home together," Brooke said with a smile. "And the boys can wait on us hand and foot."

Lennon let out a soft laugh, then pressed her hand to her chest when it started to hurt. "Congratulations."

"You know what I think?" I said when the door closed, and everything grew quiet.

Lennon leaned into me again. "Hm?"

"We should finally name that little bottle-fed calf."

Her expression was curious. "I thought we didn't name the cows?"

"I think we should name yours." I laced my fingers with hers. "There's always an exception, right? Just like I said you'd never have my last name?" I tipped her chin up and kissed her. "You're my exception."

32

LENNON

So, this was family.

I nestled into Mr. Griffith's well-loved recliner, cocooned in a stack of pillows and quilts despite the summer heat outside. A hospital tumbler of ice water, a mug of coffee, and a glass of sweet tea were perched on the side table, so I didn't have to get up if I wanted something different.

My phone buzzed in my lap. CJ had found a twenty-foot extension cord somewhere on the ranch so I could keep it plugged in beside me. I glanced down at the screen and smirked.

Ray had made a mistake. A big one.

I swiped across my phone and made my play, then turned it over on my lap and closed my eyes.

The front door opened and closed. I waited to hear the footsteps before I opened my eyes.

If it was CJ, it would be steady, purposeful strides in cowboy boots.

Mrs. Griffith usually wore sneakers, so her steps were softer.

Mr. Griffith had an offbeat pattern of walking with his walking stick.

If it was Ray, I'd hear the slide of his wheelchair against the tile and hardwood.

Cassandra's high heels had a distinct click.

Nate's gait was almost completely silent, whereas Becks stomped in like an elephant.

Christian's footfalls were heavy, but he slid his heels a little, giving his boots a distinct hiss.

But I didn't hear them. I peeled an eye open at the slide of bedroom slippers. Brooke appeared, still in her pajamas. "Hey," she said as she waddled in and slowly lowered herself onto the couch. "You up for some company?"

I checked the crossword game on my phone. Ray hadn't made a move yet. "Is your husband right behind you?"

Brooke snickered. "Yeah. He's fuming outside."

I closed my eyes again. "Where's your baby?"

"CJ's got her," Brooke said as she grabbed one of Claire's magazines and started thumbing through it. "That's the beauty of the uncles. There's always a set of hands who want to hold a cute baby."

The door opened and slammed shut, followed by the slide of Ray's wheelchair, accented by two sets of shoes: steady boots and high heels.

CJ and Cassandra, if I had to guess.

I was correct.

Cassandra strolled in looking regal and terrifying as always. CJ followed behind her with baby Olivia cradled to his chest. Ray pulled up the rear looking rather pissed.

I smirked.

"Wipe that fucking look off your face, Maddox," Ray snapped.

Cassandra glanced over her shoulder at CJ. "You're not going to yell at your brother for speaking to Lennon like that?"

CJ couldn't take his eyes off the baby in his arms. "And get bitched out by my girl? Absolutely not. Do you let Christian fight your battles?"

Cassandra inspected her nails. "Fine. You have a point."

Ray pointed a finger at me. "You're out of the game."

"And you're just jealous."

"You cheated!" he countered. "There's no way you pulled four triple word scores out of your ass without help. You can't Google words! That's the rule," Ray shouted.

"You're the one who invited me to play," I teased, pulling the game up on my phone. I dragged J, U, X, S, T, A from my row of letters and added them to the board where I'd put the word "position" on a triple word score space during my previous turn.

Cassandra and Ray's phones dinged as I racked up eighty-seven points in a single turn.

Ray let out a low growl and pitched his phone into an empty armchair. "Fuck you and your stupid vocabulary."

"Have you always been a sore loser, or is this a new trait for you?" I asked as I closed my eyes.

"He's always been that way," CJ said as he held the baby with one arm and picked up Ray's phone with the other. He pointed it at Ray. "But let's make one thing clear. If you ever speak to my woman that way again, I will dig your grave while she slices you to ribbons with a kitchen knife."

"Looks like it's back to just me and Cass playing," Ray grumbled.

Brooke laughed under her breath.

"Bummer," I said as I picked up my phone and played

around with my available letter tiles. "I was about to turn your double word score 'cap' into 'capricious.'"

Ray huffed. "What the hell, Maddox? Did you play Scrabble professionally or something?"

I looked him dead in the eye. "I was in prison for a long time. I played a lot of Scrabble."

"Better watch your mouth," Cassandra said. "She might strangle you with her chest tube."

"If I weren't getting it out tomorrow, I would," I muttered.

Ray held his hands up in surrender.

CJ settled in a chair he'd pulled next to his dad's recliner. "How are you feeling?"

"Tired," I said as I tilted my head to look at him. "I really have to pee, but I don't want to get up."

I turned my gaze away so I wouldn't have to see him watching the labored rise and fall of my chest.

CJ had barely left my side since I was discharged from the hospital. Everyone had scrambled to cover for us both but, at some point, life had to go back to normal.

Whatever that meant.

My brother had been murdered. I had been stabbed in the chest by one of my cooks. My boyfriend had killed him.

And we were supposed to move on like nothing ever happened?

The FBI had searched Julian's apartment and found the money. Most of it, at least. He had spent bits and pieces of it over the years, but had been waiting to get my brother and me out of the picture before he disappeared for good.

There was damning proof that would have exonerated me a decade ago, but it didn't matter now. I couldn't get that time back. I couldn't turn the clock back and skip being attacked when I entered the prison system. I couldn't return the years I'd spent there. I couldn't avoid the struggle of reintegrating into society as a woman with a criminal record.

I couldn't undo the knife sliding between my ribs and puncturing my lung. I couldn't undo the weird looks I got in the hospital, the suspicious treatment from the doctors and nurses whenever I needed more pain meds, and the excruciating recovery.

I wouldn't be able to change the fact that I'd never walk into the storeroom of the restaurant without reliving it over and over again. My staff would never look at me the same nor give me the respect that I had earned.

CJ leaned over and pressed a kiss to my temple. "Want me to kick everyone out so you can rest?"

"I'm fine. I've been resting for a week."

"Do you want to go sit on the porch?" CJ asked.

"Quit hovering. She'll let you know if she wants something," Ray called from the kitchen where he was pawing through the fridge.

A tight smile tugged at the corner of my mouth, and I squeezed CJ's hand. "I'm fine. Promise."

I finally relaxed when someone turned on the TV. The background noise was a reprieve from everyone staring.

CJ had passed Olivia off to Cassandra, who reacted to holding the baby the way bomb technicians handled live explosives.

"What do you need?" CJ asked softly.

I sighed. "To be able to sleep flat in a bed and not upright like a vampire."

CJ chuckled. "Maybe tomorrow."

"Go sleep in the bunkhouse tonight. I know you're exhausted."

He shook his head.

CJ had taken up residence on his parents' couch ever since I came home from the hospital, just in case I needed anything. Every morning his neck and back were more jacked up than the previous day, but he never complained. Not once.

"I'm sorry about all this," I said as I stared aimlessly at the wall.

"Stop apologizing." He laced our fingers together. "It's not your fault."

"It kind of is..."

"Stop arguing with me, slugger." He pecked my forehead. "We're just getting a head start on the 'for better or worse' part of things."

People filtered in and out all afternoon. Brooke and Ray went back to their house when Olivia started getting fussy. Christian stopped by to talk for a few minutes before taking Cassandra home with him. Becks and Nate stopped by and hung out through dinner, then went home.

I was thankful when the cacophony of opening doors and cowboy boots grew quiet.

I took advantage of the silence while CJ slipped out to check in at the bunkhouse and make sure everything had been taken care of. I had just drifted off to sleep when something shifted the blankets. Or rather, someone.

I rubbed my eyes and found CJ's mom at the end of the recliner's footrest.

"Don't mind me, sweetheart," she said quietly as she picked up a blanket that had slid halfway off my legs and laid it neatly over my lap. "Just don't want you getting cold or having to get up."

"Thanks, Mrs. G."

She chuckled. "You make me sound cool. Need anything

before I turn in for the night? I'm an early-to-bed kind of gal."

"I'm all right," I said as I traced one of the seams of the quilt pattern. "Thanks though."

Claire gave me a curious look. "You sure? I'm always here to talk if you need it."

I mulled over the thoughts that had been swimming around in my mind for the better part of the day, then decided against it. "I'm fine. Sorry I crashed your living room."

Claire took that as an invitation to sit beside me. "There's something you should know." She rested her elbow on the armrest. "CJ didn't ask if you could stay here when you got discharged. He didn't even get a chance to bring it up. I offered."

My brows furrowed.

"No one should have to go through what you did. And you certainly shouldn't have to recover without people around to help you." She patted my hand. "You know, I started getting sad when my boys grew up. The house got more and more quiet. They moved out, made their way in the world, and built their own lives. And that's the way it's supposed to be." She smiled. "But then they started bringing me daughters. Years ago, it was Gretchen and Vanessa. Gretchen passed away, bless her, and Nate and Vanessa divorced. Things got quiet again. Ray was off riding bulls, and Nathan was in the military. Nate came back from deployment all torn up over this woman he had met over there. It didn't take long for Becks to show up after Nate came home. And then Becks brought Cassandra out here, and she fell in love with Christian. Brooke stumbled onto the ranch." She chuckled. "We've just been waiting for you, dear."

"I like your family," I hedged.

"I don't think I've ever been happier," she said. "I like having a full house. I like getting to know the women my boys have fallen in love with."

Something warm blossomed between us.

I looked down at the quilt because eye contact was a little disconcerting. "You raised good men."

One of which I didn't deserve.

She smiled. "Then I'll save the stories of the four of them being complete hellions for another day. Let's just say Brooke and Ray are going to have their hands full with Seth if he's anything like his daddy."

I laughed.

"Years ago, I was having a similar chat with Cassandra. I told her that it takes a strong woman to put up with a cowboy, and I stand by that." She squeezed my arm. "I can't imagine anyone better for Carson."

Footsteps echoed through the house as CJ came in from the bunkhouse. "Hey, Momma," he said as he strolled in with his arms full. "What are you still doing up?"

"You know me," Claire said as she eased out of the chair. "I'll never pass up a chance to spend time with my girls." She patted my knee. "Hope you get some sleep, honey."

"Thanks, Mrs. G."

CJ kissed his mom on the cheek as they passed and said their goodnights.

"You ready for bed?" he asked as he dropped his haul on the couch and placed a vase of fresh-picked wildflowers on the table beside the recliner.

"I guess."

I hated the night routine of getting in and out of the recliner. I hated that I still needed CJ's help to do basic things, but he never acted inconvenienced.

He helped me up from the recliner and carried the drainage container that connected to my chest tube as we made our way to the bathroom. His eyes never left mine as he helped me onto the toilet, then waited outside until I needed help getting back up.

It was an exercise in humility for both of us.

The pride we had forged our identities in was nothing but a pile of smoldering ashes.

I brushed my teeth with my good arm, then leaned against the edge of the sink as CJ gently changed my wound dressings. The one on my side wasn't too bad. That incision had been intentional, thanks to the surgical team who repaired my lung and saved my life. The one on my chest was much more gruesome.

When I was a rookie in the kitchen, everyone always regurgitated the mantra that a sharp knife was a safe knife.

But no knife was safe when it was going into your chest.

I grimaced as CJ threaded my right arm into the sleeve of an oversized shirt. Pain, hot and incessant, lanced through my body every time I had to move it up and down.

I could kick off a pair of sweatpants, but getting them back on was twice as hard. So, I had to settle for him pulling them up my hips.

"I hope you know how much restraint I'm showing right now," he said with a devilish smirk. He knelt before me and slipped his hands up my sweatshirt, grazing my nipple piercing with the back of his knuckles.

"Sorry," I said as I looked at my week-old braid in the mirror and decided another day without taking it down wasn't unreasonable. "I'm a little out of commission at the moment."

His gold and green eyes met mine with tenderness. "Don't be sorry. But mark my words, trouble. As soon as you're back on your feet, I'm going to make you feel so damn good."

The faint memory of that night at the bar floated back through my mind. I cupped his cheek while he was still on his knees and looked him dead in those hypnotic eyes. "Counting on it, pretty boy."

33

CARSON JAMES

Jessica greeted me with a coy smile as I slipped through the restaurant's dining room and down the hallway that skirted the kitchen. Victoria, the woman Lennon had met in a past life, stood at Jessica's side. She was in the process of learning how to flip tables during service.

A month had passed since that day in the storeroom where I prayed for Lennon to keep breathing as she bled out in my arms. I had been by her side every day as she fought in the hospital. When she came home, I only left her when I knew someone else was around to help, and then I was right back.

Lennon had returned to work a few days earlier, and it nearly killed me. The thought of not having eyes on her all the time made me physically ill. She should have been resting, but she was nothing if not stubborn.

I peered through the small cut-out window in the kitchen door, and spotted Lennon.

She rocked between her feet where she stood behind the

expo line. Her chef's coat was too boxy to see if she was breathing comfortably. I spotted the dandelion in the narrow pocket on her sleeve, and smiled.

The kitchen door muffled the sound of culinary chaos, but I could still hear her calmly directing her team as the printer spat out tickets.

"You good, Chef?" Zach asked as he worked at the grill behind her back.

"Fine," Lennon said, but she didn't look like it. She looked absolutely exhausted. Sweat beaded on her forehead as she leaned on the work table for support.

Lennon had been nervous to go back to the kitchen. Partially because it was where the attack had happened, but more so because she didn't want to look weak in front of her team.

Zach dropped his utensils and sprinted around the corner. He returned in the blink of an eye, carrying a stool. "Sit, Chef."

"I'm fine," Lennon said, not giving him a second thought.

I gritted my teeth as I watched Zach scowl at her while he flipped the steaks. "We just got you back. Don't wanna lose you so soon. Sit."

With a huff, Lennon obliged and eased onto the stool.

The flurry never stopped. The cooks adjusted to Lennon guiding the madness from the stool and kept up the flow of plates flying into the dining room.

"Table twelve would like to send its compliments to the chef," a server said as he burst through the door.

Lennon tipped her head to Zach. "Go get your praise. You've earned it."

He looked surprised. "You sure?"

Fire Line

"You covered for me for weeks. I'll cover the grill for a few minutes. Go."

They traded off. Zach removed his apron and uncuffed his sleeves before heading to the dining room. Lennon worked between the front line and the grill.

My family was probably waiting for me upstairs, but I didn't care. I needed to watch her for a minute to know that she was okay.

I loved watching her work. She had an ease and confidence about herself, even in the tensest of situations. She rocked and rolled the way I did when I was riding Anarchy.

It was elemental. The purest form of her, and I loved it to my core.

Zach hurried back into the kitchen and took over his role at the grill, leaving Lennon to run the front line. I must have caught his attention, because he spotted me peering through the window and gave me a chin tip.

With Lennon in good hands, I returned the gesture and hurried to the rooftop dining room where my family was gathered.

Balloons and a congratulatory banner stretched across the wall over the long farmhouse table.

"Is Lennon coming?" Bree asked from the seat of honor.

We were celebrating her high school graduation tonight. Lennon had pulled out all the stops for my oldest niece, creating a menu of all her favorites.

"Nah, she's on the clock and I don't want to get yelled at for pulling her away," I said as I dropped into my chair.

"Smart man," Christian said.

The festivities went on as dinner was served, and we all celebrated Bree before she moved to New York for her first year of college.

I sat back in my seat, draping my arm around the empty chair beside me.

Lennon had protested this morning when I told her she should cut out of work early to join in on the family dinner at the restaurant.

She argued that it would be a bad look for her to leave her team hanging. I got where she was coming from, but at some point, we'd have to find a balance between working for the business and spending time with family.

The duo of servers tag-teaming our party dropped in to serve the graduation cake that Javi had whipped up for the occasion. Like clockwork, my mom flagged them down and asked if they could send up Chef Maddox so she could thank her for the meal.

I wondered if Lennon would send Zach instead.

Good leaders recognized good work, and Lennon was a good leader.

A few minutes later, Lennon appeared at the top of the stairs. I frowned at how her arm was hanging.

According to the few complaints she let slip, her shoulder had been killing her as she recovered.

"How was everything tonight?" she asked the same way she usually did each time my folks summoned her. But there was no nervous energy. No sizing everyone up. No guarded body language.

"Aunt Len!" Seth said as he clapped his hands. "Color?"

Ray chuckled. "I've been replaced as the favorite human coloring book."

Lennon squeezed my hand as she rounded the table and carefully hugged Bree. "Congratulations."

"Everything was divine as always, Lennon," Mom said as she raised her glass of wine to my girl.

Lennon's blush was the prettiest sunset I'd ever seen. "Thank you."

"Take a minute and join us," Christian said.

But Lennon shook her head. "I should get back down to the kitchen. I've missed enough time as it is."

We shared a chaste kiss in passing before Lennon slipped back downstairs.

When I turned my attention back to the table, everyone was glaring at me.

Bree and Gracie were each holding up their left hands and pointing to their ring fingers. Everyone else echoed the sentiment.

"Hold your horses," I said as I finished off my beer. "I'll pop the question when I'm ready. Not when y'all are ready."

Frankly, I had been ready since before the attack. But Lennon needed time to recover. I didn't want to rush things just because we were both caught up in the torrent of emotions in the aftermath.

Grumbles rose up, but quickly shifted as the attention went back to Bree.

I headed down the stairs when dinner wrapped up. The dining room was sparse, and the kitchen had begun to close.

Lennon had been given strict instructions not to do any heavy lifting, so closing up was out of the question. I found her in the office, fingers flying across the keyboard to complete a product order before she clocked out.

"Hey, beautiful."

She looked up with tired eyes. "Hey, yourself."

I lifted my keys. "You ready to go?"

Lennon huffed. "I can walk, you know."

"I know. Just figured we could go see how Kevin is doing."

Lennon looked up through her lashes. "Are you really bribing me with a cow?"

"*Your* cow," I clarified. "Your cow that you somehow convinced me to let you name 'Kevin.'"

Lennon smirked. "Are you mad that his name is Kevin or that he has a name at all?"

I rested my forearms on her desk. "Get in the truck, pretty girl. Let's go see Kevin."

Kevin was fine and happily took a bottle from me while Anarchy sniffed up and down Lennon's shoulder.

"This is weird," Lennon said with wary disgust. She stood still, trying not to flinch as Anarchy's giant horse lips fluttered over her collarbone. She had ditched her chef's coat in the truck, leaving her in a tank top and black pants. "Do you think she smells the restaurant and wants to eat me?"

"She knows you got hurt," I said as I came out of Kevin's little home in the paddock and watched Anny checking on my girl. "Horses have a good sense about those things."

Lennon's eyes widened as Anarchy nuzzled her. She placed her cheek on Anny's long nose and closed her eyes, returning the love. They were kindred spirits.

A light breeze could have knocked me over.

"You okay?" Lennon asked. She and Anarchy were staring at me.

I blinked.

"You look like you were having a stroke."

I cleared my throat. "Yep. I'm good now."

I needed to get the show on the road before I lost my fucking mind over my lady and my horse.

Lennon accepted my hand as we walked out of the barn and climbed into the truck. I slammed her door and shoved my hand in my pocket as I rounded the tailgate, checking to make sure the ring was where I had been keeping it all night.

I pulled away from the barn and headed out into the grass. Beams of light danced across the plains as I drove past the bunkhouse.

Lennon looked at me curiously. "Something the matter?"

"No?"

"Why aren't we going home?" she asked. "Do you have to go out to the herd or something?"

I draped my arm around her shoulders. "Figured we'd take a little drive before we call it a night."

Lennon settled in and rested her head on my shoulder. "Take me away, cowboy."

I chuckled. "You got the words, just not in the right order."

Her smile was soft. "I'm learning."

I reached for her hand and brought it to my lips, pressing a kiss to her palm before lacing our fingers together. "Yeah?"

"Might even get a pair of boots."

"You'd better let me go with you. Ray has his own line of boots, and if you wear anything else, it's considered family treason."

Lennon's giggle was light like a birdsong after spring rain. "Understood."

I stopped beneath that towering tree that stood in, what felt like, the middle of nowhere. It was really only a mile from the rear edge of Ray's property. I had barely cut the engine and hopped out when Lennon opened her door.

"Excuse you, ma'am. Back inside."

Lennon rolled her eyes and slammed the door shut.

I reopened it with a dramatic flourish. "That's more like it."

Lennon slid her hand into mine and followed me around to the bed of the truck. She braced her arms on the edge to push up and jump in, but paused and bit back a groan.

"Stop. Don't hurt yourself." I turned her to face me, then grabbed the back of her thighs and lifted her onto the tailgate.

Moonlight peeked out from behind a cloud, casting soft light on the spread in the back of the truck.

I had hauled a spare mattress out of the bunkhouse and covered it with soft blankets and a nest of pillows.

Lennon lifted a suspicious eyebrow. "Why does this not seem as spontaneous as you made it out to be?"

I chuckled and climbed in behind her. "Just enjoy it. It's quiet out here."

Lennon took off her shoes and wriggled under a blanket. "People are going to get suspicious when they see a truck parked in the middle of a field." She snuggled into my side as I laid down beside her. "And especially when the truck starts rocking."

"You think I brought you out here for sex?"

She tipped her chin up and nipped at my lower lip. "If you didn't bring me out for sex, then I'd say you're passing up a golden opportunity. I could be riding your dick where your guys won't hear us through the walls. But it would be just our luck that someone would stumble out this way."

I laughed. "No one's gonna catch us out here."

"You know how everyone is. They work weird hours. Cows wander off. A guest could—"

I pulled the piece of paper out of my back pocket. "Trust me. No one's coming out here."

She paused, taking the page from me and unfolding it. "Why?"

"Because I own it."

Her eyes darted back and forth as she scanned the photocopied deed. "But you sold your piece of land so they could build the lodge and restaurant."

"And I made the investors pay out the nose for it." I took the deed back and stuffed it in my pocket. "I got more than triple what it was worth because they wanted that piece so badly."

I rolled onto my side and brushed her hair away from her face. "It took a while. I had to convince Ray to sell a bit of his land for an easement to the service road on the south side. And then I had to get Christian and my dad to sell me the rest. But it's official now. Those three acres and this tree are ours."

"Yours," she said.

I shook my head and kissed her. "Ours, Len. And you know what? It's far enough from the lodge that you can't even see the lights. We get an unobstructed view, east and west, so the sunrises and sunsets are always ours."

She swallowed. "Oh, you're . . . you're saying a lot of things right now."

"Then let me say a few more."

I sat up and helped her lean against the stack of pillows.

"I'll plant you a million wildflowers, so you never open your eyes without seeing your beauty reflected back to you. I'll build you that house with a glass roof, so the stars are never far. I'll gladly give you my last name because I want you to be a part of this legacy. But I'd also take yours because you are the most important person in my life. I'd give it all to you, and I'd give it all up for you."

I shifted onto my knee and reached behind the pillows,

pulling out a ranch jacket. "And since I've been apologizing a lot over the last few months, let me do it one more time. I'm sorry it took me so long to see how badly we needed you. The ranch. My family. But mostly how badly I needed you, and I'm sorry for how much I fought it."

She ran a finger over the brand-new stitching. "I thought you wanted me to wear your jacket. I get my own?"

"You can have my jacket too, but I have something else I want you to wear." I pulled the ring out of my pocket and held it between us. "This."

34

LENNON

I gaped at the diamond as it glimmered in the moonlight. Memories flashed through my mind, reminding me of the days before my mom went to prison. Before I moved in with Justin and had to hustle my way through life. I survived the years that were stolen from me and then clawed my way out of that pit.

In my previous life, I would have pawned the ring to put gas in my car and have somewhere to sleep for a little while. Now, all I wanted was for CJ to slip it on my finger and make me his.

CJ didn't know it—or maybe he did—but he had given me so much more than a ring. He had given me a place to belong. A place to live and grow.

People to love and be loved by.

"Are you asking what I think you're asking?" I whispered, dabbing the tears streaming down my face.

CJ smiled. "Remember the first question you asked me?"

I shook my head.

"You pushed me out of the way at the bar and said, 'Do you wanna be next, cowboy?'" He slid the ring onto my left hand. "Len, I'm not the next one. I'm the last one. You and me? I know a good thing when I've got it. This is a forever kind of love. And, if you'll have me, I'd like to be your husband."

"Yes," I whispered against his mouth as I pressed my palms to his cheeks and kissed him deep and hard.

His smile was blinding as he met me in the heat of the moment, matching each bursting flame with fire of his own.

CJ worked the straps of my tank top down off my shoulders to my waist, then pulled it down my legs so I didn't have to lift my arm. My sports bra quickly followed. He tossed my pants next as he stripped me bare in the starlight.

"Look at the sky, beautiful," he whispered as he kissed his way up my leg to tug my underwear down. "See all those stars? They're all for you."

Warm night air coated my skin as he took everything off except for the ring on my finger.

It felt so foreign, but so right.

CJ started low, kissing the scars that curved and dotted my hip. He worked his way across my pelvis, ignoring my giggle when his scruff tickled a little too much. He kissed up my stomach to my breasts.

I arched and groaned when he swirled his tongue around one nipple piercing and toyed with the other between his fingers.

"You good, Len?"

"Uh-huh."

"Hurting?"

"No," I whispered as the sparks skittered across my breasts, converging in a line and flooding my core. "Give me more."

CJ nodded. The brim of his cowboy hat prodded at my neck as he obliged.

I lifted it off his head and dropped it on mine.

"What do you think you're doing, trouble?" he murmured before swirling his tongue around my nipple.

I squeezed my thighs together to ease the ache, but his hand was faster, cupping my sex and stalling my pleasure.

"You don't think I moved to Texas without a little research?" I smirked. "I'm aware of the cowboy hat rule."

CJ laughed as he kicked off his jeans and boxers, then stripped off his shirt. He scooped me up and took my place, settling me astride his hips in one smooth motion.

"Alright, Trouble. You're wearing the hat." He reached up and straightened it on my head. "Looks like you have to ride the cowboy."

His cock was thick and swollen between us as I eased up on my knees, notching the head of his dick against my entrance.

"Um . . ." I chewed on my lip as I worked the question over in my mind. "Do you want to use a condom? I mean, we can. I'm just saying . . . I'm on birth control and I've never gone without and . . . Never mind, it's stupid. We can use a condom." I knew he had some stashed in the truck.

CJ shut me up with a kiss. "Len."

I closed my eyes and tucked my head in the crook of his neck, wishing I could take back every word that had spilled out of my mouth.

He smoothed his palm up and down my spine as he shifted his dick out of the way and teased the entrance to my pussy with his finger. "Do you want me to fuck this cunt without anything between us?"

I didn't move. I didn't even breathe. I wanted it more than anything.

CJ teased my clit. "I need an answer. Yes or no."

I nodded against his shoulder.

He took his hand away, gently pushing me away from his cock. "I want to hear you say it, Len. Say the words. Tell me *exactly* what you want."

I whimpered at the distance. I wanted to be fucked. It had been so long since we'd had sex. CJ was always so careful not to hurt me as I recovered, which meant sleeping together was just sleep.

My heart was in my throat, and I couldn't get the words out.

"Need a little motivation?" he teased as he braced his thigh between the apex of my legs. "Fine. You don't get my cock until you tell me in explicit detail that you want me to fuck you bare. Now, ride my thigh."

My hips moved like they had a mind of their own; each rock and grind that teased my clit exhilarated me. Fireworks lit up every inch of my body.

CJ had a self-satisfied smirk on his face as he laced his hands to rest behind his head. "This is the best view on the entire ranch." One hand came down, and he stroked his cock.

Watching him pleasure himself was erotic.

"Please," I begged as I rolled my hips, grinding on his thigh, helpless and desperate.

"What'cha need, Trouble?" He thumbed my nipple and gave it a little pinch. "Tell me what you want and I'm more than happy to give it to you."

"Fuck me," I rasped as my pussy clenched around nothing.

"It would be my pleasure," he said, but didn't move. "How would you like to get fucked, darling? You were never this shy before."

My throat was dry. "With your cock."

He chuckled as lightning blazed up and down my spine. "Now we're getting somewhere."

"Please, Carson. *Please.*"

"I like it when you say my name. Maybe I should make you beg a little more." He swiped a finger through my pussy and teased my clit. "You needy little thing. Soaked and humping my thigh. Tell me what you want, Len, and I'll give it to you."

My chest tightened. "Fuck me bare."

"Good girl," he grunted as he grabbed my hips and yanked me forward. "Now get on my cock. Let me feel you."

I slid down, instantly filled to the hilt. "Oh my God," I choked out.

CJ cupped my cheek and kissed me. "You okay?"

"Uh-huh."

"Breathe for me," he said as he matched his inhales and exhales with mine. "Just like that. You're okay. You can breathe. I've got you."

Two of the best epiphanies I could have conjured hit me all at once.

I could breathe. I was his. For a while, those were two things I thought would never be true.

"Atta girl," he said as he rocked inside me. "Feel that? That's you and me, Trouble. This is our ever after. You ready?"

I nodded, wrapping my arms around his neck as we worked and moved as one, chasing our respective pleasures and a collective end—the way it was meant to be. Working with each other, not against.

"Goddamn, you feel incredible, beautiful." CJ planted a wet kiss on the side of my neck as his ministrations grew erratic. "I've been waiting for you my whole life."

Words failed me as I careened over the edge. He was

right behind me, slamming deep inside me as he hit the peak of ecstasy, crashing into his release.

"I love you," I whispered as soon as I caught my breath. "So much. Thank you for loving me. I know I don't deserve it." Tears streamed down my cheeks. "Good things don't happen to people like me, but my God, I am so glad I got you."

I had never cried after sex before. Not even with him. But something about this moment was sacred.

CJ kissed my lips, then my forehead. "You deserve every good thing this life has to offer. Bad things happen to good people, but the difference is that good people will have goodness ahead. You, Lennon Maddox, are good. And you're mine."

EPILOGUE
CARSON JAMES

Two Years Later

I came to a screeching halt and jumped out of the truck. Lennon had called me in a panic and asked me to come down to the house.

It didn't matter what it was about. The worry in her voice was enough to chill me to the core.

Lennon and I had been married for a year and a half, and we'd lived in the house for most of that time. There were still stacks of lumber in the yard from where I worked on projects like building the deck when time allowed. The ranch's communal pet cows, Kevin and Mickey, were napping by a mulch pile that I needed to spread in the flower beds.

I jumped over the concrete pavers that had been delivered last week, bolted to the door, and yanked it open.

The light pine floors were marred by a single black chip of wood that had been planted and sealed in the threshold —the burned piece of the lodge that had lived on my nightstand for ages. The inanimate object that used to hold all my anger and resentment. Now, it represented something else.

Our fire line.

The mark on the floor was a daily reminder. Inside these walls, it was to be a safe, peaceful place for both of us to lean on each other. A reminder that we were a team inside and outside that door. And that good things happened when we pushed through the flames, side by side.

But right now, I wasn't so sure that our sanctuary was peaceful. Not with the way Lennon was pacing in the living room.

"Oh my God!" she shrieked. "What took you so long? I've been waiting for hours!"

I checked the timestamp of the call. "It took me ten minutes, slugger. Besides, didn't you just get back from town?"

Lennon looked a little green. "Uh-huh."

I kicked off my boots in the entryway and calmly approached her. "Len, what's the matter?"

She started pacing again. "Um. So, you know how I've been kinda sick?"

"Yeah? What'd the doctor say? Food poisoning from that intern you hired? I told you that chicken looked raw."

Lennon shook her head.

"Becks said that Charlotte picked up a stomach bug. It could be that. Can't they give you some antibiotics or something?" I grabbed a glass from the cabinet and yanked open the fridge to grab a drink.

"I'm pregnant."

Those two words stopped me dead in my tracks. Slowly, I turned to face her. "You're . . ." I blinked. "What did you say?"

"Yep," she said with a manic sort of laughter. "Twins."

The glass fell from my hand and shattered across the tiled kitchen floor.

Lennon started babbling as my world spun. "Apparently, I'm pretty far along too. I told the doctor I thought I had food poisoning, and it wasn't going away, so she had me pee in a cup, and then she told me I'm pregnant. *Pregnant!*"

She dug both hands in her black and white hair. "My periods have always been irregular, so it wasn't weird that I missed a few. But when I told her and she did the math, they did an ultrasound right there and ... twins. Twins, Carson. *Two* babies. Two. *At one time!*"

I rushed around the kitchen island and pulled her into my arms, kissing her hard and deep. "Two babies?"

Lennon nodded as tears welled up in her eyes. "Oh my god. This explains why I've been such a hormonal bitch lately. I have to apologize to everyone at the restaurant."

I lifted her tank top and dropped to my knees, resting my forehead against her stomach. "You're giving me twins?"

"Giving you twins?" Lennon shrieked. "I think what you mean to say is, 'Oh my God, babe. I'm so sorry you have to push not one, but two babies out of your vagina in a few months, even though we haven't finished the house yet.'"

My God, she was beautiful when she was pissed. Then again, I didn't think she was mad, just scared. She had a habit of reacting to things that scared her by lashing out. But that didn't scare me in the slightest. She felt safe enough with me to react however she needed to.

That, or she really was pissed, and we were about to be in for a rollercoaster ride with the pregnancy hormones.

"I'll finish the spare bedrooms," I promised as I kissed her belly. "It won't take long. I'll get my brothers down here to give me a hand." I stood and pulled her into my arms.

Lennon collapsed immediately, caving into my chest. "I'm scared."

"It's okay to be scared, Len." My heart raced as I held her and rubbed her back. "You and me, slugger. We're in this together."

She sniffed. "I hope they're girls. Or at least a girl and a boy. I can't imagine raising Griffith brothers."

I chuckled. "You know, being the only one out of my siblings to have the next generation of Griffith brothers sounds pretty great."

BONUS EPILOGUE
LENNON

Nineteen Years Later

"Clay! Aiden!" I shouted up the stairs. "You're going to be late for school if you don't get a move on!"

Feet thundered overhead as my boys jumped out of bed and hurried to get dressed. I ignored their argument over who took up more bathroom real estate and poured my coffee.

The front door opened and closed, and CJ appeared in my kitchen. "Morning, beautiful."

"Is it a good morning?" I asked as I pulled the creamer out of the fridge. "Because if memory serves, I only got four hours of sleep last night."

He grinned. "If memory serves, you got three orgasms before those four hours of sleep."

I rolled my eyes and hid my smile behind a sip of coffee.

CJ stole the mug out of my hand, pinned me against the counter, and rocked his hips against mine. "How does round four sound? I can spare half an hour once the boys are gone. Get your day started right."

I snickered. "How romantic."

CJ surprised me with his hand in my hair, tugging my head back and giving me a panty-melting kiss. I squeaked at the jolt as he pried my lips open with his tongue, deepening the connection.

"Gross," Clay yelled as he careened down the stairs.

Aiden was on his heels. "What?"

"Mom and Dad are making out again," Clay grumbled.

Aiden dry heaved.

Grumbling, they quickly gathered the textbooks from the kitchen table and packed their backpacks.

Oblivious to them, CJ's lips remained locked on mine.

Our front door creaked open and slammed shut, interrupting the moment. The click of high heels echoed through the house.

"It smells like a sock in here," Cassandra said flatly, stepping into the room.

I peeled away from CJ. "Welcome to life with teenage boys, empty nester. Feel free to clean my house whenever you'd like, your Highness."

Cassandra grimaced. "Gross."

I shrugged. "Yeah, at this point I just follow them around with air freshener and try not to die in the vat of toxic laundry."

"Hi, Aunt Cass," the boys said in tandem as they raided the fridge.

"Fire twin. Earth twin. Have a productive day," Cassandra said, teasing them with her signature black cat attitude and the nicknames she had given them at birth.

"Love you," I said to Aiden as he gave me a kiss on the cheek before heading out the door.

Clay mimicked the gesture and grabbed the keys to the old truck they hated sharing. "Love you, Mom," he said.

"'Sup, Uncle Christian," Aiden said.

Christian appeared behind Cassandra. "Hey, boys."

Since we apparently had company, I started another pot of coffee. "To what do I owe the pleasure of you two in my house this early in the morning?"

"Early?" Cassandra looked at the clock. "It's almost 7:30. This is early for you?"

CJ chuckled.

"I closed the restaurant last night. So yes, this hour is decrepit, and I would like to go back to bed. To what do I owe the pleasure of having you two in my house this wicked morning?"

Christian helped himself to the coffee. "CJ, you should sit down."

I caught my husband's eye from across the room. The surprise on his face was palpable. He had no idea what was going on either.

"Everything okay?" CJ asked as he took a seat at one of the stools pushed up to the kitchen island. "You're not sick or something, are you?"

Christian looked confused, glanced at Cassandra, then realized what CJ was getting at. "What? No. No, everything's fine. There's some ranch business we wanted to talk to y'all about."

I shared a look with CJ. "Are we waiting for Nate and Ray?"

"No, I've already spoken to them," Christian said as he worked his hand over his silver beard.

CJ frowned. "Then what's this all about?"

Christian rested his forearms on the kitchen island. "I think it's time we talk about what happens when I retire."

"Retire?" I said in surprise.

Christian had never mentioned slowing down, much

less retiring. He was only in his sixties and kept the same schedule and workload as he had when I first came to the ranch.

"What's going on?" CJ asked. "Why would you retire?"

"Bree's in New York with her family. Gracie and her girlfriend are in Austin. Cass and I want to be able to visit them more."

"Then take a fucking vacation!" CJ shouted. "You're talking about retiring so you can visit the girls and your grandkids? Jesus, take some time off and stop giving me a heart attack."

Christian chuckled. "It's more than that. After Dad died, you know we had an attorney go through the wills and company deeds to transfer everything out of his name."

"Yeah?" CJ said. "I thought we had taken care of everything. Did we miss something?"

"No, but it got us thinking," Cassandra said. "If we're not around as much, someone else has to run the cattle operation, the lodge, and the restaurant."

"That's where y'all come in," Christian said. His smile was a little sad, but full of love as he looked at his brother. "Nobody loves this land more than you. And Lennon, you started with the restaurant when it first opened. You're both a perfect fit to step in and take over for Cass and me."

I held my hands up. "I'm a chef. I don't do all the hospitality administrative shit."

Cassandra turned to me. "You know this place like the back of your hand. It might be a learning curve, but you'll pick it up. Besides, you were just saying that being at the restaurant full-time was tricky with your kids' schedules. This way, we can tag team it before it's all yours."

"And everything stays in the family," Christian said. "I talked to my girls. Ray and Brooke talked to their brood.

Charlotte's living overseas. Nate and Becks are always bouncing between here and wherever she is. You have to want this life, and they don't. That's okay. We all raised our kids to go after whatever they want."

"But we also want the ranch to stay in the family," Cassandra said. "And all your boys want to do is work cattle. Hell, you've had them out there with you since they were in diapers."

I let out a slow breath as it all sank in. The look on CJ's face was an immediate yes. He had never wanted anything else.

He loved this land. He loved the life we had built here. I loved it too.

I'd only found myself on this ranch because I was running from my past. Now I was a permanent part of a place I never expected to be my home. Part of the legacy.

"We'll have to talk about it," CJ said as he scrubbed his palm down his scruff and over his mouth. He glanced at me with watery eyes. "And talk to the boys about it."

My eyebrows winged up and I laughed. "Are you fucking kidding me, Griffith? Say yes. It's everything you've ever wanted."

I thought about that charred piece of wood that CJ had insisted be put in the flooring. All those years ago, he thought he had lost his piece of the legacy. Now here he was, with his wife and boys, leading the next generation.

"You sure, Len?" CJ asked in a hushed tone.

I reached across the island and squeezed his hand. "I'm sure."

Christian and Cassandra looked at each other. "I'll call the attorneys," she said.

CJ smirked at me. "You know this makes me your boss, right?"

I cut my eyes at him. "Call yourself my boss one time and see what happens, cowboy. We know who runs the show around here."

CJ leaned across the island and kissed me. "Team."

I cupped his cheek. "That's better."

"You know this means you have to be okay with things changing, right?" Christian said. "No one knows the future. We can't predict whether things will change or stay the same."

"Whatever it takes," CJ said as he held my hand. "We work for the land and the legacy. But more than that, we do it for the family. This place has always been ours. It's always been exactly what we need, in the lean years and in the growth. We'll keep it going and growing for everyone who has the honor of calling themselves Griffiths."

COMING SOON FROM MAGGIE GATES

I was living in a house of cards. All it took was one night for my mansion to come tumbling down.

Every dream. Every goal.

Forever changed.

Either we own our mistakes, or the mistakes own us.

Coming Winter/Spring 2025

PREORDER NOW!

CURIOUS ABOUT CHEF LUCA DEROSSI?

While you're waiting for the next release in the Maggieverse, check out Luca and Maddie's workplace romance in *Poker Face*!

CLICK HERE TO READ!

Follow Maggie on social media to keep up with new book announcements, updates, and teasers!

Instagram: @authormaggiegates

Facebook: https://www.facebook.com/AuthorMaggieGates

Facebook Reader Group: Maggie Gates' Reader Group
https://www.facebook.com/groups/authormaggiegates

AUTHOR'S NOTE TO THE READER

Dear Reader,

I'm crying as I write this author's note because this series has changed my life in so many indescribable ways. As I think back to Nate and Becks's story in *The Stars Above Us*—my debut novel—I'm hit with an overwhelming sense of pride and accomplishment.

The Griffith Brothers series was a long time coming. I started writing *The Stars Above Us* nearly four years ago. In the back of my mind, I knew that the brothers would be compelling characters for a series, but I kept pushing it off. There were other stories I was more excited about. Other worlds I wanted to explore. And then it came time to finally (as Becks would say) tell their stories.

I had no idea how this series would be received, but the love has been overwhelming. It has truly been an honor to write these books.

Thank you for reading them. Thank you for sharing them with your friends, spreading the love online, and shouting about them from the rooftops!

As sad as I am to see this chapter come to a close, I am SO excited for what's next, and hope you stick around for it!

With Love and Happily-Ever-Afters,
   - **Mags**

PS. Because you're super cool, let's be friends!

ACKNOWLEDGMENTS

Landon: For being my partner in every aspect of the word. For being my colleague, my love, my biggest cheerleader, and my safe place.

Flavia, Meire, and Luci with Bookcase Literary: Thank you for your guidance, expertise, and for believing in me!

Mikayla and Mandy: For endless encouragement. For being the best friends a girl could ask for.

Kayla: For tackling all the behind the scenes work that keeps my digital life rocking and rolling! Thank you for everything!

Sam: For loving and caring for my community and being the biggest cheerleader!

Mel: for being the most incredible cover designer! This series would not have been the same without your covers!

To Jen, Megan, and the Grey's Promotions Team: Thank you SO much for all your hard work and for hyping up this book!

Kyle and Michael (Badass Attorneys): For being my email

filter and anger translator. I could never do what you two do. Your patience is unmatched. Thank you for everything!

Kayla, Sierra, Catherine, and Jen (Promo Badasses): Thank you for your hype!!

The HEA Babes: For laughs, inexplicable microtropes, and a cool place to overshare.

My Street Team: Thank you for your enthusiasm and encouragement! You all are an imperative part of my book team and I'm so grateful for every recommendation, video, and post!

My ARC Team: You guys are the greatest! Your excitement and support astounds me on a daily basis. You make me feel like the coolest human being alive. I'm so grateful for each and every one of you. Thank you for volunteering your time and platforms to boost my books!

Starbucks Baristas: You don't talk to me and never question why I'm sitting in the corner 40+ hours a week. Thank you. Also, please bring back the almond croissant. I'm begging you.

My Readers: Because naming all of you one by one would double the length of this book: You all are the reason I keep writing books. I'm thoroughly convinced that there's no greater group of people in the world. Y'all are amazing human beings! Thank you for loving these characters and getting as excited as I do about their stories! Thank you for your hype, encouragement, and excitement!

ALSO BY MAGGIE GATES

Standalone Novels

The Stars Above Us: A Steamy Military Romance

Nothing Less Than Everything: A Sports Romance

Cry About It: An Enemies to Lovers Romance

100 Lifetimes of Us: A Hot Bodyguard Romance

Pretty Things on Shelves: A Second Chance Romance

The Beaufort Poker Club Series

Poker Face: A Small Town Romance

Wild Card: A Second Chance Romance

Square Deal: A Playboy Romance

In Spades: A Small Town Billionaire Romance

Not in the Cards: A Best Friend's Brother Romance

Betting Man: A Friends to Lovers Romance

The Falls Creek Series

What Hurts Us: A Small Town Fake Engagement Romance

What Heals Us: An Age Gap Romance

What Saves Us: A Small Town Single Mom Romance

The Griffith Brothers Series

Dust Storm: A Single Dad Romance

Downpour: A Grumpy Sunshine Romance

Fire Line: An Enemies to Lovers Romance

ABOUT THE AUTHOR
MAGGIE GATES

Maggie Gates writes raw, relatable romance novels full of heat and humor. She calls North Carolina home. In her spare time, she enjoys daydreaming about her characters, jamming to country music, and eating all the BBQ and tacos she can find! Her Kindle is always within reach due to a love of small-town romances that borders on obsession.

For future book updates, follow Maggie on social media.

- facebook.com/AuthorMaggieGates
- instagram.com/authormaggiegates
- tiktok.com/@authormaggiegates

Printed in Great Britain
by Amazon